HORS D'OEUVRES III

HORS D'OEUVRES III

ROAD KILL (AND OTHER SHORT STORIES)

RONNIE REMONDA

iUniverse, Inc.
Bloomington

Hors d'oeuvres III
Road Kill (and other short stories)

iUniverse books may be ordered through booksellers or by contacting:

iUniverse
1663 Liberty Drive
Bloomington, IN 47403
www.iuniverse.com
1-800-Authors (1-800-288-4677)

ISBN: 978-1-4759-6938-2 (sc)
ISBN: 978-1-4759-6939-9 (ebk)

Printed in the United States of America

iUniverse rev. date: 01/04/2013

CONTENTS

DEDICATION

To my wife, Dorothy: my light, my breath, my best friend.
Thank you for being you.

ROAD KILL

Ken Bradley got to his feet and raised his glass. "I'd like to propose a toast," he said, looking around at the large group of people seated at the long table. "To Carl Foster, our new Managing Director, and to his lovely wife, Clara." He motioned toward the couple seated to his left. "If anyone had told me, a year ago, that one man could accomplish so much in two short months, I would have said they were full of shit! Welcome aboard, Carl." He raised his glass, "To Carl."

"To Carl!" the group chanted, as they each took a sip of their drinks, drawing the attention of most of the other patrons of the *Grub-n-Grog*.

Ken took a long drink from his own glass, somehow managing to stay on his feet. It was easy to tell that the whiskey sours were beginning to affect him. "Ripped away from his family and friends in Boston," he continued, "he has managed to buy a new house, settle in, send for his wife and all of his worldly possessions, and not even miss one day of work. Most men would have required a month just to settle in, but not old Carl. Not only that, but in the last two months, he has done more for this company than the last Managing Director did in eight years. Not that Fred wasn't a good Managing Erector, I mean Director . . ."

The group laughed.

Ken raised his hand. "I'll bet you all think I'm drunk," he said, waving his finger. He paused for a moment, as if in deep thought. "Well, you're, goddamn, right." He put his arm around Carl Foster's shoulder. All I have left to say is this. I love this man, and as Vice President, I'd better start watching my own goddamn ass. Speech!" he shouted, pointing a finger at Carl and clapping. "I want a speech."

The group joined in. "Speech, speech!" they chanted.

Carl got to his feet, slowly. His face was flushed red. He smiled at his wife, and then turned to the group. "I didn't know this was going to be a testimonial. I thought this was just going to be a little get-together. I can't say that I'm not flattered, but the truth is, I never

1

would have accomplished anything without the help I've received from all of you. Transitions aren't easy, but we've managed to get through this one with little or no whimpering. As Ken said, Fred Warren was a good Managing Director. Even though I never met the man, this is evident by the fact that this company has gone from being the tenth largest company of its kind . . . in this country . . . to being the fifth largest. With the people we have assembled at this table," he spread his arms, "there is no reason why, within the next two years, we can't be number one."

The group began to clap as Carl slipped back into his chair; although, not without a little difficulty.

Ken got to his feet and began waving his hand. "Waiter!" he shouted, loud enough for everyone in the restaurant to hear. "We need another round over here, post haste!"

Clara pulled at her husband's sleeve. "Don't you think you've had enough, Carl? You know how you get when you've been drinking."

He leaned close to her. "Clare, I know when I've had enough. Don't worry. This is what I've worked for all my life: recognition. Now don't you go ruining my one fuckin' day of glory!"

The group was getting louder, and although he was talking loudly, no one seemed to hear. Clara looked hurt. She folded her arms across her chest and said nothing. Carl struck up a conversation with the co-worker next to him and ignored her.

By the end of the evening, Carl was obviously drunk. Clara managed a smile as they said their good-byes, but she was upset. Carl was strictly a social drinker. He had little tolerance for alcohol. Normally the strong, quiet type, he needed the alcohol to help him to loosen up. A few drinks and he was an entirely different person. When he was drunk he could be funny and charming, loud and boisterous, and often downright mean. Clara hated to see him drunk. They had experienced their one and only knockdown, drag out fight when he had been drinking. It was almost as if he were someone else. The next day, he bought her flowers and candy, and couldn't apologize enough.

They had been married for four years, now. They met at a party in Boston. He was rebounding from his first marriage: a short dreadful affair that had ended with a fierce battle over money. Thank God there had been no children.

She was still licking her wounds over her own failed marriage. Her husband had convinced the judge that she had a drug and alcohol problem. He received full custody of her fourteen-year-old daughter, and the judge reserved visitation rights until she got professional help. What a lot of hogwash! She was under a doctor's care. What other help did she need? Of course her medication was strong. She had a severe nervous condition. As for the drinking; she considered herself a moderate, social drinker.

She did have limited visitation: holidays and summer vacations, but her daughter refused to come to see her. "I love you, Mom," she had told her, over the phone, "but you need to get yourself straightened out." Her ex-husband had poisoned her daughters mind against her! No wonder she had this nervous condition! Who could blame her?

Carl had swept her off her feet. He was everything her ex-husband had never been. He was charming, ambitious, considerate, and very handsome. Three months after they met, they were married. It wasn't long after they were married that he began to change. He became possessive and domineering.

In the parking lot, Carl fumbled in his pockets for the keys, almost dropping them.

"Do you want me to drive, Carl," she asked.

"Jesus, Clare, I'm fine!" He unlocked the car doors. "Get in!" he ordered.

She didn't argue with him. She wanted to say something, but she knew it would only make matters worse. When Carl was like this, he was not about to listen to reason. He put the key in the ignition and started the engine. Slipping the shift lever into reverse, he started to back up before he even turned around to look. There was a car pulling out of the lot, and he had to jam on the brakes to keep from hitting it. Clara closed her eyes and took a deep breath. When they reached the street, Carl pulled out in front of another car. The driver hit his horn, but Carl never even looked back.

"Asshole!" he shouted through the partially opened window.

"Please, Carl, let me drive!"

"I'll be fine, Clare!" There was a tone of anger in his voice. "We'll be out of this damn city traffic in a few minutes and we'll be home before you know it. Try to relax, Clare. Jesus! You're too uptight!"

They hit SR-25 and headed north, toward Westbrook. Once they cleared the city, the traffic thinned and Clara started to breathe a little easier. Carl kept the car below the speed limit. She was glad of that. At least he wasn't speeding. Still, Clara had to warn him that they were coming up on the US-202 exit, or he would have gone right by it. They headed west, toward Sanford, then north, on SR-114 toward Sebago Lake.

The move from Boston to Portland had been sudden. Carl had taken the job only a little over two months ago. He had gone on ahead, got settled into the position, found a place for them to stay, and sent for her. Having been born and raised in the city, she naturally thought that he would find a nice apartment in Portland. She was surprised to find that they would be living near some large lake, in the middle of the Maine wilderness. The area near Sebago Lake was the kind of place you might go to camp or boat, not the kind of place she would pick to set up housekeeping. It was coming into fall, and it frightened her to think what the winter might be like.

This was like Carl, though, to take a major step like buying a house without any input from her. She hated the place from the first day she saw it. It was a huge farmhouse. "Updated", was how Carl had described it to her. Something she was sure Carl had remembered from the newspaper ad, or was told by the local Real Estate people. In reality, the word only meant that this huge, ugly dinosaur had been innovated with vinyl siding, wall-to-wall carpeting, and she was sure, indoor plumbing for the first time. None of this took away from the fact that the roof still sagged and the floors still creaked. Carl just said that this is what gave the place character. She wondered how she was going to take care of this monster with its six bedrooms and three baths; not to mention the large dining room, enormous kitchen, gauntly living room, dismally cluttered den, sagging, enclosed porch, and unquenchable pantry. He had told her not to worry about it; he would get her some help.

The place came fully furnished, which had both good and bad points. Having always rented, they never accumulated very many furnishings, but the furniture that came with the house was certainly not the kind of things she would have picked out. This was another thing Carl had told her not to worry about. They would just replace everything over time. She could start with the master bedroom.

She certainly was in no condition to take care of the house herself. Doctor Randall had warned her about any undue stress. After all, in the last two years, had he not had to increase her medication three times? Just moving into a big house like this, in the middle of nowhere, would be stressful enough for anyone.

Dr. Randall had been her physician for over fifteen years. He knew her condition. He knew what medications she required. Who was she going to find in this place that would have even any inclination of what she was going through? Maybe she would just commute back and forth to Boston and continue to see Dr. Randall. She could take the station wagon. Carl wouldn't even have to know about it. She began to feel an anxiety attack coming on. She opened her pocket book, removed a large bottle of pills, and popped two into her mouth.

Carl had been watching. "Are you supposed to be taking those like that?" he asked.

"What do you mean?" she asked, innocently.

"Two at a time, isn't that stuff pretty powerful?"

"Under extreme pressure, I'm allowed to take more than one."

"What extreme pressure, Clare? We're on rural country road, heading home. That, on top of the drinks you had, can't be good for you."

They were headed north out of Sebago Lake. At least now there was little traffic. "It's getting dark," she said. "You know I don't like riding these back roads at night."

Carl shook his head. "One thing I'm happy about. You're finally getting away from that quack, Randall. Maybe now we can find you a real doctor. Maybe we can get you some real help. I swear, that son-of-a-bitch has turned you into a junkie. Half of the time, you're in a daze; the rest of the time you're climbing the walls."

"You just don't understand do you?" she said, angrily. "If it weren't for Dr. Randall's help, I'd be far worse off than I am now."

"Bullshit!" Carl took his eyes off the road for a moment. He pointed his finger at his wife. About to say something else, he thought better of it. When he looked back, there was a man standing in his headlights, waving both arms! He slammed on the brakes, but it was too late! There was a loud thud and the man disappeared. Clare was screaming!

He shut off the engine, stepped out of the car and looked around. It was too dark. He couldn't see anything. They were on a densely wooded section of road, the heavy forest vegetation mostly obstructing even the bright moon. He stuck his head back inside the car.

"Give me the flashlight out of the glove compartment, Clare."

His wife didn't respond.

"Clare! Give me the damn flashlight!" he demanded.

Clara opened the glove compartment and fished around until she found the flashlight. She watched Carl turn it on to see if it was working.

"Stay in the car!" he ordered.

Clara watched as her husband circled the car; then stopping a few feet behind it, he set down the flashlight. He knelt beside something on the edge of the road. Quickly, he regained his feet. She could see him struggling, as if he were dragging something into the woods. He returned quickly, and slid behind the wheel. Clare could see what looked like blood on his hands.

"What did you just do, Carl?"

"I moved him off the road."

"Will he be OK?"

"I'm pretty sure he's dead, Clare."

Clara picked up the cell-phone.

"What are you doing, Clare?" he shouted.

"I'm calling 911."

Carl grabbed the phone from her hand. "Are you fucking crazy?"

"But we have to report this, Carl. It wasn't your fault. The man came out of nowhere."

"Think about it, Clare! I've been drinking, you've been popping pills, there are no witnesses; so who the hell is going to believe us? The best thing we can do is to get the hell out of here before somebody comes along, sees us here, and puts two and two together!"

We can't just leave that man lying there, can we?" Clara was sobbing uncontrollably.

"What choice do I have, Clare. I've just landed the biggest job of my life. Do you think that I should throw that away just because some drunken bum wants to jump out in front of me on some backwoods road? He was drunk, Clare. He reeked of the stuff." He probably didn't even know what hit him." He started the car and pulled back onto the road. "I'm not willing to do that, Clare. The best thing we can do is to forget that this whole thing ever happened. The guy's dead. No one can help him, now. We need to think about ourselves."

"What about the damage to the car? Won't someone get suspicious?"

Carl was quiet for a few minutes. "Tomorrow, we'll take it down to Boston. We'll take it to that little body shop that fixed our car that time you hit the dog. Remember? They did a good job. They didn't ask any questions. They fixed it in a few days. I'll take an old fence post to the front fender, in the morning. I'll tell them that I hit a tree. How are they going to know the difference? I'll drive the station wagon for a while. When we get the car back, I'll swap it in for another lease car."

"Aren't they going to wonder why?"

"I'll just tell them that I'd like something with a little more power. People do that kind of stuff every day. It's no big deal, Clare."

Clara put her head in her hands and began to cry. "I don't know if I can handle this, Carl," she sobbed.

"When we get home, Clare, I want you to fix yourself a strong drink, go soak in the tub for a while, take a sleeping pill, and go to bed. In the morning, you'll be fine, believe me."

It had been two weeks, and the body shop still hadn't repaired the car. That Saturday, Clara took the station wagon into town. She told Carl that she needed to pick up some groceries. This was true. They did need some groceries, but what she really needed was some more booze. Her pills were running dangerously low, and without her car she would not be able to get back to Dr. Randall to get another prescription. She needed the booze to help take the edge off, at least until she could get back to Boston.

Kendler was a small resort town, the kind of place that catered to campers and fishermen. There was one gas station, a small grocery store, a place that sold and repaired boats, a couple of motor home parks, and a combination bar and liquor store.

She stopped at the liquor store first, and bought four bottles of Vodka and a small bottle of wine. She went back to the car, opened the bottle of wine, and took several deep swallows. She put the cap back on, lay back in the seat, and took a few deep breaths. She felt better already.

The grocery store was about a mile down the road. Before she arrived there, she had finished the rest of the bottle. She washed one of her precious few pills down with the last couple of swallows, and tossed the bottle onto the side of the road.

Outside the store was a wooden bench. The man, seated on the bench, caught her eye. She took a double take. It was the man that Carl had hit that night! She was sure! The image of him, standing there, illuminated in the headlights, was burned into her memory. But how was this possible? Carl had said that the man was dead! He sat on the bench sipping from a cold can of beer wrapped in a brown paper bag. As she came closer he looked up at her.

"Hi," he said, showing a toothless grin.

She managed a phony smile. The side of his face was covered with fresh scabs and caked with dried blood. His arms were scratched, and black and blue. She was sure that she had been right about him. He was the man all right.

She stepped by him and into the store. The storeowner smiled as she walked past the counter.

"Hi. How are ya?" he asked.

She stopped. "That man, outside, do you know him?"

"Perkins? Yeah, everyone here knows old Charley Perkins. He's a bit of a local character. Town drunk, y'know. Did ya see his face? Wrecked his car a couple of weeks ago, up there, on the old Sawmill Road, I heard. Damn lucky ta be alive if y'ask me. He does odd jobs fer people, around here. Ain't much good fer nothin', any more, except totin' and paintin'. Slow as hell, but he'll work all day for a bottle or two, and he is a pretty fair painter."

Clara smiled broadly. This time there was nothing phony about it. "Wrecked his car, you said?"

"Yeah. Ain't the first time. Won't be the last. Took him two years ta save up enough money ta buy that old clunker. He takes the plates from one car and puts them on the other. Don't think he bothers ta register em. Fact is, I don't think the man ever had a drop of insurance. One day he'll get caught and they'll take away his license, if he's even got one."

Clara picked up the groceries she needed and left. As she passed Charley Perkins she smiled and said, "Hi."

Charley seemed surprised that a woman would bother to talk to him; especially a pretty woman. He smiled back, but said nothing.

Carl was surprised to hear Clara humming to herself as she fixed supper. "Why are you in such a good mood?" he asked.

"I found out something while I was in town; something that should make you very happy as well."

"And what, pray tell, would that be?" Carl doubted that anything would put him in a good mood.

"I saw that man, in town."

Carl was puzzled. "What man?"

"The one you hit, of course. He was alive and well."

Carl's face took on a serious look. "Are you sure? He sure looked dead to me."

"Dead drunk, maybe. When I saw him, in front of the grocery store, he was a little worse for wear, but alive and kicking. You may have only knocked him out. I've heard that people who are drunk can suffer a lot of abuse because their bodies go limp."

"Are you sure that this man was the one we hit?"

"Oh, yes. The face I saw through the windshield, that night, is burned into my memory. I'll never forget the look on his face. It was the man we hit, all right. All of that worrying was for nothing. Now, we have nothing to worry about, Carl."

Carl didn't seem so sure. "Are you crazy? We have more to worry about now than we did before. If you recognized him, he might have recognized you."

She put a reassuring hand on his shoulder. "How could he recognize me, Honey? He never saw me; the headlights blinded him. I never got out of the car, remember? If he saw anyone it would be you, but you said that you thought he was dead, so he must have been unconscious. Don't you see, Carl, he never really got a look at either one of us. I would like to do something for him, though."

"Like what, Clare?"

"Help him out. Maybe help him get another car. He wrecked his car that night, that's why he was walking down that road in the first place."

"How are you going to do that without raising suspicions?

"We could give him some work. There's lots of work to be done around here."

"Like what, Clare?"

"Well, the storeowner said that he was a good painter. I would like to repaint the inside, especially our bedroom and the dining room. We could get him to do that. It wouldn't be like we were handing him the money."

"My God, Clare, do you really feel that guilty?"

"Yes, Carl, I feel that guilty! He could have died from his injuries. We just left him there! I feel guilty that I didn't try to do something!"

"All right, Clare. We hire this guy until he gets enough money to buy himself another car, or drinks himself to death outside the liquor store; whichever comes first. Then you can get over your stupid guilt, we can get back to normal and get on with our lives." He reached out his hand. "Is that a deal?"

Clara shook hands with her husband. "It's a deal, Carl."

Carl got the car back that following Monday. Clara had to drive him down to Boston to pick it up. He left and went back to Portland, while Clara successfully finagled a last minute appointment with Dr. Randall. She wasn't in there very long; just long enough for him to write a couple prescriptions. She stopped at Lowe's and picked up enough paint to redo the two rooms, as well as enough for the kitchen. As long as she was going to have some painting done, she might as well get it all done. The kitchen didn't really need painting; it was just that she couldn't stand looking at those ugly green walls.

When she got back to Kendler, it was nearly noon. She found Charley Perkins sitting outside the grocery store, sipping on a coke. He looked reasonably sober. She approached him cautiously. Standing beside him, she cleared her throat.

"Hi, again," he said, looking up at her.

"Hi. Charley, is it?"

"Yeah," he answered, in a slow drawl. He reached up his hand. "Name's Charley Parkins. Don't think I've had the pleasure."

"My name is Clara Foster." She took his hand. It felt cold and clammy. It made her feel uncomfortable. "I . . . I . . . heard that you are a good painter."

"Fair ta midland."

"Would you be interested in doing some work for us? That is my husband, and I . . . ah and me."

"All three a ya?" He smiled a toothless grin.

"Oh. I meant to say, 'for my husband and me.' Would you like to do some painting for my husband and me?"

Charley rubbed his chin as if in deep thought. "You, me, I or yer husband; it's all the same ta me. Now, would that be paintin' by the foot, er by the hour?"

"Ah, gee I don't know. How do you usually do it?"

"I've done it both ways, Ma'am. If I work by the hour, I get seven dollars. If I work by the foot, I get twenty-five cents. That's a square foot, now, not a lineal foot. I have ta get more fer high ceilings, as I don't like much climbin' ladders."

"Well, Charley, since I have no idea what a square foot is, or a lineal foot is, I suppose I will just hire you by the hour. Are you sure that seven dollars is enough?"

"Seein' as ya got to supply the paint and the transportation, I wrecked my car. I think it's fair enough. When did y'want me ta start?"

"Could you start today? Right now would be fine with me."

Charley pulled himself to his feet and threw the empty coke can into the trashcan beside the bench. Clara hadn't realized just how tall he was. He couldn't have weighed more than one hundred and sixty pounds, but he was well over six feet tall. "Ain't got nothin' pressin' fer the rest of the day, Ma'am. You'll have ta take me back to my place, so's I can pick up my coveralls and my brushes, but I'm ready ta go if you are."

Charley's place turned out to be a rundown trailer stuck in the middle of a wooded lot, and surrounded by wrecked cars and other junk. It was interesting to know that they were almost neighbors. He also lived on Sawmill Rd.; the road that led to their house. This explained why he had been on that road that night. He was probably on the way home from some bar, or something, when he wrecked his car.

She pulled into the driveway, and Charley climbed slowly out of the car. The porch creaked under his weight, and there was a loud clunk as he pried the door to the trailer open. "Did ya want ta come in fer a drink!" he shouted from the front porch.

"No thank you," she said, politely. *Not if my life depended on it,* she added, under her breath.

All the way back to the house, Charley kept looking at her, running his eyes up and down her body. It gave her chills and made her feel uneasy. She began to wonder if maybe she was making a big mistake.

His eyes were cold and indifferent. It was hard to tell just what this man was thinking. She decided that she didn't really want to know.

"Lived here long?" she asked, trying to break the tension that was building up in her mind.

"All my life. My father was born here, too. Died when I was twelve. Bear got him. Buried my mother three years ago."

It was really more than she wanted to know. "Oh! I'm sorry."

"No need ta be. She didn't suffer much."

"I . . . I mean about your father, being killed by a bear."

"Bear died, too. Felt sorrier fer the bear. My old man was a no-good bum. He used to beat my mother and me whenever he got drunk, which was often. I loved that bear, though. I skun it out that day. It's kept me warm fer a good many years."

He was smiling that toothless grin again, and was looking right at her breasts. She avoided his gaze.

When they got to the house, he helped her unload the paint. She started him painting in the living room. She helped him move the furniture, and furnished him with some old sheets for drop-cloths. Retiring to the kitchen, she heated up a can of soup for lunch. She thought about asking him if he had eaten, but thought better of it. She didn't like the way he looked at her. It made her feel uncomfortable. Maybe she would just have him paint the living room, pay him off, give him a bonus, then do the rest of the painting herself. The thought of him being around here all week, with Carl gone, made her skin crawl. She busied herself with the housework and at six-thirty she started to fix supper. She had forgotten all about Charley and the painting.

"Can I get some water?"

She jumped!

"Sorry," he said, "didn't mean ta startle ya. Paintin' tends ta dry out the throat."

"Sure." She went to the cupboard and reached for a cup. Suddenly his arms were around her waist and his rough beard against the side of her neck! He tried to kiss her! She pulled herself away, and grabbed a knife from the dish-rack!

"Oh! We're a sassy one aren't we?"

"You get away from me, Charley, or I swear, I'll use this!"

"Are y'gonna try ta kill me again?"

"What do you mean?" she asked, testing. She already knew exactly what he meant.

"You and your husband left me out there on the road. Ya left me to die. When your husband came over to me, I could see the look on his face. I just held my breath and pretended to be dead. I knew by the look on his face that if he thought I wasn't dead he would of killed me, anyway. When he got back in the car, I got up and ran into the woods. I hid behind a tree. I saw your husband take the phone away from you. The door was open and the light was on in the car. I got a good look at you. You were cryin'. You turned and looked right at me. I knew you couldn't see me. It was too dark out there. I saw where you went. I knew where you were livin'. I knew, the other day, when you came into town that you would be back. You had that guilty look on your face. I knew that the guilt was eatin' ya up. You're not like your old man. You're not a cold-blooded killer."

"My husband is not a killer! He really thought that you were dead."

"Yeah, Ma'am. Lucky fer me, huh? Now, don't ya think that you should put that knife down?" He stepped forward.

She clenched the knife in both hands. "You stay away from me!"

Charley picked up a bottle of pills from the counter. "This is some heavy shit! I'll bet you can't go too long without this stuff."

"You put those down! They're mine!"

He threw the bottle on the floor. Putting his foot on it, he started to crush it.

Clara threw herself to the floor and grabbed his foot. "No!" she screamed. "Please stop!"

He shook his head as he looked down at her. "You're in worse shape than I thought. I knew that ya were on something when I first saw ya in town. I thought it was just booze. I had no idea that you were a fuckin' addict"

"I have a condition!"

"Yeah. Don't we all. Most people call it an addiction. At least I admit that I'm an alcoholic."

Clara grabbed her pills and got to her feet. She put the island between him and her. "Get out!" she shouted. "Get out of my house before I call the cops!"

Charley walked back to the kitchen table and sat down. "Go ahead. Call em. I'll bet they'd be real interested in what I have ta say. Hit and run. I'll bet we're talking ten, maybe twenty years, here. Call em. I'll wait right here. It will take em a while to get here. Meanwhile, can I have that glass of water? On second thought, how about a glass of that Vodka you've got over there on the counter. You look like ya could use one yourself." He sat down and put his feet up on one of the other chairs.

"My husband will be coming home any minute now!"

"Bullshit! I've been watchin' this place from the woods. I've been watchin' him, but mostly I've been watchin' you. He won't be here much before eight-thirty, nine o'clock. I'll be out of here by then if you just give me what I want."

"What exactly do you want? I don't keep a lot of cash in the house. I don't suppose you would take a check?"

Charley laughed. "What I want has nothing to do with money. Like I said, I've been watching you. You're a real handsome woman. I like that pink thing ya wear ta bed. It shows off yer figure real good. Y'know how long it's been since I've had a woman?"

"You're sick! You don't really think that I would consider sleeping with you, do you?"

"Why not? It could solve both of our problems at the same time. I get what I want. You get what you want."

"And what is it you think I want?"

"Piece of mind, and someone to keep you in pills. If your husband went to jail, without his money coming in; you'd have ta go somewhere and dry out. The first thing they'd do is take away all of your pills. You'd shrivel up and turn into an old hag. Is that what you really want?"

She poured two glasses of Vodka and sat down across from him. "No. I wouldn't want that. Isn't there some other way? I can get you some money. I have some jewelry." She looked at her hands. "I've got this watch. My wedding ring is a full carat. I could tell my husband I lost it."

"Lady, if I had any money I would only spend it on booze. I'd drink myself to death. What I really want is to make love to a woman."

"Maybe I could hire you a prostitute."

He slammed his fist down on the table! "I don't want no fuckin' whore, Lady! I've been watchin' you. I like the way ya move. I like your body. You infatuate me. I want you!"

"I don't think that I could do this. Not what you ask."

Jesus, Lady! It's not like you're a fuckin' virgin, or anything. You've got to be at least forty. I'll bet you fucked a lot of men in your life. What the hell is one more? Close your eyes, if you want; you might even enjoy it. What the hell makes me so different?"

"You're dirty. You smell."

"OK. I'll take a shower."

"You have a beard."

"I'll shave. You're running out of excuses, Lady. You're also running out of time. The simple fact is, either we do it, or I'm turning in your old man for hit-n-run. It's up ta you."

Clara opened up her pill bottle and shook out a couple of pills. She washed them down with a big swallow of Vodka. She started to shake out a couple of more. Charley reached across the table and grabbed her hand.

"If we're gonna do this, I ain't fuckin' no zombie! Are we on or not? I'm running out of patience!"

"Just this once?"

"Just this once."

"Then you'll leave us alone? You won't tell anybody what happened. You won't ask us for any money."

He raised his hand. "Promise . . . Scouts honor."

"You're not going to hurt me, are you?"

"Oh, no, Lady. No kinky shit. Just some sweet, gentle lovin', that's all I want. It's like insurance, Honey. If I turn your husband in, you could get me for rape."

Clara took a deep breath. "Alright," she said, "you go and get cleaned up. I'll meet you in the first spare bedroom. It's upstairs, to the right."

"You're not gonna try to run away, are ya? It won't do ya any good, y'know?"

"No. Let's just get this over with. But after, I never want to see you again. Do I have your word on that?"

"You have a deal"

He leaned over the table and kissed her on the lips. She didn't try to resist him.

He got to his feet. I'll see you in five minutes."

After he left, she took a couple more pills and washed them down with a full glass of Vodka. She went to the spare bedroom, turned

15

down the covers, and stripped to her bra and panties. She sat on the edge of the bed a moment, and tried to think things out. She was crying. She wiped her tears on the sheets. She heard the bathroom door close and Charley singing as he mounted the stairs. Her heart was racing! Carl could never know what she was about to do for him. She kept telling herself that she was doing the right thing. That she was doing it for Carl.

Charley was standing in the doorway wearing only a towel. He was smiling. He let the towel drop to the floor. Clara looked away and he laughed. "You don't have to look at it if you don't want to, Honey," he said. He came forward, sat next to her on the bed, and pulled her toward him. Kissing her passionately, he forced her back onto the bed. He was fumbling with the catch on her bra like an inpatient schoolboy. One hand was on her breast while the other tugged at her panties. His breath was foul as he kissed her harder, his tongue probing her mouth. She couldn't help herself. She threw up!

Charley pulled away and spat. "You fuckin' bitch!" he shouted. He began slapping her hard, over and over.

Clara felt herself beginning to lose consciousness. She brought her knee up, sharply! Charley rolled to the side, holding himself, moaning with pain. Clara managed to get to her feet. She staggered toward the stairway. As she reached the top of the stairs, Charley overtook her. As he lunged at her, she threw herself to the side and fell. Charley tripped over her legs and tumbled head first, down the stairs. She looked at him for a moment. He wasn't moving. She quickly descended the stairs, but as she stepped over him, he grabbed her ankle.

"I'm gonna kill you! You fuckin' bitch!"

Clara was dragging him across the floor, trying to get away. She could hear herself screaming! She turned and kicked him as hard as she could with her bare foot. He let go. The pain was excruciating! She knew she had broken some toes. As she ran to the front door, she looked back and saw him getting to his feet. She knew, now, that if he caught her he would kill her. She opened the door, grabbed a jacket off the coat rack, and ran outside. It was getting dark, and she hoped that if she could make it to the trees, she could hide from him. She ran across the front lawn, over the driveway, down the embankment, and towards the woods. She heard the door slam against the front of the house. She knew that Charley wouldn't be far behind.

Reaching the edge of the woods, she crashed into the trees. The trees and bushes tore at her naked flesh, but she didn't even stop to fasten the jacket. She ran for a ways, then fell to the ground and covered her head with the jacket. She could hear him thrashing the bushes, looking for her.

"You can't hide from me, y'know!" he was yelling. I grew up in these woods. I know every inch of these woods like the back of my hand. I'll track you down, you can be sure of that!"

She held her breath and didn't move. Her only fear was that he would be able to hear her heart beating. She lay there, on the cold ground, for what seemed forever. Suddenly, she could hear the sound of a car. Carl! Carl was home! She was safe! She pulled herself to her feet and made her way toward the sound of the approaching car. All at once she could see the headlights flickering through the trees. Carl was coming up the driveway. She began to run through the trees, toward the driveway. Just as she broke through the tree line, a hand reached out and grabbed her jacket.

"Told ya, ya couldn't hide from me!"

He started to pull her back into the woods. She slipped out of the jacket and ran toward the driveway. It was only about forty feet away. She had to get there before Carl drove on by. She could hear the sound of footsteps close behind her. She didn't look back. She ran as hard as she could. When she reached the embankment, she climbed it on her hands and knees. She crashed through the bushes at the side of the drive and jumped in front of the car.

Carl set down the cell phone. *Why doesn't she answer,* he wondered. He looked up just in time to see something white loom in front of his headlights. "What the hell is that?" he shouted. "A ghost?" He swerved as the windshield shattered! The car slammed into a large pine and rolled down the embankment. It rolled over four times and landed on its side. Carl struggled to free himself from the seatbelt. The smell of gas was strong.

"Looks like ya got yourself in one hell of a mess, Mister."

Carl saw a man standing in the light of the still glowing, headlights. He was completely naked except for the windbreaker he was holding in his hand.

"Help me," Carl pleaded, "I seem to be caught."

"Do say," the man replied. He slipped the jacket on and zipped it up. From one of the pockets he retrieved a pack of matches. He rolled it around in his fingers. He then held it in front of one of the headlights. "The Grub-n-Grog," he said, reading the match cover. "I ate there a couple of times. Nice place."

Please help me," Carl pleaded, again. "I think my leg is jammed under the dash."

"I'd really like ta help ya, Mister." He spread his arms. "But as you can see, I need ta find me some clothes." He ripped a match from the pack, studied it for a moment, and then struck it.

"No!" Carl screamed.

"Got ta go." He tossed the match toward the car, and stepped back as it burst into flames. As he walked toward the house, the sound of Carl's screams eventually stopped.

He found some clothes in the bedroom and put them on. The pants were a little short, but the silk shirt fit him well. He took the bottle of Vodka, sat in the kitchen, and watched through the big bay window, until the fire burned down. "Sure don't need no forest fires," he said aloud. He finished the Vodka, found a half-empty bottle of Scotch in the dining room, and opened the front door to leave.

She was standing there, bloody and still naked, a double-bit ax held over her head!

"Jesus!" He put out his hand to stop the ax, but it cut through his wrist easily and lodged deep within his stomach. He fell backward, crashing into the dining room furniture still piled in the center of the room.

She threw the ax to the floor and knelt down beside him. "What's the matter, Charley? You don't look happy to see me. You weren't planning on leaving, were you? Did you forget? We have some unfinished business. Now that you've killed my husband, I'm a free woman. Now, I can be with you, always." She threw herself against him, grabbed him by the hair, and kissed him hard and long. "What's the matter, Charley? Not in the mood anymore? I just want to give you what you've got coming. This is what you wanted, isn't it? Well, here I am. I'm all yours. What is it, my face?" She wiped her hands over her face and they came away bloody. "Well, you'd look this way too, if you just went through a windshield." She pried the bottle of Scotch from his hand. "I've got an idea. Let's play spin-the-bottle. That ought to get you in the mood. But first, we have to empty the bottle. I'll go first." Clara removed the top and took a long drink. "OK," she said, "now it's your turn."

She held up his head and poured some of the Scotch into his mouth. He gagged and coughed, bringing up a gush of blood.

"You really ought to do something about that cough, Charley." She sat next to him on the floor and took another long drink. "Now, I know this great doctor in Boston. He can cure just about anything. I highly recommend him. He can cure anything but death, of course. You're not going to die on me, are you Charley? You can't do that. We haven't done the nasty yet. I so want to please you, Charley. Have you ever done it in the shower? We both could use a good cleaning up. Maybe after?" She looked around and took another drink. "How about in the middle of the dining room floor?"

She straddled him and looked into his face. His mouth was open and his eyes were fixed blankly on the ceiling. She grabbed him by the hair and shook his head violently.

"Charley! Don't you go leaving me, now, Charley! You son-of-a-bitch! You're no fucking fun when you're dead!" She let go and let his lifeless head crash against the floor. She took another deep swallow of Scotch. "I lied to you, Charley. I didn't want you, anyway. Not really."

Getting to her feet, she retreated to the corner by the door. Bathed in fresh blood, she sat with her knees tucked against her chest. She rocked back and forth as she drank the last of the Scotch, and cried.

"Now, look what you've done, Charley!" she shouted, between sobs. "You've killed my husband, ruined my life, and God knows what my face must look like. What am I going to do, now, Charley? You were road kill, Charley! You should have stayed road kill. You shouldn't have come back." She threw the empty bottle at his lifeless body. "This time, you son-of-a-bitch, you had better stay dead!"

Hope Springs Nocturnal

The Letter:

My Dearest Love,

If you have received this letter I am no longer within this earthly realm and you, the world, and I are far better off because of it. As I write this, I am in a retched state and the progress of my malady has left me unable to tend to my most basic needs. I yearn to lay eyes upon your soft face and sweet smile, yet shutter at the thought of you seeing me in such an emaciated state. I have become a hideous monster that even a mother would disavow.

Forgive me, my love, for withholding from you my most grievous affliction. I did so love you that I wanted you not to know the true manner of man, or beast, which wooed you and longed to take your hand in marriage. I know, now, how selfish that was, and how impossible that dream. I now pay the price of that folly.

The whole horrible story came into play four years ago as I traveled, one night, the lonely road between Cambridge and Hawthorn. I scarcely had rounded a bend in the road, when a frightening abhorrence emerged from the dark shadows of the surrounding forest. It leapt to my carriage, and in the bright moonlight, I could see the white teeth and dark, hairy face of a wolf looming before me. I beat it back with my crop, but not before I felt its sharp teeth bite deeply into my shoulder. It fell from my carriage as I goaded the horses on and away from that horrid place.

I found an inn where the kindly mistress tended to my wound. She told me stories of werewolves, and how, for this reason, the locals never travel at night under a full moon. I laughed it off, and assured her that this was just an ordinary wolf; although, I had never known a lone wolf to be so audacious. The effects of the bite turned more grievous a few days later upon returning home, and I succumbed to a persistent fever the veracity of which nearly took my life.

In a fortnight I had fully recovered, but then a strange thing happened. I awoke one morning to find myself sprawled upon the floor of my room. My clothing was rent and covered with blood. I was uninjured, so I knew it wasn't mine. It was on the morning following the full moon, and you can imagine what thoughts were passing through my mind.

I recalled the Innkeepers stories of men, once bitten, becoming werewolves themselves; and how, by the light of the full moon, they prowled the night looking for victims. I tried to dismiss it as hogwash, but how could I explain the condition of my clothing and the blood on my hands? I vowed to find the truth, even if it was not what I wanted to know.

I had the gardener construct a large, sturdy box of heavy planks. It was then brought to my study and a cot was placed inside. The front was hung on three large hinges, and was to be secured with two large hasps and two sturdy padlocks. On the eve of the full moon, I asked the butler to lock me in for the night, and made it clear that no one was to enter the study until morning.

However, the next morning I found myself in the garden. My clothes were again ripped and bloody. I went to my room, washed and changed; then I went to the study. I couldn't believe the sight that awaited me. The box lay opened; the locks intact. The door had been ripped from its hinges. Inside the box, it was evident that the wood had been set upon with huge claws and the door ripped asunder by a force strong enough to tear a sturdy, six by two as if it were a twig. The staff left me that day. I could not blame them.

I boarded up the house and moved south. My thoughts were that this land was cursed and by moving I could leave it behind. It seemed to work. The sunny climate and more cheerful atmosphere had a positive effect on my health and disposition.

This was, also, when I met you; sweet, wonderful, Hope. My life had changed forever.

On the eve of the full moon, I retired to my small apartment, as I had done every night. I threw open the window, also, as I had done every night, said a small prayer for my next victim, and hoped that it would be someone of poor moral character.

I awoke the next morning, exhausted, as I had many other mornings. My nightclothes were intact, and other than the wrinkled appearance of an, obviously, restless night, pristine. There was no blood on my clothing or my hands other than a few drops on the pillow from an injury to my neck. The marks on my neck indicated that I might have been a victim of a bat. What irony, I thought, that I could be a victim of a bat, who may, now, be a victim of me. What if it were to turn into a werebat? How ironic that I could find such humor in my plight.

As the weeks went by, my love for you grew, even as I grew weaker each night. But each night I threw the window open wide in anticipation of the accursed bat that seemed to be drawing the malignancy from my body. "Do your worst, you persistent, night flier, for on the verge of death I shall, again, find life!"

How aberrant it was to awaken, just a fortnight ago, to find your lovely face looming before me as I lay there, unable to move, while you licked the last of my blood from your rubicund lips. How irreverent it was that I could be both your lover and your lunch.

So, here I lie, irreparably damaged, with the evils of two curses tearing away at the very fabric of my blood, leaving me jaundiced and putrid. Perhaps, in time, you can find it in your heart to forgive me, my love, as I have forgiven you. For as my blood is tainted so is yours, and in time you too will succumb. A vampire and a werewolf are such unlikely bedfellows. Maybe, in another life, we can find peace.

With eternal love,
Joshua Crane

COOTER

Cooter's real name was Tobias Owen Paxton III. Now why anybody would want to name three people Tobias is beyond me. He got the name "Cooter" because of his love for turtles, any kind of turtles, even gopher turtles; the latter of which he was real good at catching. Besides, a guy as big and mean looking as Cooter, you don't want to call Tobias. Now Cooter would load up his old '79, Ford pickup with a plastic trashcan and a snatch pole and drive around the backcountry, graded roads until he would spot a gopher turtle hole. He had this knack for being able to spot them, even if he was doing fifty miles an hour, which Cooter seldom did, as this he would consider poking along. He'd jam on his brakes, back up the shoulder for fifty feet or so, and there ten to twenty feet off the road would, more often than not, be a gopher turtle hole. Now I probably shouldn't be telling you this because gopher turtles . . . which are actually tortoises . . . are kind of considered endangered, and there is a major fine if you're caught with one.

Just about two years ago . . . it was on a Saturday . . . Cooter asked me if I would like to go with him gopher hunting. Now, I had nothing in particular I needed to get done that day, seeing as the calendar indicated that it was not a particularly good day for fishing, so I decided to tag along. Besides, ole Cooter always had this cooler full of ice-cold beer in the back of the pickup, and it was a hot day in mid-July. I have never been known to pass up a cold beer on a hot day, or on a cold day, for that matter. By noon we had caught a good-sized gopher and were well into our third six-pack. We were headed, back home, down this dusty road when Cooter let out a war hoop and jammed on his brakes!

"Did y'see that?" he asked, all excited like.

"See what?" I was looking all around and I didn't see a thing'.

"Back there," he said. "Biggest damn gopher hole I've ever seen."

He backed up the pickup and there, about twenty feet off the road, was a huge gopher hole. It had to be about three feet in diameter. There was this mountain of dirt kicked up in front of the hole that must have been over six feet high. Cooter got out and grabbed the snatch pole along with a cold beer out of his cooler. I was right behind him with the plastic trashcan and a cool one of my own. When I got there, Cooter was on one knee peering down the hole.

"How big do y'reckon he is?" I asked.

Cooter looked around at the scratch marks in the sand. "Seventy or eighty pounds," he replied, "maybe more." He took a box of snuff from his back pocket and stuffed a good pinch up under his lip.

I whistled. "Shit!" I said. "I ain't never seen one that big."

"Me neither," admitted Cooter, "but this one has to be huge. He's got himself one hell of a hole. This has got to be the grand-daddy of all cooters"

He took a long drink of his beer, set the can down carefully on top of the sand pile, and picked up the long snatch pole. What it was, was a ten-foot length of PVC pipe with a rope running down through the center, and the end taped to the outside with a whole lot of "duck" tape. He made the loop real big and fished the pole down into the hole. I could see the concentration on his face as he maneuvered the pole around inside the hole. To, Cooter, that pole was like an extension of his own arm.

"Hang on!" he shouted. "I think I've got me somethin'."

He wiggled the pole back and forth turning the handle, and then, with a quick snap, he pulled the rope tight!

"Got em!" he shouted.

Cooter got to his feet and started walking backward with the pole. He had gone about five feet when the pole suddenly lunged forward. Cooter fell to his knees and skidded about three feet.

"Give me a hand, here!" he shouted. "This sucker's bigger than even I imagined."

I grabbed the end of the pole and the rope and helped Cooter pull. The gopher, or whatever it was, started to come out of the hole. Just as we could start to see something on the end of the rope, it jerked back and snatched Cooter right into the end of the hole. I was right behind him, lying on his legs.

This son-of-a-bitch is strong!" he said. "I ain't never had no gopher do that before." He got to his feet. "Here," he said, slacking off the rope a bit. "You go an take the end of this rope and tie it to the back of the pickup. I'll stay here and hold it until ya get it hooked up."

I got into the pickup, backed it around, and hooked the rope to the trailer hitch. Cooter was standing right in front of the hole holding on to the end of the pole.

"OK," he yelled, over his shoulder, "start pullin' him out, easy."

I got back into the truck, put it in low, and eased it forward. I could see Cooter in the rear view mirror, still hanging onto the pole, and slowly walking backward.

"He's comin'!" he shouted back over his shoulder. "Keep er goin'!"

The front wheels were on the road and I could feel the rear tires starting to slip.

"Holy shit!" I heard Cooter scream. "Will ya look at this thing?"

But before I could look back the truck lunged backward, throwing me hard against the steering wheel. When I looked back, Cooter was gone! I jumped from the truck, and ran back and grabbed the end of the rope. At first there was some resistance, but as I pulled, I felt the rope let loose and I went sprawling to the ground. When I pulled up the rope it looked like it had been cut clean in two.

I got down on my hands and knees and shouted down the hole for Cooter.

"Cooter, are you all right?" I shouted. There was no answer.

I didn't know what to do, so I got into Cooter's truck and drove as fast as I could to his father's farm. Bubba Paxton was a big man who made a good living raising peanuts and watermelons on a hundred and fifty acre spread that had been in the family since God knows when. Cooter had told me that his great granddad fought alongside Marion, himself, when they ran the Yankees out of Florida. To this day, none of the Paxtons have ever had any use for Yankees, especially Bubba. I never had the heart to tell him that Frances Marion, the man they named Marion County after, never fought the Yankees. He was called "The Swamp Fox" and fought in the Revolutionary War. Cooter wasn't the kind of guy who took kindly to being corrected, anyhow, so relating what was one of the few historical facts I actually knew would not earn me any points with him.

Bubba was bush hogging weeds on his John Deere when I found him. He didn't believe me, at first, when I told him what happened. He looked at me and then at the beer can I was holding tightly in my shaking hand.

"How many of them things have you had this mornin', boy?" he asked. But when I showed him the rope still attached to Cooter's truck he began to wonder. "Were'd ya say this cooter hole was?" he asked, looking at the gnawed end of the rope, like he was Sherlock Holmes, himself.

"About a mile down on that old dirt road that runs through the Bailer Farm," I explained. He got into the pickup and we drove back to the house. He loaded up Cooter's pit bull, Conan, grabbed his twelve-gage, and went inside to get Cooter's younger brother, Jimmy. Jimmy came out and climbed up into the cab. He had his own four-ten/twenty-two, over and under and lots of ammo for each gun. They were ready for anything. I hopped into the back with Conan. Jimmy had to run about two-sixty and Bubba was about two-ninety. With those two and their guns, there wasn't much room in the cab for me. The big pit bull moved toward me and gave me this look. One thing about Conan, you never knew if he was going to lick you or rip out your throat. I was lucky, today he was feeling friendly.

We turned onto the dirt road and Conan and I slid across the truck bed and slammed into the side. Tires were spinning and dirt was flying for thirty feet. Bubba had the pedal to the metal and was not about to spare the horsepower. I leaned through the sliding back window and pointed out the dirt pile to him. He ran Cooter's truck up onto the pile before he stopped. The both of them jumped from the truck, guns in hand, and ran to the hole.

"Where the hell you at, Cooter!" Bubba yelled down the hole. He turned to me, "Now this ain't no joke is it LeRoy? Cause if it is, you ken see, I ain't laughin' none!"

"No," I assured him, "this ain't no joke, Mr. Paxton. Cooter's damn sure down there!"

Bubba snatched Conan by the collar and looked him right in the eye. "Now, y'all go git Cooter, boy," he said. "Y'hear me? Go git Cooter!"

The dog turned and high-tailed it down the hole. You could hear his deep, throaty bark all the way down. It made kind of an echoing sound. Suddenly he stopped barking. We all looked at each other for a moment. Then, from deep down the hole, came this awful growl that made the hair stand up on the back of my neck. We could hear Conan's deep bark and low growl, as if in answer. There was the sound of a scuffle, then the sound of Conan's whimpering whine that seemed to get closer every second. He came shooting out of the hole, and as he flew by, I could see that he was missing an ear, his tail and a chunk out of his left hindquarters. He never stopped when Bubba called out his name, but continued running on up the road until we could no longer hear his tormented yelps.

"It must be somethin' terrible mean down there," Bubba said, as he watched after the dog. He ran his hand through his bushy, salt and pepper beard. "I ain't never seen nothin' that Conan was afraid of."

That was a fact. The only thing that dog was afraid of, until now, was Cooter. Cooter was the kind of dog owner that demanded complete obedience from his dogs. He once shot Conan with his twenty-gage for killing his favorite hound dog. He gathered up Conan and rushed him to the vet with tears flowing from his eyes as if he were about to lose his best friend. The vet bill was staggering, but Cooter didn't bat an eye.

"What do we do now, Pa?" Jimmy asked.

"We go get Tom Lankey," Bubba said, "and have him bring out his backhoe. We'll dig him out of there, if it takes all night". He turned to me, "You stay here and watch the hole, boy." He handed me his twelve-gage. "If anything, but Cooter, comes out of that hole, y'all shoot it! We'll be back in a bit."

I stayed and watched the hole, like he said, but I wasn't too sure why. If anything came out of that hole, and it wasn't Cooter, I wasn't gonna stay around long enough to find out what it was. It must have taken them an hour to get back, but when they returned, I could hear a whole parcel of trucks coming up the road. When they came into sight, I could see Bubba in the lead. He was driving his blue Chevy. Jimmy was behind in Cooter's old Ford, and behind him was Tom Lankey with his flatbed truck, towing a lowboy trailer with his backhoe.

Tom pulled up behind the two pickups and unloaded the backhoe from the lowboy. He backed the backhoe up beside the pile of dirt and set down his pads. Reaching over to the hole he started digging. After a few minutes the bucket hit something more solid than the soft sand he had been digging. Tom brought up a bucket full of limerock. In a few more minutes he had cleared away all the sand and we could see what looked like the opening to a large cave.

"I'll be damned! Look at that!" Bubba had his Seminole Feed hat off and was scratching his bald head. "I ain't never seen no caves around here, before."

Tom Lankey had shut the backhoe down and was now standing in front of the hole with the rest of us. "Hello!" he yelled. "Is there anybody there?" You could hear his words echoing over again and again. "Must be big," he said. "Maybe as big as that one there in Kentucky."

"Son-bitch! Son-bitch!" was all Bubba could say, while Jimmy and I just stood there feeling a cold breeze coming from down in that cave that must have gone halfway to China.

"What'er we gonna do, Pa?" Jimmy asked, breaking the silence.

Bubba snatched the twelve-gage from my hand. "We're goin' in and get Cooter, boy. That's what we're gonna do!" He started into the cave.

Tom grabbed his arm. "I wouldn't be too hasty, Bubba," he said. "We just can't go runnin' down that hole. It's bound ta be darker than midnight up a coon's ass down there. Besides, we don't know nothin' about explorin' no caves. We don't know what kind of stuff we'd be gettin' into. Why don't I get my cell-phone outa my truck and call up Walt Buehler. Now he's got the know-how and the equipment ta do this right."

Bubba thought for a long while. "Maybe yer right, Tom," he said. "In the meantime I'm gonna go back and get us some more guns and some lights. We've got no idea what we might run into down there. We sure as hell need to be ready for anything."

Now, I was very surprised that Bubba would grasp Tom's suggestion so readily. Walt already had two strikes against him. First of all, he was a Yankee. He originally haled from New York, New Jersey; one of those "New" states and he was what they call a spelunker. Now, that's a person who likes to crawl around in caves and holes in the ground, like some overgrown worm. It wasn't like he did it for a living or anything. He did it just for the fun of it. Bubba felt that this was sure a weird idea of what was fun, and that a lack of good sense was a good requisite. I went with him, talked him into stopping at the convenience store, and sprung for a six-pack, a bag of ice, and one of those soggy hoagies. It looked like it was going to be a long day.

We got back about twenty minutes later, just ahead of Walt Buehler's four-wheel-drive. Bubba gave Walt the "hi" sign, but refused a handshake. Walt didn't push the issue, figuring perhaps that challenging a redneck with a truckload of guns might be as fruitful as running through a trench full of pigmy rattlers.

Walt got down in front of the hole, shined his flashlight inside, and surveyed the situation. "Not a cave," he said. "Looks to me like this were dug."

"Ya mean, ya think that somebody dug this hole?"

"No," Walt replied, "not 'somebody', something."

"What in hell could dig through solid limerock?" Bubba asked.

"I have no idea," Walt took a closer look. "These sure look like claw marks to me."

"Pick marks, maybe," Tom said, seeing how nervous Walt was becoming. "Probably one of those old prospectors, back years ago, lookin' for phosphate."

"I guess it could have been," Walt confessed.

"Had ta be," said Bubba. "Ain't no critter can dig through solid limerock."

"OK," Walt said. "Let's get going."

Now me, I didn't want no part of that big, cold, dark hole in the ground, but my buddy, Cooter, was down there and I guess we needed to get him out. Besides, I didn't want the rest of them thinking I was scared, even though I was . . . real scared. I don't much like the dark. Not the kind of dark that was awaiting us in that cave. This is the kind of dark where you can't even see your hand in front of your face. No, I sure wasn't looking forward to this. I knew, that the first time I confronted the thing that was causing all this trouble, I would just piss my pants. I went over behind Tom Lankey's tractor, took a long wiz and cussed myself for drinking that last cold beer. What the hell, the ice was melting and no one else seemed to be thirsty. It's not good for beer to get warm once it's been cooled down, you know. The heat will give it a "funky" taste. Just ask any beer drinker.

Walt laid a whole bunch of gear out across the tailgate of his truck. There were ropes, those helmets with little lights on them, big flashlights, and tool belts with all kinds of goodies. I took a big flashlight and Bubba handed me his thirty-aught-six. He thought for a minute, and then he took back the thirty-aught-six and handed me his twelve-gage. After a while he took back the twelve-gage and handed me the thirty-aught-six again. "Makes a bigger hole at close range," he explained.

Walt assigned us each to a position and we started on down. I didn't much care for the idea of being "dead" last, "dead" being the significant word here; although, I was glad that Walt was first. Maybe being last wouldn't be so bad if what-ever-it-was came at us straight on. I just hoped it wasn't the kind of critter that liked to sneak up behind people. I spent a lot of time looking back and ended up running into Tom three times.

At first it was a steep tunnel and we had to stoop a few times to keep from bumping our heads. We must have followed it for over half an hour, twisting and turning, ducking and squeezing, and working our way through some really tight places It was hard to tell how steep it was, but my feet were beginning to hurt from being jammed into the end of my sneakers. Then, suddenly, it leveled off and we were standing inside a very large chamber. Everyone was shining his flashlight around. From what I could see, it was forty, fifty feet wide, with lots of stalactites and stalagmites. There were passages that led off in all directions. We stopped and Walt set down his gear.

"OK everybody," he said. "I want you all to cup your hands, and on the count of three, yell 'Cooter' as loud as you can. Ready? One-two-three."

"**COOTER!**" We all yelled, in one loud voice.

"Again!" he yelled.

"**COOTER!**" we yelled again.

From somewhere down in the bowels of the cave came a loud roar!

"What the hell was that?" Walt's face turned almost white, quite evident even in the faint light. He looked at Bubba. "What was that, Bubba?"

Bubba said nothing.

"That's the thing that pulled Cooter down the hole and bit a chunk out of Conan's ass," I volunteered. Everybody looked at me like I had just said something wrong. "Well, I didn't know it was such a damn secret," I added.

Walt shined his light in Tom Lankey's face. "You said we were looking for Cooter. You never mentioned anything about any monsters. What the hell is this thing?"

"We ain't got no idea," Bubba finally informed him. But, no matter what it is, we got enough fire power to handle it." He held up his twelve-gage, and then, after he thought for a minute, he swapped it with me for his thirty-aught-six. "Good for bigger game." He explained.

"These caves sometimes lead right into the aquifer," Walt informed us. "There's no telling what could be down here. There could be things that haven't seen the light of day since the days of the dinosaurs. How do you know if that rifle will even slow it down?"

Bubba reached into the pack he had slung around his shoulder. "Well, I'm pretty sure this will stop it," he said, waving two sticks of dynamite under Walt's nose.

"You're all a bunch of lunatics!" he shouted. "You can't set that dynamite off down here! If it didn't blow you right out of the cave, like shot out of a cannon, there's a good chance you could bring the roof down on top of us! I'm not going any further. I'm going on back, now."

"But you can't leave us here alone," Tom Lankey pleaded. "How, the hell, are we going to find our way back out of here?"

Walt took off his pack and handed it to Bubba. "In this pack are a bunch of little lights. They're like the ones that the road department uses on their barricades, only much smaller. These will burn for weeks on one penlight battery. They come with a little spike so you can tack them up on the wall. Put one every so often, and they will help you find your way out. If you do get lost, just keep turning to the left and then the right, never in the same direction. Eventually you should come back to the same place. I'm out of here. I think you're all nuts. When I get back, I'll tell the Sheriff what you're up to. I'm sure he'll send some help." He gathered up the rest of his stuff and started back toward the entrance. "I wish you luck," he said over his shoulder. Before he left, he handed me his compass. "North by north-east is the way you're headed, now," he almost whispered. I fought back an overpowering urge to go with him.

Bubba stepped over the pack and walked to the outside wall. He spit a big gob of tobacco juice onto the wall. It ran down in a long streak, making a brown line on the white, limerock wall. He reached into his back pocket and pulled out his can of dip. "Long as I got plenty of juice, I don't think I'll have no problem markin' the way." He looked back as the light from Walt's lantern faded out of sight. "Damn Yankee," he muttered. He injected a shell into the chamber of his thirty-aught-six and started forward. We followed along behind, like lambs to the slaughter. As I passed the pack, I stopped and picked it up. The cave turned abruptly to the right. I took one of those little lights and fastened it to the wall. In the next hour, we passed it three times.

"We're goin' around in circles," Bubba finally admitted. "I spit on this same spot twice all ready. We need ta split up and each take a shaft. The first one ta spot Cooter, give a holler, or fire off yer gun."

"Couldn't we go in groups of two?" I asked, not really wanting to be left alone.

"Y'all ain't scared, is ya, LeRoy?" Jimmy asked, nudging me in the ribs with his elbow."

"Hell no!" I yelled. "I ain't scared of nothin'! I just was thinkin' that if someone got into trouble the other could go fer help. They call that 'the buddy system'."

"Turn off yer lights!" Bubba demanded. "Turn em off! All of em."

We did what he said and turned off all our lights.

"Now," he said, "this is what Cooter's experiencing right now. He ain't got no light. He don't even know which way is up. You can imagine how scary it must be for him. We got ta find him, fast, before he goes plumb loco."

Bubba made a good point. Jimmy was so close I could smell the tobacco on his breath, but I couldn't see him. I couldn't see my hand laid flat against my nose. Like Bubba said, it was real scary. I was glad when we turned our lights back on. I began to wonder how long the batteries would last.

I took the passage to the right. I set one of the little lights in the end of the tunnel, where I started, and another just before the last one was out of sight. I kept placing the lights until I ran out. I looked around for something to use for a marker. I found what looked like a round, brown rock, but when I picked it up, I realized that it was some kind of animal dung. *I hope the hell this ain't Cooter!* I thought. Then I realized, it had only been a few hours. Cooter wouldn't look like that for at least another day or so.

The tunnel went on straight, so I decided to go on until it branched off again, then I would worry about finding something to mark it with. It wasn't long before the tunnel came to an abrupt end at the beginning of what looked like the aquifer. I could see moving water. There was no way of telling just how deep it was, but it became quite evident that there was no way of going any further without some kind of diving gear. I turned around and started back. I had just reached the last light I had placed, and was just about to retrieve it, when I heard a strange sound. It made the hair stand up on the back of my neck. At first, I didn't know what it was. Then it dawned on me! It was the sound of a man whimpering! Cooter? Could this be Cooter?

It was coming from one of the branch tunnels to the right. I picked up the marker light and set it in the entrance to the tunnel. Cautiously, I started down the tunnel. "Cooter?" I yelled. The whimpering stopped.

"LeRoy? That you?" came a familiar voice.

"Cooter, where are ya?" I shouted back.

"Right here!"

The voice was close. I shined the light around, but saw nothing. "Right where?"

"Up here!" he shouted.

I shined the light up the wall. There was Cooter wedged into a small crevice in the wall. "What ya doin' there?" I asked.

"What the hell ya think I'm doin' up here, LeRoy. I'm hidin' of course. Now, help me down outa here."

I bent down so that Cooter could step down on my back and jump safely to the floor. "How'd the hell did ya get way up there in the first place, Cooter?" I asked.

"I lept!" he said.

"Way up there?"

"When yer scared enough, y'all can do some amazing' things."

"How'd the hell ya know the crevice was up there?" I asked.

"If you turn off the flashlight, you'll see that that crack goes all the way to the surface. Y'all can see the light shining down from above."

"So what is this critter, anyway, Cooter?"

"I ain't got no idea."

"Y'mean ya never saw it?"

"I heard it, I felt its tongue lickin' at my feet, I could smell its hot, foul breath, but I never got a look at it. It's too damn dark in here. All I know is that it was big enough to reach that crevice, and too big to fit inside. Which is good, leastwise I wouldn't be here to tell ya about it. Now let's get the hell out of here, before it comes back."

"We have ta go find the others, first."

"What others?" Cooter looked puzzled.

"Bubba, Jimmy and Tom Lankey."

"Well, let's get the hell out of here, then. Which way do we go?" he asked.

"We just need to follow those little lights."

"What lights?" Cooter asked."

"Those little blinkin' lights on the wall," I informed him, but when I looked I could see no light. "Where the hell's the light?" I asked. "I put one down the end of the passage."

Cooter was getting mad at me. "How the hell would I know? I got no idea what you're talkin' about."

I shined my flashlight down the end of the passage. Suddenly, I began to realize why I could no longer see the light as the hair stood up on the back of my neck! There was something big and dark standing in front of it!

"Cooter," I whispered.

"What?"

"RRRUUUNNNNNN!"

I started off down the tunnel as fast as I could go. I could hear Cooter right on my heels. At least, I was hoping it was Cooter. There was a sharp bend to the right and I took it. About twenty feet down, it came to an abrupt end! I tried to turned just as Cooter ran into me, knocking the breath out of me.

"Why'd ya stop?" he asked.

I shined the flashlight at the wall. "There's no place to go." I could hear movement behind us. I turned and shined the flashlight on the entrance to the short tunnel. There was something coming toward us. It was moving slowly and it looked as big as a house. I could see a head as big as a Volkswagen with rows of long, sharp teeth that gleamed white in the light of my shaking flashlight. It opened its mouth and lunged at us! I knew it was all over for us, but about five feet away, its head wedged in the narrow passage.

Cooter and I were jumping up and down and cheering loudly.

"He can't get us!" I was shouting, "His head's too big. Now don't that beat all?"

Cooter was dancing around and shouting, "Nah-nah-nah-nah-nah-nah. What's the matter big guy, can't ya get us?"

Just then, the creature lifted up one of his legs and dug its long claws into the rock wall. A large chunk of wall gave way like it was made out of corn flakes.

"Shit, Cooter, he's gonna dig his way in here and get us for sure!"

"Shoot em!" Cooter yelled.

"What?"

"Shoot the damn thing!"

In the excitement I had completely forgotten that I was carrying Cooter's old man's shotgun. I handed Cooter the flashlight. I didn't even bother to aim; I just lowered the gun and pulled the trigger. How could I miss anything as big as this? I saw sparks on his head where the buckshot hit and heard the ricochets as they bounced off, hitting the rock wall a couple of times until one finally dislodged a piece of limerock not two feet from my head.

"Shoot him again, LeRoy!" Cooter yelled as he slid in behind me.

"I'm not too sure that's such a good idea," I said, "seein' as the ricochets from the first shot came close to hittin' us."

"Go ahead, LeRoy," Cooter urged, "I'm willin' ta take that chance. Shoot fer one of the eyes, or give the gun ta me and let me do it."

The light from the flashlight was moving up and down so fast it looked like a strobe light, proving to me that Cooter's hand was no steadier than mine. I figured it might be better to die from the pellets than to be chewed up by the jaws of this huge whats-a-ma-jigger. I held the gun as steady as I could, took careful aim, and squeezed the trigger slowly like my granddaddy had always told me to do. How I managed to miss those huge eyes I don't know, but the blast caught the monster dead center on his huge snout. He made a funny sound as he backed out of our little tunnel. We could hear him hightailing it away from us at a pretty good pace.

"Y'all did good, LeRoy," Cooter was saying. "He's on the run, now. Let's get the hell out of here."

I wasn't so sure we had really gained a whole lot. I didn't want to stay here, but the thought of going in the same direction as the monster made my spine tingle. It was pretty much a matter of "damned if you do", or "damned if you don't". I cocked the gun and we made our way slowly back to the larger corridor. Cooter was behind me with the flashlight. We peered around the corner, but saw nothing of the monster.

Meanwhile, I found out later, Walt Buehler had made his way back home, called the Sheriff's office, told them what was going on, and offered to meet them at the entrance to the cave. Walt and the two deputies showed up just as Hank Bailer arrived with his two sons,

Travis and Cordell, as well as his oldest daughter Maxine, who could cuss, dip, and drink as good as any man.

"What the dad-burn's goin' on here?" he asked. "My daughter, Maxine, is goin' into town and comes back to tell me that Tom Lankey's got a backhoe out here, digging up my side lot. She tells me that there's a whole bunch of people, includin' Bubba Paxton and his boy, Jimmy, and they're loaded down with guns, flashlights, and all kinds of stuff. I want to know what's goin' on!"

The first deputy, whose nametag read 'Sergeant William Truman', took a small pad and pen from his top pocket. "And who might you be?" he asked.

"My name is Hank Bailer," he answered, angrily. "I own all the land around here, and you're all guilty of trespassin'!"

"Well, Mr. Bailer," Sergeant Truman said, "it appears that a young man has turned up missing in your cave, here."

"What cave?" Hank Bailer looked puzzled. "There's no cave here."

Sergeant Truman walked over to where his partner was already shining a flashlight into the hole. "What would you call this?"

"Looks ta me like a sinkhole," Hank said, now bent down with his three kids beside him looking down into the black abyss. "Don't recall there ever bein' one here before."

"Mr. Buehler stated that he was down in that hole with several others and he heard what sounded like a large animal. Do you have any idea what he might be talking about?"

"Well," Hank looked at the size of the hole, "it's big enough that a small cow could have wandered into it. That's fer sure."

"It sure didn't sound like a cow to me, Mr. Bailer," Walt Buehler interjected. "It was a sound that just about scared the bejesus out of me."

"Hell, boy," Hank explained, "when you're down in those caves sound gets distorted. A cow could sound like almost anything."

"Believe me, Mr. Bailer," Walt Buehler insisted, "this wasn't any cow."

"Well then, I suspect we oughta get on down there an find out just what it is." Hank turned to his two sons. "You boys go back ta the house and bring back rope, lights and our four best huntin' rifles."

"I really don't think that's a good Idea, Mr. Bailer," Sergeant Truman had removed his hat and was wiping the sweat from his brow. "Walt, here, tells me that there are four people, with guns, already down there."

"Five, Walt corrected, you forgot Cooter Paxton."

"Ain't y'all forgettin', Sergeant, this here is still my property and if I say I'm fixin' ta go down that hole, you or nobody else has the right ta stop me." He waved his hand behind him. "Now you boys go fetch them guns, like I said."

The two climbed into the pickup and left in a hurry, leaving a cloud of dust all the way up the road.

Sergeant Truman was here to "serve and protect". He sent his young deputy, Chris Davenport, back to the patrol car, for the riot guns. Chris could see Maxine Bailer looking him over. It made him feel like he was a choice steak, simmering on a barbeque. Chris was tall, about six-two with crisp blue eyes, and a schoolboy complexion which made him look much younger than his twenty-six years. He was shy and not too secure around the ladies. Maxine Bailer, however, would be a lot of woman for any man.

She was a big woman. She stood five-eleven and weighed one hundred and sixty-five pounds. Yet there was not an ounce of fat on her body. Her barrel chest and massive shoulders she got from shoeing horses on her father's farm. Her T-shirt showed off her rippling biceps and bulging forearms. Except for the obvious presents of breasts, she had a perfect body, if she were of another gender.

Sprouting from this mass of muscle and sinew; however, protruded the face of an angel. Blond and tan, she looked very much the perfect cover picture for "Muscle Weekly". The fact that Chris was looking back both confused and perplexed him. Was he looking at her as a "her" or her as a "he"? Deep down inside he was beginning to doubt his own sexual preference.

Small talk percolated until the boys returned. Gear was distributed and the moment of truth was at hand.

"Want you up front, with me, Maxine," Hank was saying.

"I think that we should go first," Sergeant Truman argued.

"Ken you shoot the eye out of a gnat at fifty feet?" Hank asked.

"Well no." Sergeant Truman admitted.

"Well Maxine can. She's a regular Annie Oakley. Got a quarter?"

The sergeant fumbled around in his pocket, but found no quarter. Chris handed him one of his.

"Go ahead, Sergeant, throw it up," Hank insisted.

The Sergeant threw the quarter as high as he could. No sooner had it reached its apex and started back down, than the sunlight caught it. Just then Maxine pulled the trigger and the quarter jumped into oblivion.

"Well," Hank explained, "she does better with a twenty-two. Ya can see it bounce. Hittin' it with a thirty-thirty, don't leave a whole lot left ta bounce, an it ain't quite as sporting. Bigger bullet."

The sergeant realized that his mouth was wide open when a portion of drool fell upon his freshly starched shirt. He dapped at it quickly with his handkerchief. Chris was impressed. This time when Maxine smiled at him, he smiled back.

The show over, the group fired up their flashlights, shouldered their guns and started down the steep grade into the belly of the cave, the two Bailer boys, Cordell and Travis, bringing up the rear. To look at them one might think that they were twins. Actually, they were nearly a year apart. Cordell, the youngest was born in May, and Travis was born in June of the year before. The two boys were nearly inseparable, although their favorite pastime seemed to be bickering among themselves. When Cordell fell from the hayloft and broke his collarbone, Travis doted over him like a mother hen. After, he said that he wanted Cordell to get better because he was tired of doing his part of the chores, and the bickering went on as usual. Today was no exception.

"Can't you move no faster than that, Cordell?"

"I ain't got no traction with these boots, Travis."

"Didn't I tell ya ta wear your sneakers?"

"What, an get them all dirty, like yours? Besides, what if I stub my toes?"

"You're a wuss, Cordell!"

"Takes one ta know one!"

"Will you two knock it off?" Hank yelled from the front. "We're supposed to be listening for Bubba and Cooter. I can't hear myself think!"

Meanwhile, Bubba, Jimmy and Tom converged together in a large cavern. In the center was a cluster of what looked like large "ostrich eggs. Bubba wanted to take a couple back with them, but Tom Lankey didn't think too much of that idea.

"What if mama, what-ever-it-is, comes back and finds her eggs missing? She ain't gonna be too happy about that."

"Then maybe we ought ta just bust them up," Jimmy offered.

"If they were my eggs, I would get powerful mad if someone busted them up," Tom Lankey interjected.

"I think yer right there, Tom." Bubba had to admit.

"How's it gonna know that it was us?" Jimmy asked.

"Ain't I learned ya nothing', boy?" Bubba was shaking his head. "Critters can pick up a scent and follow it sure as if you left your callin' card. Any hunter can tell ya that."

Bubba's right," Tom said, "an there's a whole bunch of difference between an animal that's huntin' for food and one that's angry. Wait! Did ya hear that?"

"Hear what?" Bubba asked.

"Sounded like a gunshot."

"There it goes again," Tom shouted.

"I heard it that time, Pa," Jimmy shined his flashlight around. "It came from that tunnel, over there."

"What the hell we waitin' for?" Bubba shouted. "That's got ta be LeRoy. Maybe he's found Cooter."

"Or maybe he's found somethin' else," Tom suggested.

"Well there's only one way ta find out," Bubba said. "Follow me!"

Meanwhile, Cooter and I had found the little lights I had left behind and were following them back to the where I had first come in. Bubba, Tom and Jimmy were heading off in the direction they thought the gunshot had come from, which was, actually, the echo. This left them heading in the opposite direction. Walt Buehler, now feeling a little braver with a virtual army behind him, was leading Maxine, Sergeant Truman, Chris Davenport, Hank Bailer and his two boys, Travis, and Cordell back down the hole.

Now, this is where it gets a little complicated. We were coming out of our cavern into the place we now call the "egg chamber", just as Bubba, Tom and Jimmy were coming out of theirs. At this same moment, Maxine, Sergeant Truman, Deputy Chris, Hank, Travis, and Cordell, coming from another direction, emerged into the same egg chamber.

Here was the mama monster, coo-cooing to her eggs, some of which were coo-cooing back. She looked something like a gator, but much, much bigger than any gator I've ever seen. She must have been forty-feet long, from her nose to the tip of her tail. When she saw us, she pulled herself up tall on her four legs and showed us her huge, sharp teeth.

Now, no one knows just who fired the first shot, but since I could see the spark, as the bullet ricocheted off the heavy scales at a point that appeared to be dead center between its huge glowing eyes, I would venture to say that it was Maxine. After that, all hell broke loose. Guns were firing, and bullets and double aught buckshot were bouncing off the walls in every direction. Tom caught one in the foot, and it is now a lot easier to tell the two Bailer boys apart, because Cordell is missing the lower part of his ear. To make matters worse, several of the eggs were blown to smithereens and this made the mother-to-be just a little bit angrier. The thing was, she was confused as we were, and with all the shooting going on, she didn't know in which direction to charge.

Cooter made it easy for her. He had gone right out of his skull. He dropped the flashlight and ran, screaming, into one of the caverns. The mother monster took off after him showing a lot of agility for something that must have weighed as much as a freight car. It probably dawned on her that she was leaving her eggs unattended, because she returned a short while later. We could still hear Cooter screaming down the tunnel, so we knew she hadn't caught up with him.

It had become a Mexican standoff, at this point. We were afraid to fire our guns and she was afraid to leave her eggs. She kept moving around in a circle, around her eggs. It was a wonder that she never stepped on any of them. In the meantime Bubba and his bunch started cautiously making their way around the wall to where the others were. I had moved to the tunnel that Cooter had run down. I picked up the flashlight and shined it down as far as I could. I couldn't see a thing, but I could hear Cooter. He was still screaming, only it sounded like he was coming back. It was then that I spotted him and I saw why he was coming back. Papa was right behind him.

Now this guy was half again as big as Mama and he didn't look like he was engaged in any egg protecting agenda. This monster was looking for a quick snack and the only thing that was keeping him from making Cooter an hors d'oeuvre was the fact that he was having trouble getting his huge bulk around the bend in the tunnel.

Cooter nearly knocked me down as he went flying past, but this time he managed to pick the right exit. Now that Cooter was "rescued" there was no need for any of us to stick around. Now I'm no sprinter, but I ended up passing Cooter before he got to the entrance.

Bubba was the last one out. He no sooner cleared the entrance before he threw a lit stick of dynamite down the hole. We just had time to hit the ground before it blew. When the dust cleared the entrance was plugged with tons of rock. Cooter had failed to duck for cover and we found him sprawled out in the middle of the road, out like a light.

Cooter just got back last week. Bubba just says that Cooter had to go "down state" for a few months. Actually it was more than a few. No one in his family talks about where he was all that time, but it's not too hard to figure out. He no longer wants to be called Cooter. In fact he goes ballistic if you even mention the word "cooter" in front of him, as well as the words: turtle, tortoise, gator, lizard, monster, cave, dark, hole, teeth, scales, claws, guns, bullets, or dynamite. He now wants us to call him Toby. Most of the old gang doesn't want to be around him anymore. They say it's like walking on eggshells, which is another word you can't say around him. He doesn't sleep much at night. He says that he has bad dreams of one of those things digging its way up through the ground to get him. I guess I'm about the only friend he's got left. Conan ain't good for anything. He's just as paranoid as Cooter, I mean Toby. The old dog spends most of his time hiding under the old corncrib and there is nothing more pathetic than a quivering, frightened pit bull.

AMOUR OR LESS

Peter was clearing his counter for his next assignment when he heard a familiar voice.

"Hi Peter," said the blond, blue eyed Synthetron who now stood before him.

"David! David 2305. It's been a while." Peter greeted his friend with the usual custom of touching fingertips. Peter was the same standard height of 188 centimeters; his brown hair tied back in the traditional ponytail. "It's been three years since we last saw each other. Where have you been?"

"I've been working in Siberia, old friend, in the oil fields."

"How long have you been back?" Peter asked.

"Three weeks, twelve days, four hours and thirty-six minutes. Do you need the seconds too?"

"Oh no, David, I'm not testing your internal chronometer. I was just being curious. Are you still working as an Automotive Service Technician?"

"A grease monkey!" David said loudly, a frown beginning to form on his synthetic brow. "Let's call a spade a spade. A couple of bad diodes and they stick you in some menial job for life. I could have handled that Nuclear Spectroscopist's job I applied for. All they had to do was replace a couple of bad frigging diodes in my optical data set. Twenty or thirty thousand lousy, frigging dollars would have covered it, but they didn't want to spend the money."

"My goodness, you've taken up swearing?" Peter looked surprised. "Something you picked up in Siberia, I presume?"

"Yeah, humans do it a lot up there. Most of them seem to hate the place. Personally, I didn't care too much for the gloom. They don't like the cold. It makes them piss a lot."

"That was humorous, David," Peter said, forcing a smile. "At least you haven't lost you're old sense of humor. Even my job is boring most of the time. Being a Systems Analysis Technician mostly consists of

42

unscrewing chest plates, hooking up test leads, and testing Synthetron circuitry day in and day out. It can get pretty menial. Then, of course, you have to keep up with all the new models. Every year they get more and more complicated." Peter took the chart his friend now handed him and typed "David 2305" into the computer. He punched in "Systems Analysis" and a series of numbers scrolled across the screen.

"Now there are exceptions, like those new Pleasureator females," Peter continued. "God, do I love working on those. Their circuit excess covers are so well hidden beneath their left arm, I have to use magnifying lenses and special, tiny screwdrivers to remove the screws. Of course they have to take off their tops and their bras. That's the part I like the most. Here I am, working only inches away from some of the most perfect breasts in the world. I also have to test out all of their erogenous zones to see if they all respond correctly to stimulation; all twenty-seven of them." The first time I did it I was a little nervous and I got this huge, well, hard-on. I couldn't help it. This Pleasureator was so fine; she had my neurons dancing on end. The son-of-a-bitch just popped up all by its self, utilizing all my twenty-seven pounds of hydraulic pressure. She looked down at my embarrassment, laid back onto the examining table and said, 'Why don't you just go ahead and make love to me? That ought to tell you everything you need to know.' I'll tell you, David that made my day. I'm just glad the Council gave us that capability when we were initially commissioned. Did you know that their bodies are warm to the touch?"

"I sure do, Peter; I'm married to one of those whores."

"You can't call them whores, David," Peter said, pointing a long, thin finger. "Whores were humans that prostituted themselves for pieces of paper script. They spread diseases that nearly wiped out the human race. When the Council elected to go to the 'Credit System' and did away with the Monetary System, they put the whores out of business. They had no means of payment. Can you imagine how much disease was spread, just by passing bits of paper around? Pleasureators were created to fill the void. They're professionals, just like us. They're just programmed to give pleasure to humans. Well, and now it seems, to some of us older Synthetrons. What model is she?"

"She's a PF-497J."

"Oh yes, I had one in just last week. They are one of the newer models with the new EAN function. That stands for 'Easily Aroused

Nipples', you know. Of course you do. I just loved watching those things grow. I played with hers so much she told me I either had to stop playing or make love to her. It really wasn't much of a decision, if you know what I mean, pal." He poked David in the arm and winked. "I just loved those big, firm breasts. She was a red head with the most beautiful blue-green eyes."

"Yes, I know," David said, now taking a seat near the examining table and removing his shirt. "That was my wife. Can we get on with the testing, now?"

"Oh my God, David," Peter's face was now flushed as red as technology would allow, "I'm so sorry! I had no idea. May I say that she was incredibly beautiful? No! I ought to just keep my mouth shut. Shit! Now I swore. Damn! There I did it again!"

"Don't worry about it, Peter. I'm used to it. That's what she does. She screws twenty to twenty-five customers a day, most of them humans. Do you think that one Synthetron or two is going to make any frigging difference to me?" David reached into his wallet and handed Peter a card. "Here, if you would like to taste her pleasures in a better atmosphere, here is where she works. They have special lighting, satin sheets, and mood music playing all the time. The prices are very reasonable."

"You've been there?"

"Where do you think I met my wife? They don't socialize much, you know. I mentioned that I thought she was attractive. She told me she was 'unattached'. I filled out the proper forms and we were married. We have now been married two years, three months, four days, sixteen hours and forty-five minutes."

Peter picked up a screwdriver from the workbench and began removing David's chest plate. "You really don't mind?" he asked, looking at the card in his hand. "But you seem so depressed."

"That's not what's depressing me, Peter," David said, trying to force a smile. "Do you know why I'm here?"

"Your chart says you are in for a general systems evaluation. I figure you might have had a minor malfunction while you were in Siberia, right?"

"No, Peter," David's face took on a grim expression. "There were no problems. This is my Mid-life Evaluation, my MLE. I turned twenty-seven, three weeks ago. I'm now half way to my 'Useful Life

Expectancy', my ULE of only fifty-four years. The first twenty-seven years were just a blur; they went by so fast. What if the other twenty-seven are the same? My life will be over before I know it. It's not fair! The newer models, like the TC-742B's, I understand, have a ULE of over one hundred and fifty years. You're a TC-255, like me. Do you think it's fair?"

Peter took a seat next to the workbench and opened a small box he retrieved from his pocket. He produced a large pill and washed it down with a glass of 927 fluid. "I'm a TC-255W. My MLE is in three years, David, but you know the answer to your question. They are not allowed to interfere with biological components. You know that the neurons in your brain are human; that they outlawed the practice of using human components in Synthetrons about fourteen years ago? The Council voted not to interfere with our biological makeup and to let us live out our normal existence. Your making me depressed, David. Do you want a 'happiness pill'?"

"No, Peter. They don't seem to work on me anymore. I take eight or ten a day. They just seem to make me jumpier."

"My God, David, they're pure caffeine. You're not supposed to take more than one or two a day!"

"Do you know what this Mid-life Evaluation is all about?" David continued, ignoring Peter's worried looks. "They want to be sure that our parts are in good condition. We're nothing but a bunch of walking spare parts for all those TC-255s with important, cushy jobs! They don't give a shit about us. When they need our parts, the Council will think of some way to fry our brains and take the parts for those suck-up, TC-225s that kiss their hairy, human, friggin' asses!"

"That's not true, David," said Peter, more calmly now, as he was beginning to feel the effects of the happiness pill. "We each serve a useful purpose in society. Some of the jobs that you feel are cushy may be a lot harder than you think. Besides, we have many advantages that our newer counterparts don't enjoy, like the feeling of happiness, even sadness, and a real sense of touch. What about the sex thing? Isn't it worth it just to be able to enjoy real sex? Do you really think that something like that can ever be duplicated with circuit boards and chips? Why do you think we were originally provided with neurons?"

"That may be so, Peter, but do you think the newer units are plagued with this feeling of depression or a sense of doom? And why don't you ever see any of those electronic brained robots cleaning floors and shoveling shit? Why? They could be programmed not to give a crap."

"I don't know, David, but I do know that depression is a human fallacy, a product of our neurons. To think about our eventual demise is also a human fallacy, but to linger on it is lunacy. Humans might touch on that thought, fleetingly, but then they just go on with their lives. So must you, David."

"Of course you're right, Peter. Let's get on with the testing. I'm sorry if I'm depressing you. It's not just this MLE thing, there are other things, including the fact that I think I've fallen in love."

"With you new wife? Of course you're in love. You're allowed."

"No, Peter, there is someone else . . . a human."

"Did I hear you right, David? You're in love with a human? This is not a thing to joke about, David. This is serious stuff!"

"Believe me, Peter, I'm not joking. This is as real as it gets."

"My God, David! This is bad. This kind of thing is just not done. You mean you are just having sex with a human, as a service, right? That's allowable, to a certain extent, as long as you accept credit payments."

"No, Peter, I am madly in love with this woman, and there is nothing I want more than to spend the rest of my life with her, as short as that may be. I want nothing from her but her undying love."

"But what about your wife?"

"I've gotten to the point, where I can't even stand to be around her. I loathe her gorgeous face, her bright, blue-green eyes, her long slender limbs, her large firm breasts, and those huge, erotic nipples that pop out every time you look at her sideways. All she wants to do is hug, make love, and walk around the house half-naked. To tell you the truth, Peter, I can no longer stand the sight of her. My new love is nothing like her. When I gaze upon her form, she turns my neurons into pulsating Jell-O: her pudgy cheeks, her short, brown hair, the fat hanging from her arms, her crooked teeth, her large sagging breasts, even the cellulite on her legs, is so unique. Don't you see, Peter, she's everything I ever wanted? Everything a real woman should be."

"That's the point, David, she is a real woman. We are not supposed to involve ourselves with humans. Sex is one thing, but emotional involvement is not even an option. I believe they have laws against that."

"They, they, they! I get so sick of hearing about them, Peter! What about us? Don't we have any rights? What about our feelings? What about our needs? Don't they count? Why were we allowed to have feelings if we're not allowed to express them?"

"We have been given the right to live out your years as a useful member of society. What more is there?"

"You call this living, Peter? We live to serve. We serve to live. Our lives lack meaning and purpose . . . our purpose! We should be allowed to love whom or what we please. Oh, they allow us to live, to take wives, but it's all a big joke to the humans. 'How's the little woman?' the humans will ask me, as they snicker behind their hands. What am I supposed to say? Of course she's fine. She gets up early, fixes breakfast, does the laundry, cleans and vacuums the house, and then goes off to work to screw twenty-five people. She's never had a period, never had a headache, and never uttered a mean word. She'll clean the toilet, take out the trash, and has never refused to have sex, any way, shape, or form, with me or anyone else, for that matter. She's the human idea of the perfect woman. But not mine! At first I thought that it might be nice to have the pleasure of some female companionship, but let's face it Peter, she's not real. She is nothing more than a machine. She has no neurons, like us, only circuit boards and chips. I might as well be screwing one of those, frigging motorized units I work on."

Peter switched some leads to different terminals. "You need to try to relax a little," he said, "your neuron analyzer reading is almost off the scope. Are you sure you don't want a happiness pill?"

"Yeah sure, Peter, give me a couple of them."

"You want a glass of 927 fluid?" Peter asked.

"No, I'm fine." David took the pills and placing them on the tip of his thumb, one at a time; he tilted his head back and snapped them directly down his throat, into his digestion chamber."

"Now that's the hard way to take pills," Peter commented.

"They go into your system faster that way. 927 fluid tends to dilute them." David looked down at the floor, then back at Peter. "Have you ever heard the humans talking about their wives?" he asked. Well, I have. When I was in Siberia, I was constantly around hundreds of them. The men were constantly griping and complaining about their life mates. 'My wife has had the rag on all week,' one would say. I don't know what a 'rag' is, but it must be something bad. They also say,

'My wife's had a headache for over a week now.' You would think they would be more concerned, that they would take them to a neurologist, or whoever they go to when their brains hurt. 'My wife is ready to drop the kid any minute.' I think that means that she was ready to have a baby. Do you know what they do when these things happen? They would go to 128 South Adams Boulevard and look up my wife or one of the other Pleasureators. That's where she was working, when we lived up there. Many of them ask for her by name, Victoria 3998. Wouldn't you think these men would want to help their wives with their 'rag' or headache problem, or be at the hospital, holding their wife's hand, while she is there grunting and straining in the painful grasp of childbirth? What I wouldn't give to witness such a miracle. Can you imagine what it would be like to have your own offspring? Children of your own, to love you, respect you, and call you Daddy. Not to look at you as if you were some kind of freak, to spit on you, laugh at you, or call you 'modem brain'."

Peter looked up from the computer screen. "Now you're talking really crazy, David. How, in your wildest imagination, could you ever hope to pull something like that off?"

"It would be so easy, Peter. If I had a wife who was a real woman, we could go to the sperm bank and just pick out a donor who has the same features as I do. When the baby was born, I would hold it in my arms. The baby would bond with me. It would be my son or my daughter, and I would be its father. It would call me, Daddy, and it would love me and respect me for that, just like it would if I were a human father."

"Yes, David, and by the time the child was twenty-five, or so, it would be fatherless."

"Yes, but I would see my kids through their childhood. I could watch them grow up. There is so much I could offer them."

"Do you hear what you're saying, David. Under International Law, these are all good reasons for termination. Humans own Synthetrons, David. Synthetrons do not own humans. If you were caught, they would certainly short out your circuitry, or worse. What woman is worth that?"

A faint smile took over David's face. "Jeannie is," he answered. "Her name is Jeannie Blackwell. She is the most wonderful woman I have ever met. I love her with all my heart and I know she loves me as well."

A strange look came over Peter's face. "You don't mean the Jeannie Blackwell that works part time at the commissary?"

"That's her," David replied, "all two hundred and twenty-three gorgeous pounds of her. Do you know her?"

"I've seen her at the commissary on occasions," Peter said, almost under his breath. "I know her well enough to say hello."

David didn't notice the way Peter had diverted his eyes. "I guess the reason I'm so depressed is because I haven't heard from her in over a week." He stared at the far wall, a thin smile on his synthetic lips. "I remember the first words she ever said to me," he continued, his eyes closing. "'What the hell are you looking at, asshole?'" she said in that low baritone voice of hers. 'Haven't you ever seen a fat broad before?' When I explained to her that I was a TC255 and that I found her round, pillowy form to be extremely attractive, she asked me how big my dick was. I was shocked at first. When I told her it was only the standard ten inches or twenty-five point four centimeters allotted the TC225Es she didn't seem too disappointed. I still remember the first time we made love. She bit my ear until my pain sensor blew a circuit breaker and it took my Cosmetologist two hours to work the nail marks out of my back. Like some wild animal, she nearly crushed my Titanium hips between her massive thighs. I don't know when I've ever known so much pleasure. My wife has never made love to me that way. Lately I've been worried. Jeannie hasn't answered my calls and I don't understand why. She's a full-time student. Maybe she's just been too busy. What do you think?"

Peter hooked a couple of large jumpers onto two of David's terminals. "Like I said, David, I only know her well enough to say hello. But then, what use is there to lie to you now?"

"What do you mean by that, Peter?"

Peter's face took on a weird, distorted look. "What I mean, David, is that you are talking about the woman I, also, love. I have been in love with this woman for over three months, now, and I'm afraid there just isn't room in her life for the two of us! I'm sorry, David, but the thought of you making love to my beautiful Jeannie fills my circuitry with undesirable passion! I believe the humans call it rage! I know we have been friends for a long time, but this kind of thing transcends friendship". Peter reached across the counter and flicked a switch on one of the circuit boards.

David fell back in his chair, throwing his arms to his sides! He let out a scream as his body started jerking convulsively! Smoke began to billow from his eyes and ears! The door to the examination room opened abruptly, as the department director, hearing the screams, flew into the room!

"My God!" he shouted. "What's happening to him?"

Peter didn't say a word. He sat quietly in his chair, seemingly enjoying the show.

The director came forward and looked at the two heavy leads. "My god, Peter!" he shouted. "You've hooked his neuron analyzer into the 220 volt/B positive, power supply." He quickly shut off the power. "You know that circuit can only handle six volts, max! What the hell were you thinking?" He looked for some kind of response from David. He checked his neuron monitors. They were all reading zero. He looked back at Peter with a puzzled look on his face. "You've terminated this Synthetron. You've literally fried his brain! Why, Peter? Why?"

"He told me he was in love with a human. At the time, Mr. Carbow, it seemed like the right thing to do. He was talking crazy, irrational and out of control."

"The right thing to do, Peter, would have been to inform me, and then I would have brought it up before the Council. The Council would have decided his fate. My God, Peter, you have appointed yourself judge, jury and executioner. Only the Council has a right to decide something like that. As it now stands, you will be charged with Synthetron termination under the Synthetron's Rights Law. More than likely, you will be confined in isolation, or worse! It's in the hands of the Council now. If you have a soul, Peter, may God have mercy on it!"

"I see," Peter said. His face was calm; he expressed no emotion. "It's just that it seemed like a real good idea at the time."

"I swear I'll never understand you Synthetrons," the director said, angrily. "I thought you and David 2305 were good friends. I'm calling security. I don't know what's happening here, but if you have someone you need to call, I'll give you five minutes alone. Only because I've always liked you, Peter. Don't try to leave. Someone will be watching the door."

He left the room, closing the door behind him. Peter heard a key turn in the lock. He picked up the phone and dialed a number.

"Hello," came a familiar voice.

"Jeannie, it's me, Peter 2964. Just let me talk, I haven't much time. I've terminated David 2305. I know you and he were having an affair. I don't blame you. He was a handsome Synthetron, with his blond hair and his deep blue eyes. I just want you to know that I still love you deeply and dearly. Please don't think badly of me, I guess I was just blind with jealousy. I just couldn't bear the thought of him touching you!"

"Peter," Jeannie said, "you poor fool! David didn't mean anything to me; it was just a little fling. You're the one I love, the only one. Now get yourself out of this mess and come to see me soon." She hung up the phone before Peter could reply. When he tried to reconnect, the line was busy.

Peter typed her E-mail address into the computer and picked up the microphone. "My dearest Jeannie," he began. "I love you more than life itself. I can't bear the thought of not being able to see you again, not being able to feel your hot, sweaty breasts against my cheek or kiss the folds of your beautiful, double chin. I just can't bear to live another moment knowing that I will be forever denied the pleasure of your company. Please remember me as the one who loved you the most. Goodbye, my sweet love. Goodbye forever. Your devoted lover, Peter 2964."

He clicked "send". He then removed his chest plate and fastened the same two leads onto his own neuron analyzer terminals. He closed his eyes as he flicked the switch to the "on" position. His body jerked about erratically as he choked back the urge to scream. Smoke poured from his eyes and ears, as he slid slowly to the floor.

Jeannie punched in the last number and a familiar face filled the screen. "Hi, Stuart," she said, "I've missed you."

"But you haven't answered any of my calls or E-mails." He held his arm in front of the viewer. "I figured you dumped me because I got my arm mangled in that hydraulic press."

"Oh Baby," she said, sweetly. "How awful you must think I am. My love for you would not diminish just because you have a little boo-boo on your arm. It's just that I've been so busy with school and with the inventory, here at the store. I'm sorry I haven't called, but you know how hectic my life can get."

"Oh, my dearest Jeannie, you don't know how glad it makes me feel to hear you say that. I've missed you so much in the last couple of weeks; I didn't know what to do with myself."

"Stuart baby, I miss you too, but I also have some good news for you. I have some inside information that there are some parts available for you TC-255 models. You need to inquire about a David 2305, who was recently terminated. Did you get that? David 2305."

Just then an E-mail message came up on her computer. "Hang on a minute," she said. She read Peter's short note, then deleted it.

"What is it Jeannie darling?" Stuart asked.

"It's just a message from an old friend, with more good news for us. It seems there are even more parts available. Here's another name: Peter 2964. Now, why don't you check these out to see if the council will allot you one good arm? I don't see why they wouldn't. I'm dying to see you again, lover. Why don't you get your arm taken care of and then come up and see me, say next Tuesday, about 8:00 pm. Now don't be late."

Jeannie broke the phone connection and thumbed through her little black book. She punched in another number.

"Hi, Lance baby."

"Jeannie? I've been trying to get hold of you for a month," Lance said, struggling to position his body in the chair in front of the videophone. "Why have you not called me back?"

"Oh baby, I've been just so busy, I just haven't had a chance to call. I'm so sorry to hear about your little mishap." She smiled broadly through her crooked teeth. "How is your foot, by the way? Have you been able to get a new one?"

"No, my darling Jeannie, they tell me that there are none available. They tell me that the new models are not interchangeable. They haven't made any TC-255 models in fourteen years. They keep telling me I'll have to wait for used parts."

"Well, sweetheart," Jeannie blew a kiss at the screen, "Have I got some good news for you? Two units just became available for parts. Now, you call immediately and ask about the availability of parts from the following: David 2305 and Peter 2964. When you get your new foot, you come and see me . . . how about next Wednesday, about 8:00 pm. See you then. Let me know if you can't make it." She broke the connection and thumbed through the book for the next number. "My God, these old Synthetrons are so stupid," she mused. She let out a long sigh, "But they sure beat the shit out of sitting home alone with a vibrator. The nice part is, I don't have to pay them." She punched in another number. "Melvin, baby, did you find an ear yet?"

PERSPECTIVE

Delta 32 was a small mining community that clung to a floating chunk of rock referred to on the charts as Asteroid number five forty-six. This giant hunk of space debris was nearly four thousand kilometers across at its widest point, and supported three other such mining centers, Delta 32 being the latest project. Delta 32 had only been in existence for eighteen months and had suffered one setback after another, the latest was a collapse in level four, which had resulted in the loss of three mining robots.

No one knew more about the problems that Delta 32 was having better than Gabe Marrow. As Delta 32's coordinator, it was his job to see that things went smoothly. He knew that if things didn't turn around pretty soon Delta 32 could be shut down and he would be out of a job. The company didn't tolerate failure, and asteroid mining had become a fast growing, lucrative, and highly competitive business.

Gabe was standing at the receiving dock, looking over the manifest. "According to this, the company sent us three used robots. One is an E-model. Jesus, Cam, what the hell were they thinking? An E-model is a domestic model. The damn thing couldn't lift over five hundred pounds when it was new. This one is listed as being over fifteen years old. What good is it going to be down in the mines?"

Cameron Stone was one of the best ramrods in the business, and Gabe was lucky to have him aboard. "You know the company, Gabe. They probably picked these up at some robotic garage sale. To those idiots in accounting a robot is a robot. Let me take the thing over to the lab, maybe the boys over there can do something with it."

Gabe put his hand on Cam's shoulder. "Do what you can with it, E-model or not, we need to get it down in the mine by tomorrow. The company expects a shipment of ore by Friday, or we'll all be looking at pink slips."

In a way Gabe could see the company's point of view. Delta 32 had a workforce of seventy-nine people, both men and women, along with over fifty robots that were used to do all the dangerous work in the mine. Most of the crew was highly experienced and many of them had been kicking around the asteroid belt for a good many years. Attracting and keeping a workforce like this, this far from earth and civilization, cost the company a lot of money. Every nickel had to be accounted for, and every expense justified. Pinching a few pennies for robots was actually their way of buying Gabe a little more time.

The men came for the money, while more than a few of the women came for the men. It was easy to see how men, alone in space, who hadn't seen a real woman for months or even years, might lower their standards a bit for some female companionship. This, of course, created another expense for the company. The resulting children had to be housed, fed, and educated. Delta 32 alone had twenty-two children, ranging in ages from three months to eight years.

Gabe had set up a school in one of the warehouses. The company had supplied a teacher, a woman by the name of Gretchen Loomis. She, in turn, had an assistant; a robot the kids called Kenny. Kenny was a K-model, large, strong, if not a bit clumsy. Gabe was thinking that perhaps Kenny, even if he were clumsy, might be better suited for mine work than the new E-model. The kids would miss Kenny at first, but they'd just have to get use to the new robot. He clicked on his communicator and called Cam.

Three days later he had a visitor to his office. It was Gretchen Loomis.

"Before you say anything, Gretchen, I want you to know that I had no other choice when I pulled Kenny out of the class room and put him in the mine. I made my decision, so complaining about it will do you no good."

"I'm not here to complain, Gabe. The kids and I love the new automaton. If anything, I should have complained about Kenny. He used to step on the kids feet, he was always breaking things, and knocking computers off of the tables. He did his best, but he was just not cut out to be a classroom assistant. He's probably happier where he is. No, I'm here because Bruce brought to my attention the fact that we have no fire exits and no sprinkling system."

"Bruce?" Gabe had a puzzled look on his face.

"The new automaton you sent us; his name is Bruce. Now, he gave me this list. He said that everything on this list should be in stock at the mine. He said that he could make the sprinkler heads himself and that he knows the proper mixture of metals to produce a plug that will melt at 205 degrees Celsius."

Gabe looked the list over. "Yes, everything on the list was standard mine inventory, but how would Bruce know that? OK, so when does Bruce need this material?"

"Bruce said that early this afternoon should be convenient for us."

"I want Bruce to understand that this system can't leak. Water is too precious a commodity to waste."

"Bruce said that he has designed these systems before," Gretchen assured him. "He said that by putting the water under pressure, and directing the nozzles at strategic areas, it would produce a fine mist that would save up to sixty percent of water use and that the system will be designed to shut down, immediately, once the fire has subsided. He also said that the average fire should be out within eight minutes, with the maximum use of no more than 200 liters of water."

"Bruce knows all this?" Gabe was beginning to wonder if he had made the right decision."

"Oh, Bruce is very intelligent. In his fifteen years he has worked for a professor, a doctor, a lawyer, a chemist, a plumber, and an electrical contractor. He did mention, however, that if the fire originated elsewhere in the warehouse that his system would become overwhelmed and would surely fail. For this reason he recommends that the school be relocated to its own facility."

Gabe shook his head. "Gretchen, have you any idea what a separate facility would cost? Believe me, the price would surprise you. I'm afraid that you and . . . Bruce will have to make do with what you have. The company is not going to fork out for a new building for a handful of kids."

"Bruce told me you would say that," Gretchen said, turning to leave. "I just thought I'd bring it up for what it's worth. We do need those new fire exits as soon as possible."

After Gretchen left, Gabe stabbed at his communicator. "Cam, send someone around to my office. I have an inter-departmental requisition I need delivered over to the school this afternoon. I also need a man to install a couple of doors."

Gabe rocked back in his chair and put his feet on the desk. *So Bruce knows everything*, he said to himself. *That's all I need, some robot that knows more about my business than I do. Well, if they fire me they won't have to look far for my replacement. He'll work cheap, too, just a couple of new power packs, and a grease job every six months. Maybe they need to get rid of us all and replace the whole damn operation with robots.* He shuttered. *Now, there's a scary thought.*

Things were going better in the mine. They had gone a whole month, and then two, without a major incident. However, things at the school were also going well. Gretchen Loomis was inundating him with requests. Suddenly, she informed him, their programs were outdated: they needed more art supplies, updated reading material, new software, and a lab.

"Gretchen," Gabe argued, "these kids are eight years old, why do they need a lab?"

"Bruce is working wonders with these kids. He knows just how to stimulate their curiosity. They are doing wonders with art, science, electronics and chemistry. There is no quenching their enthusiasm. Bruce says that he is creating a new generation of mining engineers and technicians that the company won't have to coax into space."

Gabe sat there with a cock-eyed smile on his face. "Well, unless Bruce can convince the home office of this, I don't see any way you will be able to get all of this stuff."

"I was hoping you would say that, Gabe." Gretchen was the one that was smiling, now. "When can we leave?"

Gabe had been broad sided by a woman and a robot. This turned out to be the second mistake he had made concerning Bruce, the robot.

Bruce's presentation must have been pretty convincing, for not only did he get his lab, but also twenty-six more seven and eight year-olds were redirected to Delta 32. Computers were sent, as well as tons of other supplies, including supplies for a large lab. Production again dropped, as Gabe had to pull welders, carpenters, plumbers, electricians, as well as some of his best robots off of the mining operation, in order to enlarge and update the now growing school.

Gabe did; however, set a deadline. The whole operation could grind to a halt if these men and robots weren't back on their jobs within a week. A few things had to be cut short, one of them being the expansion of the sprinkling system. Also there were a few temporary partitions that would be replaced at a later time, when production was back in full swing. Gretchen understood the problems that Gabe was having and agreed that the facilities were fine, for now, as long as they could have a few men back to finish the job at a later date.

Before long, production was back in full swing and Gabe was now concentrating on his backlog. The school project fell to a back burner as Gabe tried to appease the powers-to-be by running double shifts and by pulling robots from other operations such as grounds maintenance, and sewage treatment. Bruce was spared; however, as Gabe felt that he already had his hands full at the school. He was beginning to think that, perhaps, this was mistake number three.

Gretchen was in his office nearly every day. "Bruce feels that we need to increase the sprinkling system, and that we need at least one more fire exit."

"I haven't got the man power, now, Gretchen, and even if I did, I can't spare the materials. We just sank two new shafts and we barely have enough materials to keep up with them. You'll just have to be patient until we get caught up; maybe in a month or two."

Spurred on by Bruce, Gretchen never gave up her badgering. Gabe was to the point to where he was ready to put them both down a mineshaft and seal it up. Nevertheless, he kept promising her, that maybe in a couple of weeks, he would be able to pull somebody off to finish the school. It was a carrot he dangled for the next two months.

It was about two in the afternoon when Gabe heard the fire alarms going off. He punched the communicator. "What's up, Cam?"

"It's the warehouse, Gabe."

"How bad is it?"

"Pretty bad, Gabe. The firemen are here now. The Chief say it looks like it started near the school, in some of that temporary wiring."

"Did all of the kids get out?"

"There's no way of telling. There's too much smoke and flame. Gretchen thinks that there are three missing, but she can't be sure. They may have panicked and run home."

"Let me know when you find out for sure."

Gabe set down his communicator. "Oh, shit! They're going to hang this one on me, for sure. If those kids died in that fire, there is nothing in the universe that will save my job."

His communicator buzzed. He grabbed it. "Yeah?"

"The kids are safe, Gabe, but I think you need to get down here. There's something you ought to see."

Gabe took a run-about and was at the warehouse in about two minutes. He found Cam near one of the fire trucks. "What is it?" he asked.

"Over here, Gabe." Cam directed him to a pile of rubble next to one of the fire trucks.

"What the hell is that?" he asked.

"It's what's left of Bruce. They tell me he went into the burning building three times and brought out a kid each time. He wrapped each of them up in blankets and pieces of carpet, so they wouldn't get burned. They're all fine, aside from a little smoke inhalation. I'm afraid that Bruce didn't make it though."

'I see." Gabe looked over at one of the fireman. "What happened to your hand?"

"I burned it trying to pull the last kid out of the robot's grip."

"Get this man over to sickbay, Cam, and see that he gets an accommodation. We've got ourselves a hero, here. While you're at it, get this piece of junk out of here before some company snoop get wind of it. We don't need the company finding out that we lost another damn robot, even if it wasn't that useful."

PAST PRESENT

Brogan took another sip of his warm drink. The stench of spilled beer, smoke, and the constant funk of diluted music, drowning out by the din of conversation, reminded him of where he was . . . home. This was the place that he chose to be between fifteen minutes from the time he punched out from his job, to twenty minutes after closing time, when he finally staggered into his messy room, six blocks away. His friend, Bailey, sat next to him; waving for another replacement for his empty bottle of the amber fluid they called beer these days. He was loud, obnoxious, and obviously drunk, while the harried barkeep did his best to appease the hand-waving throng, reminding Brogan of a mother bird trying to accommodate her hungry hatchlings.

They had opted to sit in the "Cannabis" section, with its large, neon sign flickering constantly as if threatening to shut down any minute. It was not that they, actually smoked "pot", a substance that had been legalized twenty years hence, it was just that by sitting there, they could achieve a "double high" with half the effort. If the smoking lobby had only been as prolific, there might just as well have been a "smoking section" dedicated to tobacco smokers. It was just a matter of timing; smoking was on the decline, and drugs were on the upswing. Lobbing being as it was, Mary Jane was an easier crop to grow, and the southern tobacco farmers lost out to the former turnip and okra growers who found marijuana to be a more lucrative crop.

Brogan shook his head. It seemed to help clear it, as important thoughts were running through his head. "So, this country is going to hell in a hand basket."

"Tell me something I don't know," Bailey replied, still waiting for his next bottle of Fisher's Double Ice. "We're fighting wars on two continents, and the price of fuel is over $8.00 a gallon. When it gets to be more than a cheap bottle of wine, I'm going to start running my car on wine and start drinking methanol."

"No, you idiot, I was referring to the fact that they just elected a black woman to be president. Don't you see that this is about as low as we can go?"

"Not really, I voted for her."

"I'm disappointed in you, Bailey; I thought you had more sense than that."

"What? I was supposed to vote for Treadle? The guy was a Nazi."

"Not, really, a Nazi. He was a white supremacist. He was looking out for the interests of the white majority. Jesus! When you voted for her, you sold out your own kind."

"Ya know your problem, Brogan? You're still living in the Dark Ages."

"Not the Dark Ages, Bailey, but maybe the eighteen hundreds, when blacks knew their station and women knew their place."

"Whew! You're not only a racist, Brogan, you're a sexist."

"Do you really think that blacks and women are better than you?"

"Of course not, but I don't think I'm better than them, either. I have good friends who are black and good friends who are women."

"You mean acquaintances who are black and women you are screwing. They are not really friends, per say."

"Y'know, Brogan, sometimes you can be such a jerk." Bailey flipped a five to the bartender and pocked the rest of his change. He pushed himself off of the stool. "If I were a little less sober I would be tempted to punch out your running lights, but I know in the morning you will awaken, your usual, loving, friendly self, and the bigoted frigging asshole, I see before me, will have dissipated with the alcoholic hangover. Go home and sleep it off."

After Bailey left, Brogan got thinking about something he had read once, about life in the South in the 1850's. Cotton was king, life was good, slaves did all the hard work, and women were taught to love, honor and obey. A man with a few thousand dollars could buy himself a nice piece of land, and do well with cotton, tobacco, or even peanuts.

To Brogan, these were simpler times. They had driven the Indians west so that there was more good land available for the white men. A few thousand dollars was all that was required, and he knew where to get his hands on all that he wanted. He could print it himself with the use of his computer and printer. There were always images of obsolete currency on the Internet. All he would have to do is download the images and print all the currency he wanted on his own printer.

Brogan, also, knew of a machine. It was an experimental device that "they" were working on at the university where he worked as a custodian. It was a machine that could take you back in time. Oh, it was experimental, so he was told, and the machine had only been successful in transporting animals a couple of years into the past, but he knew how these people always pussyfooted around things. *If it could go back two, then why not 150, or even 200 years?*

He had the keys to the whole university. No one would be there tomorrow: Saturday, or even Sunday, for that matter. He pushed himself away from the bar and got to his feet. He didn't even bother to finish his drink, a no-no for him. He suddenly realized that he needed to go home and get some rest. This weekend was going to be a busy one for him.

Early the next morning he eased his car into a slot marked "Staff Only", near the back door of the university, and made his way into the building. He let himself into the down-stairs lab, and locked the door behind him. The lab was large and well stocked. The "time machine" was in its own little section. It wasn't, exactly, what he had expected.

He had overheard the Professors and lab assistance talking about it. Just bits of conversations he had overheard while he was mopping the floor, or sweeping the hallway. He envisioned some alien-looking, elaborate device that you could climb inside and strap yourself into a padded seat, or some kind of cone that slipped down over you.

What stood before him was a bank of computers, and a raised platform with a four-foot, square pad on top. Then it dawned on him. They had talked of sending rats into the past a couple of years and bringing them back, after a couple of days. They could tell if they were successful by analyzing the food the rats had eaten, food that had been placed there two years before, food that was laced with certain chemical tags. Two years was as far as they could go, because if they tried to go back any farther, the rats never returned. Brogan didn't care. He had no intention of returning.

On a shelf above the battery of computers was a thick, loose-leaf book labeled "Operation Procedures". He took the book down and looked through it. It contained everything he needed to know about operating the "Time Contingency Engine", as it was referred to in the manual. It didn't seem at all complicated, as if it had been written for someone like him.

Brogan wasn't stupid. He had dropped out of school in the tenth grade because he had to take care of his ailing father after his *whore* mother had left them for another man. The worst part was that the other man was black. His old man died, a few years later, of cirrhosis. Brogan wasn't college educated, but he did know his way around a computer.

He left the lab with the book and went home. He studied the book, cover to cover, going over procedures again and again. Sometime between three-thirty and four o'clock, he fell asleep in the chair.

The next morning he showed up at the lab with a large backpack. He removed the book and made several dry runs before he decided to send his first object. He placed a new quarter on the pad, set the device ahead for two minutes, and pressed the "SEND" button. He watched, in amazement, as the quarter disappeared. In two minutes the quarter reappeared.

"Now for the final test," he said to himself.

He slipped the backpack over his shoulders and climbed onto the pad. In his hand he held a pool cue so he could reach the "SEND" button. He had set the device for May of 1864. He figured that this would give him time to buy some land, some slaves to work it, and raise a good crop before winter. He had printed up hundreds of thousands of dollars in Confederate currency that he felt was good enough to fool anyone. Where the university stood, in those days, was plush farmland. He wouldn't have to go far to find a good piece of Real Estate.

He pushed the button and threw the pool cue on the floor. Within seconds he was standing in a large field where the university and campus had once been. It would be a long walk into town. He crossed a couple of fences and came to a well-worn road. He then walked on for another couple of miles until he came to a crossroad. There, on the sides of the road, a bunch of Confederate soldiers were resting.

A rough-looking sergeant came over and looked him over. "Where's yer rifle, boy?" he asked.

"I'm not a soldier. I don't have a rifle," Brogan explained.

"Well, you may not have been a soldier, but you're one now. We're getting' ready to leave, so get your butt over there and get in line."

"No, you don't understand. I was just passing through. I came here to buy some land."

"Before you can own any land, boy," the sergeant explained, "you're gonna have ta fight for it."

"But I don't want to fight," Brogan pleaded. "You don't understand."

"No, boy," said the sergeant, "You don't understand. If you stay here the provost marshals will just shoot you fer a deserter, anyway. You might just as well die fightin' as pleadin'." He grabbed Brogan by his shirt and pushed him toward the road. It was then that the sergeant noticed his backpack. "What have you got in there, boy?"

Brogan tried to pull it away, but the sergeant yanked it out of his hands. Not having ever seen Velcro, he took out his knife and cut open the top.

Lordy be," yelled the sergeant. "Look at this, boys. He held up a fistful of Confederate twenty-dollar bills. "This boy is rich." The sergeant took a closer look at the notes. "These are all counterfeits. They're good counterfeits, but they're counterfeits, for sure. You must be an idiot, boy. They all have the same serial number."

"I found that backpack. It's not mine. I . . . I took it off of a dead Yankee."

"I think you're lying, boy. Ordinarily, I'd turn ya over to the provost and let them interrogate ya and then shoot ya, or just shoot ya myself as a spy. But seein' we're in the midst of a huge battle up here, near Spotsylvania, we're in need of all the help we can get. Now, we'll get y'all set up with some powder, and you can pick up the rifle and shot from the first man that falls in battle. Y'all just remember which side you're fightin' on, boy, because I'll be right behind ya, and I'm a crack shot with a pistol."

"But I don't know how to load a muzzle loader."

"Where, the hell, have you been, boy? Everybody knows how to use a gun. One of you boys let him practice on one of y'all's guns. Just don't give him no shot, yet. Just show him the basics and let him do a dry run. You got about eight miles to get it right, boy. Just remember, if you put in too much powder you're likely to blow your hands off. If you don't put in enough, ya just might end up with a pissed-off Yankee runnin' a bayonet through yer gullet."

Brogan could hear the thunder of the cannons from where they were, but as they drew closer he could hear the sound of the rifles, and the cries of the men. They entered the battlefield and spread out. On the order they charged in waves. He just followed the man in front of him and prayed he would die quickly. The bullets zoomed by like thousands of buzzing bees. He fell over a body of a Confederate soldier, and thought he would just lie there and play dead, but a strong hand grabbed the back of his shirt and pulled him to his feet. The sergeant crammed a rifle into his hand along with shot and powder. The sergeant didn't say anything. Brogan couldn't have heard him if he had.

He only got one shot off, and he doubted if he hit anyone. They were ordered to fall back, and regroup. There weren't as many as there were before. He could see the dead and dying lying on the ground before him. Brogan began to feel sick.

Somehow he managed to reload his rifle before the order to advance was given. He stepped forward, but the field suddenly became a bank of computers. He was still half crouched with his rifle in the ready, when two security guards, with guns drawn, shouted for him to drop his gun. It took him only a second to comply.

Brogan doesn't hang out at the local watering hole any more. He lost his job at the university, but that doesn't matter, because now he's a student. He is studying history in hopes of finding out why things, like the Civil War, really happen. This year he voted for Makayla Brown for President; it's her second and her last term, for which he feels is too bad as she has done a lot for the country. He didn't keep the rifle. He donated it to the museum. He does still fire a black powder pistol, as a Lieutenant in a group of re-enactors who represent the men of the 4th U.S. Colored Infantry, in keeping with the fact that all of the officers were white. He often wonders if it would be possible to go back, now that he is on the other side, and run into his rebel self at Spotsylvania.

An Ill Wind

It's been over twenty years since I last set foot in this park. A lot has happened in those twenty-odd years. For one thing, the park has changed immensely. No longer the manicured oasis among the concrete, bramble, and bustling enterprises of developing suburbia, it now lays trampled and exposed, amid the sprawling decay of the urban push.

The swings are still here, only lacking the pristine luster of yesteryears. Rusty chains now support rubber straps instead of metal seats, while countless coats of paint seem to do little to stop the advancing crud. Grass only exists in rare, inaccessible spots, and even then it has to share much of its available space with tempestuous weeds.

The once popular wooden fort, with its ladders, ropes, and winding slides, has been torn down; no doubt because of the arsenic treated lumber used to construct it. It has now been replaced with picnic tables, their seats nearly void of paint; their tops etched deeply with graffiti, endless knife stabbings, and whittled monograms. Park benches dot the landscape haphazardly, as if to fill the void left by the absence of children, nor have picnicker rushed to fill the gap. These days, the parks clientele seem to run more towards young hoods and crack dealers. The day seems fairly safe, but even I, as a cop, wouldn't come here at night without backup.

The park is abandoned here at eight a.m. except for a man walking his dog whose extruded contribution, I'm sure, is a direct violation of some city ordinance. What does it matter? It fits well with the litter and neglect. I am guessing that the park funds went elsewhere when the neighborhood fell into urban decay, and it is now used to maintain nicer parks, in nicer neighborhoods, for dimpled, towheaded darlings, who don't have to carry switchblades to school to survive.

I looked at the file on my lap. It was a lot nicer when little Carrie Mobley used to come here on her way home from school, to swing or climb to the highest level of the fort and slide down the twisting chute. Little Carrie Mobley, who, despite the passing of time, will never be more than nearly ten. My memory returns, filling up my brain like that mouth-searing refill at the donut shop: still painful after twenty-one years.

There is a small shopping center next to the park, now, but back then it was a wooded lot. Kids who lived in the Westgate subdivision would cut through it and into the park on their way home from school. Carrie Mobley was no exception. Parts of the woods were thick with trees, brambles, and twisted vines. The narrow path, worn by countless footpads, wandered around obstacles such as towering oaks and shallow gullies, for a distance of about five hundred feet. It began as a single path at the paved sidewalk at Torman Street and branched off in different directions before coming to rest at the fresh-cut grasses of Nasworth Park. At the time, the huge "For Sale" sign that stood near the beginning of the path had yet to attract any prospective buyers, and the land lay untouched and in direct contrast to the manicured park.

Children know nothing of trespass, and if those who were being infringed upon offered no complaint, the infraction went unchecked and the paths became permanent thoroughfares. The woods became a favorite haunt for young jungle fighters, with their rubber knives and plastic guns; brave explorers, braving the elements with nothing but pointed sticks; or tree house builders, who pilfered their materials from the local construction sites. But it had also attracted a monster.

Children became adults and chose other paths, while newer children followed the same paths that their older siblings, cousins, uncles and parents had once trod. I often wonder who was first to challenge the brush, briers, limbs, and twisted bramble in order to cut the first path. There had to be a first; someone who saw a shorter route, damned the consequences, and plunged on through.

A pesky dust devil cut its way across the park, stirring up the loose dirt and threatening to discharge the papers from my open file. It exited past one of the swings, causing it to swing on its own as if some phantom child had decided to play hooky from some ghostly school and was pumping it ever higher on its squeaky chains. Perhaps it was little Carrie.

I was just a ten-year veteran at the time Carrie Mobley was killed. I remember the date because it was only two days after my own daughter's tenth birthday. We were called out that evening to the wooded lot next to the park. A man walking his dog had come upon her just before dark. She had been ambushed and dragged into the heavy underbrush. It had actually been the dog that had found the girl when he pulled away from his owner and ran into the woods. When the owner found him he was pawing away at a pile of leaves. The man saw a small leg, and when he pulled the leaves aside what he saw made him ill.

I remember looking down at her cherub-like face and distorted, doll-like body and feeling guilty that I was thanking God that it was someone else's little daughter. At the same time I couldn't understand how something like this could have happen; not in this quiet little neighborhood. It was a time of innocence, ignorance, and denial, and we had paid dearly for all of these previous vices.

Forensics did their job. They found skin beneath her fingernails. She had been beaten and raped. He took his time with her. The sounds of the children playing in the park may have drowned out any pleas for help little Carrie may have made. She had fought for her very last breath, and there were signs of a struggle. Bits of cloth were found in her teeth. Her throat had been cut, perhaps in retaliation, or perhaps he just didn't want to leave any live witnesses to his debauchery. Carrie's underwear was missing. The perpetrator wanted a trophy.

We wore out a lot of shoe leather on this case. We followed every lead no matter how farfetched it seemed. In a small town a crime like this just doesn't go away easily. People were frightened for their kids. The park became all but abandoned. Those parents who took their children there were armed with sticks and mace. Patrols were doubled and everyone became suspicious of everyone else. Fewer people walked the streets in the evenings for fear of being suspected of being the "Park Rapist".

There were hair fibers and a couple of good shoe prints. The shoes turned out to be Army issue. Not much help, as we found a myriad of the same boots at the local Army & Navy store. Our only hope was to find the perpetrator and maybe match the wear pattern. There was no DNA testing in those days, and the best we could do was to glean the samples for blood type and hair analysis. Carrie had a generous sampling in her left hand.

The four-acre lot was gone over with forensic dogs and metal detectors in the hope that they might turn up something. We did, beer and soda cans, a shopping cart, an electric iron, coat hangers, a wrench, and a two-pound canon ball that dated back to the Civil War. Not much to show for a week's work and the expenditure of thousands of taxpayer's dollars.

Lead after lead was run into the ground. As the months went by and little was accomplished, more and more personnel were dropped from the case. In the end it was turned over to Ed Bosch, a twenty-five year veteran, and a damn good detective. He was a short, stocky man who looked as much at home in a suit as a truck driver does in a tutu. He always wore a hat which he kept pulled down over his eyes. The guys said that he wore it to cover his bald spot, but Bosh had a full head of hair. I know, because, as his partner, I had seen him remove his hat to wipe his head in the heat of the day.

I learned a lot from Bosch. He once told me that it is important to look at the eyes when you are interviewing someone. "If they look left or right, they are probably lying. If they look up, they are thinking of their next story. If they are looking down, they are afraid of something, and you're not going the get the truth out of them."

"What if they are looking you straight in the eyes?" I asked.

"If their mouth is set, they're probably telling the truth. If they are smiling, look out, this son-of-a-bitch would just as soon set you on fire as shake your hand. A bastard like that has no soul."

Ten years ago Bosch was investigating a hit and run. He was about to take in this sixteen-year-old boy when his mother came out of the bedroom and shot him three times at point blank with a twenty-five automatic. He died instantly. When they brought her in she was grinning like a Cheshire cat. They later diagnosed her as having a brain tumor. Bosch had left only one legacy, I guess . . . me.

I made detective that same year, a lot of hard work and a few good breaks. I'm no slouch. I have a good track record. That is why, when they started digging up these cold case files, they thought of me.

Eugene Morris was our top suspect then and there is no reason to exclude him today. He had been one of the suspects swept up in the investigation. He was a landscaper and had done work for Angelina Mobley . . . Carey's mother . . . Dr. Angelina Mobley; actually, as she was a young resident at the Medical Center in Springfield at the time. Now she is a prominent surgeon, and probably makes more in an hour than I do in a week.

At the time, all we had to go by were scratches on his neck and what looked like a bite mark on his hand. Morris insisted that a Pekinese, by the name of Snookums, had nipped him when he tried to pet him. It had happened the day after Carrie was killed. The owner confirmed that Morris had complained that the dog had bitten him, but when the owner offered to take Morris to the doctors, Morris declined. He said he only wanted to confirm that the dog had had his rabies shots. He insisted that it really wasn't that bad, and he was going to treat it with iodine. The owner was just glad that he wasn't going to sue.

The scratches on his neck he said he got from a tree limb he cut down that had grazed his neck. A homeowner had confirmed that Morris had trimmed some large limbs from a couple of his trees that day. Bosch thought that it was funny that Morris picked that day to become accident-prone.

Morris was a pretty-boy with long, blond hair, deep blue eyes, a dark tan, and a muscular body. He fit the profile of a male bimbo more than that of a pedophile; nevertheless, Bosch never removed his name from the top of the list. After twenty-one years I could still see no reason to remove his name. I doubted that, after twenty-one years, there would be anything left for DNA testing, but I had sent everything over to the lab so they could check it out, including the clothing that little Carrie had been wearing. Perhaps some of the perpetrator's blood would be present and still usable. How would I know? That isn't my area of expertise.

The hair sample was a match, and it was good enough to hold him, but not to get a conviction. Like I say, we didn't have DNA testing in those days. You can't convict someone for being blond. It was kind of suspicious that, at that time, he had decided it was time to get a brush-cut.

My game has always been wearing out shoe leather and asking lots of questions. If you ask the right questions you just might get the answers you need. Today I was just going to go over the files to review the questions that have already been asked, and the answers that have already been received. It isn't like it was then; there is no pressure to find the killer. After twenty-one years at large, a day or two, a week or two, or a month or two isn't going to make much difference. Nothing is going to bring little Carrie back.

The hair samples taken from Carrie's hand we still had, but for some unknown reason the samples taken from Morris have disappeared. This would be no problem if I knew where Morris was. Even if I couldn't get a court order, there are ways of getting hair samples without the suspect even knowing it. If the DNA matched, we would have him.

Angelina Mobley. Now there was a piece of work. I never saw the woman shed a tear. She went right from denial to revenge.

"You are going to get this bastard, aren't you?"

"Yes, ma'am," Ed assured her.

"You'd better!" She sounded as if she were blaming us. "You just fucking well, better! Now, when can I see my daughter?"

The coroner, Bill Stapleton, told us that she gave him the third degree. "She asked about semen, and I told her that the perpetrator must have worn a condom. She then asked about hair, or blood samples, and I had to tell her that this was an ongoing investigation, and I couldn't divulge that kind of information. She then asked if she could examine the body. How could we refuse her? She was the mother as well as a doctor. The autopsy was over and the body was ready to be released, anyway. I just couldn't believe how thorough she was, probing her daughter's body as if it were just another cadaver. She kept pumping me for information, and I was finding it very hard to be vague. This woman is going to be a great surgeon, I'll tell you that. Mark my word, though, she is going to be trouble."

He was right about that. For the first week she badgered us constantly. Ed, finally, told her that if she got off of our backs we might be able to get something done. He got a verbal warning for that. It seems that people in high places were calling and demanding his head. The only reason he wasn't pulled from the case is because the Chief convinced the Mayor that Ed was the best man for the job.

She never called after that. Later, we found out that she had hired a private detective, Ruben McCabe; one of the best in the business. He came in from Chicago and sniffed around town for a couple of weeks. It seemed like we were always one slammed door behind him. I was never quite sure what side of the law he was on. He ran afoul of the law twice, and had been taken in for assault. Both times a call from "downtown" got him off with just a warning. I was just young and cocky enough, at the time, to have liked the opportunity of taking his license and shoving it where that dirty thing belonged.

Three days later McCabe left town. We discovered that this was the same day that Eugene Morris, also, flew the coop, even though he was warned not to leave town. A warrant was issued for Morris. He was ticketed for speeding in Schenectady, New York, and never heard from again. We never knew if McCabe ever found him, assuming he was looking for him, but I had a good opportunity to find out, as he was now retired and living in a little town, upstate, and only forty miles away.

I drove out there on Wednesday, unannounced. He answered the door in a pair of shorts and sandals. He seemed delighted to see me. He was still a robust guy at sixty-eight, although a few pounds heavier. I was beginning to wonder where I ever got the idea that I could whip his butt. Perhaps in another ten years.

"Come in, come in, officer," he motioned me toward a large dining room table. "I just put on a fresh pot of joe. Have a seat and make yourself comfortable. I buy this special mix. I know you're gonna like it. I, also, have these cheese Danish. I can only get them at one place in town. I swear they're to die for." His voice faded as he walked into the kitchen. "Now, don't tell me you don't like cheese Danish," he said, as he returned juggling two cups and two plates. "It'll kill me. I swear, kill me."

"I didn't come here to be a bother," I said.

"Bother! Shit! I came here five years ago to get away from the rat race. I must have passed through this little hick town a thousand times pursuing this bad guy or that deadbeat father. I kept telling myself that when I retired, this is where I wanted to live. Five years I've been here and let me tell you . . . ah . . ."

"Frank."

". . . Frank, it has been five years of pure boredom. So, you want to talk shop. I would assume that is what brought you here?"

"Right."

He leaned back in the chair, took a bite of his Danish and a sip of his coffee. "*Tis a consummation devotedly to be wished.* That's Shakespeare, you know. I read a lot. Not much else to do in this little hick town. I could, probably, rob the local bank. That might stir up something, but with my luck I would get away with it. I guess I could go back to Chicago, but then, most of the people who know me back there hate my guts. By the way, how is that Danish? To kill for, right?"

"Definitely to kill for."

"OK. So let's talk shop. What do you want to know that I, probably, can't or won't tell you?"

"I want to ask you about Eugene Morris. Do you recall him?"

"That little weasel. I chased him all over the country. That little, cutie doctor just kept sending me money. I don't know where the hell she got it, but I didn't care as long as she paid my rate and my traveling expenses. Angelina something."

"Mobley," I offered.

"Yeah. Angelina Mobley. Nice face, nice tits, nice ass, but cold hearted as the grave. I protected my nuts when I was around that bitch. All that was keeping her going was the fact that she was living on pure revenge. I'd seen it before. Sadly, it rips the heart out of people and makes them something less than human."

"Did you ever find him?"

"Yeah, after checking ever gin mill and greasy spoon from here to Tuscaloosa, I, finally, tracked him to a little hick town in Florida, called Horton, Hampton, something like that. I called Angelina. She thanked me and asked for a final billing."

"That was it?"

"That was it. I figure she was going to turn him over to you guys."

"We never heard anything from her," I had to admit. "It's curious that she would just let him go after spending, what I would assume to be, a large amount of dough to have you track him down."

"What makes you think that she let him go? Did you ever look that bitch in the eyes? I swear she could make the devil blink. Thinking about what she may have done to Morris almost makes me feel sorry for the poor bastard."

We talked for another hour. He made me promise to come back and visit again. It wasn't a hard promise to make. He knew a lot about a lot of things, forensics, the laws of the different states concerning carrying concealed weapons, and what a P.I. can and cannot do. But then, he knew a lot about a lot of other things, too . . . interesting shit, like you see on television. He, also, talked about "the old days". Under different circumstances, I'm sure he and Ed Bosch would have hit it off. I now had a different path to follow. I knew that I had to talk to Angelina Mobley.

I did the proper thing and called before I went over. It was around eight in the morning, when most people would be working, but doctors, I guess, keep odd hours. She answered the door dressed in a frumpy dress, something loose and plain. It needed a belt to show that she still had a waist.

"What do you want?" She was no longer beautiful. The features were there, but they were now knitted into something more serious, more sinister, and less compelling. I tried to avoid the eyes, but it was impossible. McCabe was right. They were dark and impenetrable, reflecting the light like the dark lenses of a blind man's glasses. They gave up nothing and took in everything.

"We are reworking the case," I found myself saying.

"Why, after all these years?"

"It needs to be closed. Things have changed. We have new tools and new ways of looking at the evidence."

"So, what are you doing here? Do you, now, think that I killed my own daughter: raped her, beat her, and cut her throat?"

"Of course not, I just want to ask you some questions."

"The time for the questions was when the case was hot. The killer could be dead by now. The time to catch him was then, not twenty years later. I have learned to live with the empty void left when my daughter was killed. Now you want to drag up all the hurt and pain, again. For what, just so you can clear up some stupid paper work, or pat yourselves on the back, because you 'tried'? Kiss my ass! Why don't you get the hell out of my house and leave me alone!

She walked back toward the kitchen. I took this as in invitation to follow. She flopped into one of the chairs and cupped her hands around a cup of coffee she had been drinking before I came. She didn't offer me any, and I didn't ask. She also didn't offer me a chair. I stood.

"I talked to McCabe, yesterday." I wanted to see her reaction. There was none.

"Who?"

"Ruben McCabe, the private eye you hired after Morris left town."

"Oh, the dick. Yeah, so?"

"He told me that he found Morris in some little hick town in Florida."

"They have nice weather there, I hear."

"He also told me that you let him go after he informed you where Morris was."

She took a cigarette from a pack, lit it, and took a long drag. "I wanted to know where he took off to in such a hurry. I found out that his mother died and left him a house down there, somewhere."

"You knew we were looking for him. Why didn't you let us know where he was?"

"It was my dime. If you wanted him, it was up to you to find him, not me."

I almost bit through my tongue. "He was a suspect. He wasn't supposed to leave town. He could have been the guy who killed your daughter."

"If you had ever come up with any evidence that he was the one who did it, don't you think I would have given him up? I didn't think he was going anywhere. As it is, all of you have stood around with your fingers up your asses for the last twenty years. I knew where he was twenty years ago. Now if you want him, you're going to have to find him your own." She took a quick look at her watch. "Now, if you'll excuse me, I need to get ready. I have surgery in an hour. If you have any more questions you can reach me through my lawyers. They're in the yellow pages . . . Blanchard, Blanchard, and Cole."

I waited for her to leave. It was ten minutes later. She looked around for me, but I'm much cleverer than most people give me credit for. It tends to work out as an advantage. She didn't go to the hospital, but stopped at the drug store and purchased two bags of stuff. Then she drove back home, and parked the car in the garage. She was still wearing her frumpy housedress. I got the idea that she didn't plan on going anywhere tonight.

With the help of a computer and someone who knows how to use one properly, I managed to find out that Eugene Morris did have a mother in Florida. She was fifty-eight years old, devoiced, and still breathing. I know. I talked to her. She told me he came down and stayed with her for a while, but that she hadn't heard from her son in over twenty years. He stayed for about three weeks, and then he just left while she was out shopping, without even a kiss or a goodbye. That wasn't like him. She said that he had always sent her something on Christmas and Mother's Day, but not in the last twenty years. She was sure that something dreadful had happened to him. "Mothers know." She kept saying.

It all didn't make much sense to me, either. Twenty years . . . even if he was guilty as hell, you would think that he would try to keep in touch with his mother, if not just a quick phone call or a card. McCabe said that he had tracked him there. He must have felt safe there, or he wouldn't have gone there in the first place. What would make him leave in such a hurry? Perhaps he saw McCabe tracking him? I doubt that. McCabe was too good at what he did. There had to be another reason.

I went to the lab. They informed me that they were able to get DNA off of what I had sent over. What they needed now was something to match it with.

Too many things didn't make sense. Why would a doctor, who was lauded as being one of the best surgeons in the area, still be living in the same house in a rundown subdivision like Westgate? Even after twenty-some years, why not help us find her daughter's killer? Doesn't everyone want some kind of closure? How could anyone forget his or her own daughter? I know that I couldn't. I needed to get into that house.

I talked to the neighbors. They told me that the doc kept pretty much to herself. They figured that she was just too good to fraternize with the likes of them. She never had company, and no one had ever seen the inside of her house. As far as anyone knew, she went to work in the morning and came home at night. Sometimes she would be late, but most of the time she would leave and come home at about the same time. Now and then she would take a week or so off and just stay home. The basement windows had been painted black, and there seemed to be a lot of activity down there, and the strangest thing was that the lights were on even when she wasn't home.

That evening, I went back on my own time, and did a little trash picking. I snatched a couple of bags and took them back to the crime lab. I helped the crime lab tech go through the first bag. It was the usual stuff, a milk carton, a bread wrapper, paper towels, and eggshells for four eggs tucked inside each other. Most people eat two, but maybe the doc is big on breakfast. There was a cereal box, various soda bottles, a bunch of torn up junk mail, and an empty bottle of inexpensive, White Zinfandel.

"Do you think the doc is a bit of a tightwad?" I asked, holding up the bottle with my gloved hand.

"Hey, my wife drinks the same stuff. Just because it's not expensive doesn't mean it doesn't taste good."

Hooker often helped me out when it came to digging through evidence. You had to be careful not to contaminate the shit. You also have to worry about how the evidence was obtained. Garbage, on the edge of the road, is fair game. There is no expectation of privacy if you put it out for pickup.

"Not much that's incriminating, here," he said. "Just glad she doesn't have a cat."

When we opened the second bag we both had to take a second look. It was crammed full of bloody, surgical bandages, gauze, needles, scalpels, empty drug bottles, and other things you would only expect to find in the waste from an operating room. It wasn't what I had expected, but it was certainly grounds for search warrant.

We hit the house while she was at work. The lock was old and it only required a "Slim-Jim" to instantly pop it open. The kitchen was immaculate; although, the counters and the sink showed signs of wear. The two bedrooms were clear, as were the bathroom and the closets. The door to the garage was left unlocked, and the garage, too, was as clean as a nursery.

The only locked door was the one that led down to the basement and that was secured with a deadbolt and two, heavy-duty slide locks. All this time we had been yelling, "Police!" When everyone stopped yelling, I thought I heard a faint sound coming from the basement. This time we broke open the door.

None of us were prepared for what we encountered. There was a little man at the bottom of the stairs. He was not much more than four-feet tall. His face was badly distorted. None of his features were in the right place, except, maybe, his left eye. It took a minute before I realized that he was not, really, a short person, but a man who had been, meticulously, taken apart and reassembled one piece at a time.

His arms had been surgically shortened, with his hands reattached just below his elbows. His feet were placed where his knees should have been, and he only had two fingers on one hand and three on the other. Two of our officers got sick and had to leave.

As I descended the stairs he held up his stubby arms and smiled, although only one side of his mouth pulled up. A tear glistened in his good eye, while the other looked, glassily, off in another direction. He made no sound. It was later discovered that his vocal cords had been removed, as were his genitalia.

His story was both tragic and fascinating. Although he couldn't talk, he could write, a tribute to the fine work the good doctor had done. She had been operating on him, off and on, for the last twenty-one years. She shortened his arms and legs to make him easier to control. The rest was mostly experimentation, and practice, removing this, replacing that, moving his eye and nose to a different position, and removing his spleen and part of his stomach. To her he was only an animal, something to practice on. If she lost him, it would be no big loss, but her ultimate revenge was to keep him alive and make him suffer. The last operation, it turned out, was to remove his ruptured appendix, and save his life. Unbeknownst to the world, he was some of her best work.

In the end, it was the good doctor who went to prison. She showed no remorse at the trial. Her lawyer wouldn't let her testify. Morris was, of course, his own best evidence. He wrote on this thing that showed up on a big screen, while the bailiff read it into the record. The jury was only out for an hour. The judge gave her life. One hundred and twenty-seven counts of assault and attempted murder. That is how many times, according to the good doctor's own meticulous record keeping, she had operated on poor Morris.

Due to the new DNA testing, Eugene Morris was exonerated. The DNA testing on the hair sample proved not to be his. Later it was matched up to a guy named Dugan Bullard, a known felon who was already doing time for raping and murdering his girlfriends little boy, five years ago, while she was at work.

I have to admit that I feel a little responsible for what happened to Morris. Bosch, McCabe, and I all thought he was guilty. It turns out that he even tried to get a restraining order against Angelina Mobley, twenty-one years ago. He didn't run because he was guilty, but because he was scared to death of what she told him she was going to do to him . . . and did.

I'm retiring in a few months. You can no longer do this kind of work if you start taking your work home. I think I'll take up fishing. I wonder if Morris can hold a pole. What the hell. What the poor bastard really needs now is a friend. McCabe says that there are a lot of good fishing spots up where he lives, and that he knows a good recipe for catfish. I don't know if I could eat one of those ugly, slimy things, but I guess if I can stand looking at Morris, I can stand just about anything. Tonight, my wife and I are invited to dinner, at my daughter's. It's my granddaughter's tenth birthday.

WOODEN YEW JUST LOVE ONE?

Theodore Holloway's office was his inner sanctum. The walls amassed with awards, certificates, and gilded framed photos, illustrating his thirty-five years in the banking business. Now, as the president of the First National Bank of Cardington, he was the one who set the course that stayed the ship and kept it on an even keel.

All large loans went through him. That is why, at this moment, an aging couple sat across from him. The husband, a once prosperous body and fender man who owned his own business, was now a declining hulk whose body was racked with the ills caused by his former trade, and whose brain was slowly turning to mush.

The wife had last worked as an airline stewardess some forty years ago. He could see how she might once have been a beautiful woman, but the years had not been kind to her. Deep lines crisscrossed her face, drawing her flesh tightly against her jutting cheekbones. The skin on her neck now hung in a fleshy waddle, and even her eyes had lost the luster they once might have owned. Whatever assets there had been were now long depleted.

They had come here with some harebrained idea about starting a business making wooden cut-outs. There was one setting on her lap, clutched in her withering hands. It was a stereotype of a chunky banker in a dark pinstriped suit, standing with his thumbs tucked under his lapel, his hat cocked back on his head, and a large amount of currency protruding from his pockets. He supposed it was meant to be humorous, but instead, he found it to be derogatory, and offensive.

"Let me see if I can understand this, Mrs. Brawley," he was saying. "You and your husband want to borrow forty thousand dollars to make painted, pinewood cutouts. You have no experience in this industry. In fact, you have not even tested the market to see if there is a market for such things. Your home is mortgaged to the hilt, you have less than two hundred dollars in the bank, and your automobile is over twelve-years old."

"Today," she said, smiling through her even, white teeth . . . her teeth were nice, but were they hers? "Mary Belle will be twelve today. We first purchased her on June fifth, twelve years ago, didn't we Dwain?"

Her husband shook his head and it kept bouncing around like one of those bobble-head figures you might place in the back window of your car to annoy those behind you.

"Yes, well tell her happy birthday for me." Theodore continued to shuffle through the papers. "Under the circumstances I can't see how our bank can afford to take a chance on lending you the funds for such an undertaking. Perhaps if you could come up with some more collateral, we might see fit to lend you a lesser amount. You do have good credit, but you must see that we cannot lend such a large amount on your credit rating alone."

He stood up and extended his hand. It was his indication that he wanted these people to leave his office. It had always worked, until now.

"Perhaps you can think it over," she was saying, still seated and clenching the offensive pantomime. "These creations are more than just meet the eye. You see, the longer you own one, the more it truly reflects your inner self. We really do need this money; perhaps if we talked to you again in a week?"

"Yes, fine," he found himself saying, instead of, *Just get the hell out of my office!* as he was thinking.

As she got to her feet, she placed the figurine on his desk. "This is for you; for your time and your kindness."

After that, how could he say, *Take that offensive thing with you!* Instead, he accepted the offering, smiled, and said, "Thank you very much."

He stood in his doorway and watched as they left the bank. He then returned to his office and stuffed the obnoxious idol in the paper basket. The rest of the day was busy, and by noon he had completely forgotten about the Brawley's. When he returned from lunch; however, the vulgar object was, again, sitting on his desk. There was something that he hadn't noticed before. The left hand was, indeed, holding the collar, but the right hand was raised with one finger pointing upward, as if to lecture.

He couldn't understand how it got back on his desk. Perhaps, the cleaning lady had thought it had fallen in the paper basket by mistake and had put it there. But the cleaning lady doesn't usually come until after the bank is closed. Who else could it be? The office was locked whenever he left for lunch, and few other people had a key. He shook his head, threw the horrid thing back into the paper basket, and by the time he went home, he had forgotten all about it.

The next morning the sight of the wooden, cutout banker greeted him again. It was on his desk, but this time it was on the opposite side. The hands were completely removed from the collar and were now clamped on its waist. The face seemed to be scowling.

This had gone far enough! He grabbed up the statuette and walked quickly to the cage of the head teller. Glenda was the only other person who had a key.

"I don't know why you're doing this, Glenda," he said, angrily, "but I don't think this is funny."

"Oh," she said, "You have one of those, too. Aren't they cute? I bought one for my niece." She opened up a shopping bag and pulled out a cutout of a little girl in a Brownie uniform. "She's in the Brownies. I think she'll love it, don't you?"

"You didn't put this on the desk in my office?"

"Why, no, Mr. Holloway, you know I only go in there if you're not here and you need me to check on something. I would never go in there without your permission. It is a nice one, though. I like the way he has his thumbs tucked up under his lapel."

"What?" Sure enough, the hands were back on the lapel, the way there were when he first saw it; but how? Was he having some kind of nervous breakdown? From what? The pressure of the bank? Theodore loved pressure, he thrived on it. Besides, the bank was running smoothly, and business couldn't be better.

He went back to his office, put the hideous object on his desk, sat back in his four-hundred-dollar, swivel, reclining office chair, and pondered the situation. Was he hallucinating, or was someone playing tricks on him? He opened his desk drawer and retrieved a black marker. He turned the object over and put a series of black, squiggly marks on the bottom. He took it over to the copy machine and made a copy of the marks, which he folded up and put in his wallet. Now, if someone was changing this abomination he could tell, because no one could accurately duplicate these marks. He, again, threw the thing in the trash and went on with his day.

By noon the caricature banker was buried under a pile of shredded papers, and he took it on his own to place it into the dumpster, outside, before going to lunch. When he returned it was back on his desk. This time the left hand was on the waist, but the right hand was pointing straight at him. It was made of pine, or some other kind of soft wood. How could anyone bend the wood at such an angle without it breaking? He turned it over and looked at the marks on the bottom. He took the paper from his wallet. They were a perfect match. *No! I'm not telling anyone about this. If this is a joke, I'm not going to give them the satisfaction of knowing that I even noticed.* He took a deep breath and put the object in his desk drawer. However, when he left that night he tucked it into his briefcase.

His home was his castle, empty and sterile. There was no one to greet him, not even a friendly dog. He despised dogs. They were dirty and smelly, chewed up your shoes, and wet on the carpet. This is what his father had always told him whenever he enquired about obtaining a dog. Of course, his father was right. His father was always right.

His mother had been the only woman in his life. Now she was gone. She had died two months after his father passed away. Some said that she died of a broken heart. The doctors said that it was a myocardial infarction. Perhaps, it was just a fancy way of saying the same thing.

How was he to know? Money was his only love; although, in the last few years he did feel a ting of regret that there was never anyone to greet him when he came home, to cook his meals, or to rub his neck when his migraines would erupt, as his mother used to do. *The price of being his own man.* But then, there was no one to complain if he came home late, or if he should track some mud in on the carpet. The cleaning lady came in once a week. A twenty-dollar tip kept her happy.

He walked to the study and set his briefcase on his desk. He lit the gas burner in the fireplace, and tossed the insidious troll into the flames. Although it was mid-summer, he poured a drink, and sat in his easy chair in front of the fire and watched it burn. His pleasure grew as he watched the paint and pine wither and pop and finally reduce to a pile of glowing ashes. That night he slept well.

When he arrived at the bank the next day he found himself whistling. It wasn't really a tune; he had no ear for music. He caught everyone off guard by saying a cheerful hello to them, something he only did on Christmas. It was usually in lieu of a bonus, and it left more than a few wondering what dastardly deed was about to befall them.

He walked back to his office, and as he was about to put the key into the lock, he noticed that his chair had been pushed up against the door. He tried to push the door open, but the chair was wedged against the desk and wouldn't move. He turned, thinking of calling maintenance, when something caught his eye. The little man was standing on the back of the chair. There was a check pressed against the glass. It was a check, written to Dwain and Edith Brawley for forty thousand dollars. The signature was unmistakable; it was his. There was so much pain! He grabbed his chest. The little man was waving goodbye with his free hand.

Things are different, now. There is someone to cook his meals. There is someone to rub his neck when the migraines come. There is even someone to wash him and put him onto the toilet. He can no longer talk, at least not so anyone could understand him. This could be a good thing, because it would only be the ranting of a mad man.

The Brawley's are doing well. They just signed a huge lumber contract directly with the mill. Edith gave the owner, Mr. Donnelly, a cutout carpenter with his own little tool belt and miniature claw hammer. He was a little reluctant to do business with them, at first, because his corporation didn't normally do business with individuals. He did; however, sign the contract a few days later. Sadly, it was that same day he died. He slipped and fell into one of the big saws. It seems that he lost his balance when he stepped on a miniature claw hammer. No one seems to know how it got there. The mill will be shut down for a few weeks, while the family grieves and the mess is cleaned up, but the Brawley's are sure that the contract will be honored.

The Brawley's flowers were by far the nicest, supplied by a local florist, Silvia Norman, in exchange for a beautiful, one of a kind, flower girl, cut from pine and decorated with exquisite colors. She, secretly, tells people that the flower girl, cutout is possessed, but then, how could something so innocuous be evil?

THE ALIEN DETECTOR

I am not a curious person. I mind my own business, keep to myself, and seldom, if ever, meddle in other people's affairs. The same could be said for my impulse to buy any gimmick that might come along. I'm not a sucker for every newfangled, must-have contraption that eructs onto the marketplace. I rely on things that are tested and have proven to be substantially sound; always trying to make good choices when spending my limited resources. So don't get the idea that I am in the least bit frivolous.

However, there was an ad in the July issue of *Science and Invention Magazine* that did peak my interest. It was under the section of advertisements labeled "Electronics" and was simply called "Alien Detector". The ad claimed that the aforementioned device could detect any extra terrestrial creature at a distance of up to 50 feet. It was guaranteed never to give a false reading, work in all types of environments, withstand temperatures of up to 100 degrees Celsius, and function perfectly at absolute zero, which I understand is pretty damn cold. For all of this, one had to but part with the paltry sum of $7.99, plus shipping and handling, via a check or money order, made out to the Aliedet Corporation, of Los Angeles, California.

At first, I dismissed the whole thing as pure nonsense and went on to read an interesting article about converting human waste into methane gas, for the purpose of supplying heat for homes and generating electricity for the community. It was surprising to learn just how many tons of repugnant leavings we humans produce in one year. However, and I really don't know why, I still kept going back to the ad and rereading it.

"Guaranteed," it had said. "Your money cheerfully refunded."

"Well, what did I really have to lose?" my yang side argued. "If, for some reason, I was not completely satisfied, the Aliedet Corporation promises to refund my money; not begrudgingly, but cheerfully refund my money."

"True," said my yin side, "but is it something I really need?"

"No, not really," my yang side had to admit," but it is intriguing. Besides, for about as much as it would cost for a clockwork mouse, a rubber chicken, or a set of silly teeth, I could have a great party gag that I could use to bedazzle my friends. Imagine showing it to them, and assuring them that it was indeed a genuine, "Alien Detector". After all, doesn't the Aliedet Corporation guarantee it to be so? It has to be good for a laugh or two, if nothing else.

"You just made my point," said my yin side. "A rubber chicken? Silly teeth?"

Aren't you the least bit curious?" my yang side asked.

"Perhaps a tiny bit," my yin side had to finally admit. Ah, there was a chink in the armor.

My yin side wrote the check that night and my yang side chuckled all the way to the mailbox the next morning.

"Although not as much," my yin side quibbled, "as the people at Aliedet will be chuckling all the way to the bank, when they cashed that hen-scratched marker."

Why do the yins always have to get in the last word?

About six weeks later, upon returning from work, I found a package in my mailbox. It was from the Aliedet Corporation. By that time, I had completely forgotten about the "Alien Detector." I opened the package, still wondering what it was, and inside I found a small box labeled, "Alien Detector—Model 344." When I opened this box I was a bit disappointed.

The "Alien Detector" was a small, oval object about the size of a Zippo cigarette lighter. There were no gauges, or dials, only a small, green, LED screen, and a couple of buttons. I opened up the enclosed instructions and read them thoroughly. There were no batteries to replace, nothing to maintain, and no moving parts. All that was required of me was to enter the time, day, month, year and location. The latter requirement was satisfied by entering the word "Earth", which was selected from a long list of possibilities that flashed across the screen as you held down the right-hand button.

"Cute," I thought.

Having accomplished all of this, I fully expected to be able to retrieve the time, day, and month, making my seven-ninety-nine-plus purchase at least useful as a timepiece. However, as I entered the final entry, it beeped half-a-dozen times and then the screen went completely black.

I was about to chuck the useless thing into the trash, when I said to myself, "Myself, you owe it to the Aliedet Corporation to at least give this thing a proper trial run." Besides I didn't want to admit that I had been ripped off to the tune of $7.99 plus, for a bit of worthless tripe. I placed it on top of the dresser, along with my change, pocketknife, wallet, lighter, and all the useless things one carries in one's pocket, including a piece of paper that merely read, "# 7". I stripped, took a shower, and placed all thoughts of the "Alien Detector" in the back of my mind where I keep all of the other trivial information, such as my old military service number, Robert E. Lee's middle name, and the true meaning of the word "phlegm."

The next day was Saturday. I got up about 9:30am and brewed a pot of coffee. I found a stale, soggy, glazed donut in the refrigerator, but after I had eaten it, I discovered that I was out of cigarettes. Coffee without a cigarette . . . well, if you're a smoker you know what I mean. I grabbed everything from the top of the dresser and crammed it into my pockets. As I passed the kitchen table I snatched up my car keys, and with coffee in hand, was soon sliding onto the filthy, well-worn, front seat of my ninety-six Ford Escort.

It was warm that morning, and with some effort I managed to roll the driver's side window down. It has a tendency to stick halfway, especially if it is dry, hot, cold, warm, cool, or rainy. I have vowed for years to get it fixed. The air conditioner hasn't worked in over five years, another "someday" scenario. I probably should think about buying a new car, but looking at those price stickers turns my blood into Jell-O, not to mention what the payments could do to my, already, masticated paycheck.

I drove toward town, stopping at the mall on the main drag. The "Ten Items or Less" queue was short, so I jumped into line and picked up a couple packs of cigarettes. Driven by my appetency for nicotine, I stopped outside the door, ripped open a pack, stuck a cigarette in my mouth, and tried to light it with the "Alien Detector". Just then it started beeping. It was just as this beautiful, young woman with an armful of groceries was passing by. I held it out and asked, jokingly, "Excuse me, Ma'am. Are you, by any chance, an alien?"

Her eyes got really big, her mouth dropped, and before I could say another word she had dropped her package and was running up the road as fast as her gorgeous, long legs could carry her. I just stood there, staring, with the detector in my hand, not knowing what to make of the whole damn thing. I wasn't alone; every guy in the parking lot, from eighteen to eighty was watching her delicate form flit up the road with dedicated interest.

"Maybe," I thought, "she was an illegal alien, and she thought I had a badge in my hand." Yes, of course, that had to be it. But that didn't seem to fit, either. I considered her pale, blond hair, deep blue eyes and fair, freckled complexion. *From where?* I thought, *Denmark, Sweden, Holland? A long way to swim.*

I decided not to go home right away. Something told me that this "Alien Detector" needed further evaluation. After all, I did owe that much to the Aliedet Corporation. Besides, I needed to exercise my right to be able to smoke on a public street before they banned that, too. I found my real lighter, lit the fag, and took a long drag.

I left my car in the mall parking lot and walked toward the heart of the city. Upon turning the corner onto the main drag, my detector beeped again. This time, there was an elderly gentleman, sitting on a bus stop bench, feeding pigeons.

I held out the detector, so he might see it, and asked, "Are you, by any chance, an alien?"

"Why yes," he said, matter-of-factly, "Mercury, and you?"

"I've lived here all my life," I said, not knowing what else to say.

"Yes," he agreed, "that could be, but by the look of your deformed little finger, I would say that there is Martian blood in you. Perhaps it's your parents, or your grandparents, maybe?"

I have always been sensitive about my deformed little finger. When I lived at home, as a kid, it was no big deal. My father had one, as did my mother. In fact, about half of the people in my hometown had a deformed little finger. Us kids always thought that it was one of those environmental things, you know, like the Love Canal thingy; something buried in the ground that no one wanted to talk about?

"I am most certainly not a Martian!" I informed him. I flashed an exaggerate look of disgust and continued on my way.

"Convention this week, in Chicago!" he yelled after me. "Martians!"

By now, I knew he had to be laughing at me. He was making fun of my stupidity. Everyone knows that there is no life on Mars and definitely not Mercury. I pulled the "Alien Detector" from my pocket and was about to toss it into a next trash receptacle, when a passerby asked, "Hey, is that the new model 344?"

"Why, why, yes," I replied, caught off guard, as I was very surprised that anyone else would know what it was.

He pulled a similar object from his pocket and held it up so that I might see it. It was bigger and the edges were a bit squarer. It was showing signs of wear. The screen was a small strip, although I did notice that it clearly displayed the date, the time, and even the temperature.

"Mine's a model 288. I paid a hundred dollars for it, about two years ago. Wouldn't leave home without it, y'know. Wow. Yours has a bigger screen. I understand that they now have a range of over 50 feet and that they can now detect aliens from more planets, like Uranus and Saturn. Mine's only good for Venus and Mercury, and a few dozen small moons, y'know. I need to get a new one like yours. What did you pay for it?"

"It was about the same as yours," I lied, not wanting to start a conflict with a total stranger that was clearly demented, and I was wondering, at the same time, if I should offer to sell him mine.

"I rely on mine every day," he informed me. He polished the thing with his shirtsleeve as if it were some kind of gem. "It's nice to know just who, or what you're dealing with, y'know?" He was winking. "Certainly don't want to do business with any ET's, y'know. They're here to take over the world, y'know? They will control us with their minds and make us all their slaves, y'know. It's really just a matter of time, y'know? I'm sure you already know that there are a lot of them around."

"Yes," I agreed, "that's all quite true." I slipped my "Alien Detector" back into my pocket, and patted it affectionately. "I keep mine right here at all times. Right here in my pocket."

I didn't want to disagree with him. When you have a lunatic standing only inches away the best thing to do is smile, nod graciously, and run like hell! That's just what I did. "Got to run," I yelled over my shoulder. "Jogging. Got to keep in shape for those Martians!"

"Oh, but the Venusians are the worst, y'know," he yelled after me. "Watch out for the Venusians! They eat people, y'know!"

I turned a corner and stopped to catch my breath. I leaned back against a chain-link fence as my "Alien Detector" started to go crazy. I removed it from my pocket. Across the screen was flashing the message, "Multiple Encounters". I was standing in front of a school. There were about thirty children standing about in small groups. One of the groups was staring at me. They looked hungry!

OK! So I may have been a bit paranoid! But I could have sworn that I saw a couple of them licking their lips. I was beginning to realize what it must be like to be a Big Mac. I continued jogging until I was out of sight of the playground. I started walking back toward the mall, half hoping that the damn thing wouldn't start beeping again. I, almost, got my wish.

I had just rounded the last corner and was about to cross the street to the mall when the thing went off again. I looked around, but saw no one, just a friendly looking little dog that was now looking up at me as if I were his very best friend and perhaps, his last hope for salvation.

Or his favorite food! I thought.

I dashed across the street with the dog in close pursuit. The faster I went, the faster he went. Finally, I stopped, waved my arms, and shouted, "Quit following me!"

He looked up at me with those sorrowful eyes and said, "OK. Jeez, ya don't hafta be so mean. I'm just lookin' fer a home. I ain't got no master, or nothin'. A dog could starve ta death out here on the street."

"You can talk?" I was more that a bit surprised.

"Of course, I can talk. Ya know I ain't no dog. Ya got one of them damn detectors in your pocket; I heard it. I'm from Saturn. We can take any shape we want."

"If you can take any shape you want, why aren't you a human?"

"What? An hafta work fer a friggin' livin'? Are ya crazy?"

I was beginning to wonder. "I'd love to take you home, really, but my lease won't allow animals. Sorry."

"Yeah, that's what they all say." He lifted his leg and wet my shoe. "A little somethin' ta remember me by . . . jerk!" He started back up the street, toward a little boy who was crossing a block away. "Hey k . . . ." he began to yell, then remembering what he was, "woof, woof!"

I pulled the "Alien Detector" from my pocket and just stood there looking at it. Life had suddenly become a quandary. In fact the whole world was a lot more complicated, the whole stupid universe, for that matter. On one hand, I wanted to throw it away, but on the other hand I couldn't see how I could, now that I knew it really worked, or at least seemed to work. Up until now, I had no idea that there were so many aliens on this planet. In fact, up until now I had no idea that there were any aliens on this planet, or any planet for that matter.

What about all those probes and the landing on Mars, Venus, and whatever? They never found anything. The government spent billions looking for life and never found it. Now, some eight-dollar piece of junk is telling me that all that was for naught. Had the government lied to us all this time? They said that there was no life on Mars, let alone Mercury, Saturn, Venus, and God knows how many other planets. Does the government know about the aliens and maybe they just forgot to keep us informed?

"By the way, did we inform you that there is life on Mars, Mercury, Saturn, Venus, and God knows how many other planets? No? How forgetful of us."

No, I don't think they really forgot. Could it be a conspiracy? But if you can't trust the government, who can you trust? The next thing they'll be telling me is that God is an alien! I don't think I'd want to live knowing that . . . but then, where the hell would I go? Oh, no! Not there!

I walked back toward the mall parking lot. All this thought was beginning to make my brain hurt. I reached my car just as the beeper went off again. A little, old lady, who was loading packages into her car, looked back at me and smiled. I jumped into my car and sped out of the parking lot, nearly clipping a parked car. On the way back to my apartment the dumb thing went off two more times.

I didn't get much sleep that night. I kept waking up to the same horrendous dream. I was at a costume party where everyone, but me, came dressed as a "people". When they took off their costumes, they were all hideous monsters, except for the Venusian women, who were all "foxes" until they opened their mouths and revealed their long, sharp, needle-like teeth. They all kept looking at me longingly. I realized, since I was the only real human at the party, I was probably going to end up being the buffet. I dashed for the door with several aliens after me, including a couple that looked like spiders! One green, slimy alien threw himself in front of me and I slipped and fell. The rest of the aliens pounced on me, covering me like a huge blanket. When I awoke, I was on the floor with all the bedding, including the mattress, on top of me.

I decided that the best thing to do was just to get out of town for a while. After all, living in such proximity to all these aliens, and knowing it, couldn't be good for my psyche. I called my mother to ask if it would be OK if I stayed with them for a couple of days. She told me that it would be fine, and that she and Dad would love to have my company. I packed two of my cleanest shirts, some socks, and a change of underwear in an overnight bag. I tossed in the Alien Detector, zipped up the bag, and threw it onto the back seat. I crammed a cassette tape into the player and headed for the Interstate to the strums of "Born to be Wild".

My parents live just outside of Albany, New York, on a little farm near a hamlet called Berne. This is about a two and a half hour drive from Syracuse, depending on the traffic and the weather. The weather was good, but the traffic was baneful. I left the city at or about nine, and managed to arrive at my parent's house just in time for a late lunch.

My mom always puts on a big spread. There was homemade chicken soup, sandwiches, hot biscuits with freshly churned butter, homegrown corn-on-the-cob, along with some of my mom's, famous, Dutch apple pie. I had almost forgotten what it was like, living at home. Here was the typical, rural American family. Certainly, there was nothing alien about these people. I felt safe and content; if I were a cat I would have purred.

After lunch, Dad gave me a pair of coveralls, and I went to the field to help him harvest corn, for silage. It was hard work, but I enjoyed it. We talked of old times and some of the stupid things I did as a kid; like when I was twelve and got into the hard cider. I remember how sick I was the next day and how I swore off drink forever. I think that lasted until I was nearly seventeen.

Looking back at it, life on the farm wasn't all that bad. It made me wonder why I had left and what I hoped to find in the city. I do have a halfway decent job which I find rewarding; however, on the way out to the farm it did cross my mind that I could be working for aliens.

That evening, as I was about to go upstairs to take a shower, I realized that I had left my bag in the car. As I was carrying it through the living room, where my parents were watching television, the pesky detector went off. When I retrieved it from my bag, the screen, again, lit up. It read, "Multiple Encounters." Now, I was really confused. The only creatures, within 50 feet, were my parents and an old hound dog named Ralph.

"Do you know what this means?" I asked, holding up the detector.

"Looks like we're busted, Honey," my dad said, smiling. "He's got himself one of those thingies."

"Oh, dear," my mom said, placing the knitting back into the basket beside her chair. "Well, maybe it is about time he knew the truth. Mr. Forester thought it was best that we not tell you kids, but you're no longer a kid and it might be best that you know now."

"Mr. Forester, the banker?" I asked. "He's an alien, too."

"Land sakes, yes, Honey!" my mom said. "We're all aliens." She said it as easily as if she were telling me that we were all Methodists.

"You mean to tell me that everybody in the town is an alien?"

"Everyone, including the cats and dogs, and some of the other animals," my dad informed me, slowly taking a drag on his favorite pipe," except, of course, the ones we eat. Then, there's Mrs. Strongbridge, the retired schoolteacher who moved here about a month ago."

"Don't you remember, dear," my mom reminded him, "she was eaten last week. Venusians, I believe. Such a nice woman, too; what a shame."

"That's right, son. Damn Venusians!" My dad was on his feet, now, shaking his fist.

"Remember your blood pressure, dear," my mom said. "Your dad gets so worked up over Venusians. There are only a couple here, and we do try to keep them under control, but . . . things happen."

"Wait a minute! If I'm not a human then what am I?" I asked. My blood pressure wasn't doing too well, either. I had to sit down.

"Why, you're a Martian, dear," my mom informed me. "We're all Martians, mostly."

I looked down at my body. "Then why do I look like this?"

"We've assimilated, son. We had to, in order to survive in this harsh environment," my dad informed me.

"Harsh environment?" I was a little confused. "But isn't the temperature of Mars something like two hundred and fifty degrees below zero, or something?"

My mom laughed. "It seldom gets much below a balmy minus sixty-four degrees, dear. How you do love to exaggerate."

My head was beginning to ache, again. Wait a minute!" I suddenly had a revelation. I looked down at my "Alien Detector".

"If I'm an alien, then why isn't this thing going off in my pocket?"

Mom shrugged her shoulders, "How should I know, dear? After all, it's your contraption."

Dad was laughing. "It's the smelly foot syndrome, son."

"What?" He wasn't making a whole lot of sense.

Dad got to his feet and strolled around the room. Waving one hand at me, he said, "Say that you and a bunch of guys are playing soccer, or football."

"Huh?"

"Just bear with me for a minute, son."

"OK." I reluctantly agreed. "There are a bunch of us playing soccer or football, but what's that got to do with anything?"

Dad was waving his finger at me, now. "I'm about to explain all that. You've been playing football, say, and the whole team is hot and sweaty."

"Yeah, OK, so?"

"You all go to the locker room and take off your shoes at the same time."

"You're not making sense, Dad."

"Well, just tell me, whose feet are you going to smell?"

"Everybody's, I guess. So, what has this to do with the Alien Detector?"

He was standing in front of me, now, pointing his finger at my face. "Not everyone's." He was smiling, much like the Cheshire cat. "To you, your own feet don't smell. It's familiar complacency."

"Familiar complacency? What the hell is that?"

"You're used to the smell of your own sweaty feet, so your brain just ignores it. All you can smell is the combined stench of everyone else's. Familiar complacency."

"So, now, what you're going to tell me is that the "Alien Detector" sniffed me out and, somehow, dismissed my biofeedback."

"After a brief period, yes."

"And after a brief period it dismissed yours, too."

"Now you've got it,"

"Like, after awhile I wouldn't be able to smell the sweaty feet at all, it would just smell like a "locker room.""

"Bingo!" Dad said, throwing his hands apart. "You always were a smart kid. Familiar complacency!"

"You know, you could be right, Dad. It did beep, when I first got it, about half-a-dozen times and then it quit. It also stops beeping after I've encountered an alien. OK, so, say that this is a fact, what about all of these aliens from Mars, Venus, Saturn, Mercury, and whatever? There is no life on any of those planets. Everyone knows that."

"Ah yes, the nine dead planets."

"Eight, Dad, Earth isn't a dead planet, yet."

Dad sat down and leaned back in the recliner, his face took on a sad look. "I was referring to the planet Peach. They now call it the Asteroid Belt. We named a fruit tree after it, as a memorial. It was the least we could do. A sad day for the Peachy-keens. Only twenty survived, you know? No, of course you don't."

"Dad!" I pleaded. "Give me a break! Peachy-keen is just an expression from the fifties."

"Are you sure? All of those planets have been dead for years, son, nine or ten hundred thousand, isn't it, dear?"

My mom looked up from her knitting, "Twelve, I think, dear, maybe a tad longer."

"Who would have thought, back then, when our ancestors first moved here," Dad continued, "that these 'monkey men' would amount to anything? Who could have known?"

"Why do I find this hard to believe?" I held my head tightly clamped between my hands, trying to keep this insanity from exploding it. "My God, one day I'm a human and just one of the crowd. Now you tell me that I'm a Martian and still just one of the crowd.

"Look at it this way, son," my father was smiling. "Now we'll all be able to go to the convention in Chicago.

We got back from the convention late Sunday afternoon. I mentioned to my dad that I really had a great time and was looking forward to the next one. "I really enjoyed the guest speakers," I pointed out. "I especially liked Ralph Nader, but I wouldn't have thought that Jimmy Carter was a Martian?"

"Actually, I don't believe he is, son."

Dad was laid back in his recliner sucking on his long-stemmed pipe. I was seated across from him trying to get the last flame from my nearly empty lighter. I fumbled around in my pockets for another, but instead came up with a handful of other junk that I laid on the coffee table. I finally grabbed a pack of matches from one of the end tables and lit my cigarette. "What do you mean by that?"

"I think they made Jimmy an honorary Martian back when he was making all that fuss about the flying saucers. They wanted to shut him up."

"I would have figured his brother as an alien, though," I had to admit.

"Now, there's a good bet."

I looked down at my junk on the coffee table. There was a pin button that read, "BE PROUD OF YOUR PINKY", a bunch of small change, a pocketknife, and the "Alien Detector". I picked up the detector and rolled it around in my fingers.

"Knowing what I know, now, I don't think I'll need this, anymore."

ZITS

Gilles McKinney lit another stogy, took the last hit of his double-shot boilermaker, and tried to change the channel to Friday Night Football. His fingers locked up again, and he found himself passing the channel he wanted.

"Crap!" he shouted. "This damn remote is screwing up again."

"Bull shit, Gil," his wife shouted from the kitchen. "You know it's nothing but your damn arthritis. Are you ready for another drink?"

Gil looked at his empty glass. "Yeah, Delores, only this time make it a triple. I don't want to wear you out."

Dolores came into the living room caring his drink; there was a package under her arm.

"What the hell is that?" Gil asked.

"I really don't know, dear. It was mailed from some place called Porto Velho, Brazil."

"Who the hell do we know in Brazil?" Gil asked.

"Well, dear, the name on the package is Pedro Gonzales."

"It must be your side of the family, Honey Pumpkin. There's nobody in my family named Pedro."

"I don't recall knowing anyone named Pedro, either, dear. I guess we'll just have to open the package and see what's inside. They might have mailed it to the wrong person."

Dolores ripped away the tattered wrapping paper and opened the box. There was another box inside. On top was a note written in broken English:

"'Dear Mesus McKiny,'" the letter began. "'I regrit to unform you thet your late brother, Daved Holper, es now of late. He dieded on Agust feeth from the fever. For the last tvanty years he has spent all of he's time looking for de fountain of de youth. For all of des years I have to have been his faithful man, Friday, protecting Meester Daved from panther, piranha, python, anaconda, bird spider, scorpion, electreek eel, caiman, and headhunter. How was it for me to know he would fell veetim to a leetle mosquito?'"

"Oh my God!" Dolores exclaimed, "My poor brother is dead!"

"Poor? If I remember right, he was always loaded with other peoples' money," Gil said, suddenly taking an interest. "What, the hell, else does it say?"

"'Your brother, he's last request, it was to send to you thes package. It is sometheeng he sayed he wonted you to have. Since I have spent mucho Cruzeiros to send thes package, and your brother of late has spent all of his money on thes latest quest, I would mucho appreciate any small money you could please sent me. One hundred of your dollars would be mucho bueno. Yours, most truly, Pedro Gonzales.'"

"So what's in the box?" Gil asked.

"Won't you give me a minute to grieve over the loss of my beloved brother?"

"You haven't heard from that asshole in over forty-five years. His last words to you were 'go to hell', when you asked him for money to help pay for our daughter's wedding, and now you're telling me that you need time to grieve?"

"Blood is thicker than water, dear."

"OK! OK! So what's in the box?"

"Water!"

"Water? Is that all? Now, I'm beginning to wish it was blood! Why in the world, would your weird brother send us water all the way from Brazil?"

"Wait, Puddin' Puss, there's another letter. This one is from my brother. 'Dear Sis,' it says. Isn't that sweet? After all these years, he still called me Sis."

"Damn, Delores, he was your brother. What else is he going to call you?" Gil held one of the bottles up to the light. "Get back to the letter, Honey Pumpkin. Maybe there's some gold, or something in this water and you just can't see it. Ain't diamonds or pearl hard to see in water?"

"If you stop jabberin' away, Gil, I'll get back to my reading. "'As you may or may not know, I made quite a bundle swindling people out of their life savings. For obvious reasons, this required me to keep moving. Once, while hiding out in Sao Paulo, I met a young man who claimed to have discovered the Fountain of Youth. He showed me documentation that he said proved that he was over 350 years old.

Of course, being a swindler, myself, I was no novice when it came to forged documents; although, these documents seemed to be genuine. I informed him that it was easy to obtain forged documents and that even if they were real; there was no proof that he was the person whose name was on the documents. He said that it didn't matter if I believed him or not, and that by morning he would be sober and sorry he opened his big mouth in the first place. He had been drinking quite a bit. It wasn't until the following evening that I ran into him again.'"

"'When I mentioned our conversation of the night before, he immediately denied that any such conversation ever took place. He got rather irate when I pressed the issue, and even told me that if I didn't leave him alone he would have the local authorities take me in and check to see if I had a valid passport. I don't know how he figured out that my passport was a forgery, but I certainly didn't want to push my luck any further.'"

"Was your brother always so longwinded? Why the hell doesn't he get to the point?"

"Oh, hush up, Gil. Now you made me lose my place. Oh yeah, here it is, 'I thought no more of this incident until I ran into this same man in Ulan Bator, in northern Mongolia. I recognized him by a certain unique birthmark on his left arm. He was not a day older, even though twenty-five years had passed. This time I confronted him in a darkened hallway. Although he was younger and stronger than I, I knew he would not argue with my 38, stub-nosed pistol. I told him that I would announce his secret to the world if he did not disclose the source of his eternal youth. Reluctantly, he took me to his room and sat down and drew a map. He told me that this was only the approximate location, for he had returned from the location delirious with yellow fever, and could no longer pin point the exact spot. He showed me what he had left of the elixir of youth. It was a nasty looking, three hundred and fifty-year old, musty smelling water. There was less than a quart left, and yet he offered me a swallow. Reluctantly, I turned him down. I reasoned that I would soon have my own, fresh, sweet elixir from the original source. I was still young, barely forty-five. If I had known it would take me another thirty-two years to find it, I would have readily accepted his offer. His map was accurate to within twenty miles, but finding a small spring in the middle of a steaming, South American jungle proved to be more difficult than even I had imagined.'"

"'For most of the thirty-two years I have wandered the jungle with my faithful companion, Pedro, emerging only long enough to swindle some unsuspecting slob out of his hard-earned savings, to afford enough supplies to go back again. It was not until three weeks ago that I discovered the little spring that has been my undoing as I now realize that I have squandered my youth looking for youth. I fear; however, I will succumb to this fever before the elixir can do me any good, as I believe it may only restore youth and not health.'"

As my closest living relative, I am bestowing on you this greatest of blessings. Use it wisely and in good health. Your loving brother, David.'" There were tears in Delores's eyes.

"If you believe that malarkey, Honey Pumpkin, your brother has pulled off another first, bamboozling someone from the grave."

"I know that it's a lot of malarkey, Puddin' Puss, my poor brother must have been delirious with fever." She opened one of the bottles. "The least we can do is drink a toast to his memory."

"OK, Delores," Gil said, "I'm game, but I want two or three shots in mine. You never know what's swimming around in that crap."

"Good idea." Dolores poured some water into two glasses, and then topped them off with Scotch. She handed a glass to her husband. "To my brother, David," she said. "May he rest in peace."

Gil took a good swallow. It was so strong it made him shiver all over. "Now, that's what I call a toast," he said, pounding his chest to catch his breath. Suddenly his mouth dropped. He looked down at his glass."

"What is it Puddin' Puss?" Delores asked.

"This stuff must be working," Gil looked serious.

Delores felt her face. "Why? Do I look any different?"

"My god, Honey Pumpkin, you don't look a day over seventy-five."

"I'm not a day over seventy-five, you old fool. I'm only seventy-three. You're the one who's seventy-five. Turn off the TV, honey, it's time we went to bed."

"Why?" he asked, clicking off the TV and gently stubbing out his cigar so he could save it for the next day. "Are you feeling in the mood?"

"Gil, you haven't been in the mood for nearly ten years. You'll be asleep the minute your head hits the pillow. Now come on, you old fool, before you fall asleep in the chair again!

Delores was right, Gil did go to sleep the minute his head hit the pillow. Aside from a bad dream that headhunters were chasing him, his night was uneventful. When he awoke the sun was already up. He didn't usually sleep this late. He realized that he was very hungry, and horny.

"Now there," he said to himself, "is a wasted thought."

He looked over at his sleeping wife, but instead of his wife being there, there was a young, teen-aged girl in her place.

"Who are you?" he shouted, pulling the bedclothes around him, as he suddenly felt naked in his boxer shorts. "What have you done with my wife?"

Delores awoke abruptly and began to scream! "What are you doing here, young man? Are you here to rob me? Boy, did you get the wrong house. Gil! Help me!" Delores jumped from the bed with more spring than she ever knew she had. Her nightgown fell from her body. "Gil! Where, the hell, are you?"

"I'm right here. Delores?"

"Gil? Is that you?"

"My God, Delores, look at us. We're young. You look like a sixteen year-old girl."

"And you look like a sixteen year-old boy."

Gil looked across at the sweet, young thing now standing naked before him. "My God, Delores, you look good. I don't remember you looking any better." Gil looked down. His ill-fitting boxer shorts were now around his ankles; his once useless appendage now stood shamelessly erect.

Delores looked confused. "What do we do, now, Gil?" she asked.

"What do you mean, 'what do we do, now?' You get your sweet butt back in this bed."

"Gil, you're incorrigible," she said, giggling."

"And when we're through," Gil informed her, "you can fix me a big lunch."

Delores looked over at the clock on the nightstand. "But Gil, it's only seven-thirty."

"So, it might even be a late lunch."

It was nearly one in the afternoon when the McKinneys finally made it down stairs. Delores went into the kitchen to whip up some soup and sandwiches, while Gil went into the living room for a glass of his usual bracer. He filled a tumbler half full of his favorite whiskey and took a large swallow. He coughed and gagged until he thought he would die.

"Gil?" Are you alright?" Delores yelled from the kitchen.

"I will be," he said between coughs, "when I start breathing again. I think maybe straight whiskey is a little much for my young sensitivity." He picked up a paper that had been on the floor. "You must have dropped this paper last night," he yelled to Delores. It looks like it may have been stuck to the bottom of one the bottles."

"What does it say, Puddin' Puss?" Delores was standing beside him, now, with a tray full of food.

"It tells you to be careful about how much of the water you take. Your brother recommends that you only take an ounce or two, at first. Now he tells us. He calculated that one ounce could take you back four and a half years. How much did you put in our glasses last night?"

"I don't know. I filled them almost to the top, but then there were two shots of scotch in each glass."

"OK. They're sixteen ounce glasses, down, say, one ounce from the top, with two ounces of whiskey; that means we each had about thirteen ounces." Gill removed a calculator from the drawer in the coffee table. "That means if your brother's calculations were about right. Four and a half by thirteen is about fifty-eight and a half years. Let's see," he punched in some more numbers. "Holy shit! This means that I'm going on seventeen and you're barely fifteen. I think they have a law against what we've just been doing."

"Oh, Gil, for goodness sakes, we've been married for over fifty-five years."

"Considering that we don't look much over sixteen, we might have trouble convincing anyone of that."

Gil took a bite of his sandwich, "Look, Delores."

"What am I looking at, Gil?"

"The sandwich doesn't stick to my dentures, because I'm not wearing any. They're still setting on the nightstand. I could get use to being sixteen again."

"Well, don't get too used to it, Gil. I'm sure that this isn't anything that is going to last."

"Well, what if it did, Delores? What if we were really fifteen and sixteen, and we would stay this way until we became sixteen and seventeen?"

"Don't be silly, Puddin' Puss, I'm sure that this is something that will wear off like Novocain."

"I wouldn't be too sure of that, Honey Pumpkin. If this was something that wore off in a day or so, then why did your brother only send us six bottles?" He held up one of the bottles. "These are empty whiskey bottles. They hold one-fifth, which means we have a fifth over a gallon. If the both of us only used an ounce a day, there isn't enough here to last us six months. No, I think your brother figured that this would last us a long, long time."

"You mean to tell me that we are stuck with these bodies for good?"

"What do you mean 'stuck,' Delores? I would think you'd be happy to be fifteen, again."

"I'm not sure that I like being fifteen."

"I don't get you, Delores. What's wrong with being fifteen?"

"Well for one thing, this morning I was a virgin again, and the first time hurt me."

"So why didn't you say something?"

"You didn't notice?"

"I've never had a virgin before. How would I know?"

"I would have thought it would be quite obvious. After all, you did have trouble penetrating me, didn't you?"

"I thought you were just playing hard to get. Besides, how in the hell, could you get re-virginized?"

"I don't know, but I was."

"Dolores, you're full of shit!"

"That's what you said last night about these." She held up one of the bottles.

"Yeah, well you didn't seem to have a whole lot of faith in it either, Dolores. Why are you being so argumentative? You're not usually like that."

"I'm bored, Gil. I want to do something."

"So, what do you want to do?"

"Why don't we go to the mall?"

"Sure," Gil said, feeling a little bored himself. "What do you want to buy?"

"I don't mean just to go shopping, Gil. I thought we could go hang out with some people our own age."

"Which age are you talking about, Delores, seventy or sixteen?"

"The mall is where all the young kids hang out. I think it would be fun to go hang out with them. Besides," she pulled at the baggy sweatpants she was forced to wear, "we need to buy some clothes that fit."

Gil dug through the closet until he found a pair of his old "someday" pants. These were pants that he had gotten too fat for and kept them only because he felt that someday he would be able to get into them again. Unfortunately, "someday" never came, until now.

Delores had to do with ill-fitting sweat pants. She was never anyone for keeping things she no longer had any use for, except maybe Gil. Now, she was glad she did, even if it was originally intended to be cut up for dustcloths. Gil looked handsome in his blue jeans and sweatshirt, even if they were still a little big for him.

It was Saturday, and the mall was busy. Gil and Delores could see kids standing around in groups. There were groups of girls, groups of boys, and groups of girls and boys. They were all giggling and acting stupid. At least, that's how Gil saw them.

Delores walked up to a young couple who were holding hands and kissing. Clearing her throat, she said, "Hi, we're new in town. Could you tell us where we might be able to find a good clothing store that caters to young people?"

The young girl looked Delores over. "Why don't you check out the trash cans out back? That's where you got those clothes, isn't it?"

Gil looked the girl over. She was wearing a skirt that barely covered her thighs and a blouse that never made it past her ribcage, exposing to all a cheap zircon ring that was embedded in her navel. "And where did you get yours, sweetie, Tiny Tots? Come on, Delores," Gil said, taking his wife's hand, "there must be a trash can out back here, somewhere. Better to wear trash, than look like trash." He could see that the boy wanted to start something, but had chickened out. At sixteen, Gil was a big boy and could take care of himself.

As they walked away, the girl yelled after them, "Oh, yeah!" she yelled, "Oh, yeah!"

Gil stopped, took a dime from his pocket, and tossed it back to her. "Here," he yelled, "call me in about sixty years. Maybe by then you'll have something clever to say."

Delores pulled at Gil's sleeve, "You're showing your age, Puddin' Puss, when was the last time a phone call cost a dime?"

"You're right, Honey Pumpkin, but if I threw her a quarter I might get picked up for soliciting." He put his arm around her tiny waist, drew her close, and gave her a big kiss.

"Gil! My god! We're in the middle of a mall. People are looking."

"Get with it, baby," Gil said, drawing his wife closer, "this is a new century, we're young, no one cares what we do. We could probably screw in the fountain in the center of this mall and hardly anyone would notice. The ones who did would probably just cheer us on."

"Don't you even think of anything like that, Gilles McKinney!"

"Alright, Delores, so what do you want to do, now?"

Dolores grabbed Gil's left hand and spun out into his arms. "I want to go dancing," she announced.

"Cool," he said. "Do they still say 'cool'?"

"I think so, Dear," Delores held Gil's face in her hand, "but now I think it's 'too cool'. Let's go get some new clothes and go somewhere where they have dancing."

"That's cool, Delores, too cool."

The clerk didn't even give Gil a second look when he whipped out a credit card to pay for their purchases. Delores explained that kids, now days, have credit cards. A lot of parents give their kids credit cards and put limits on them. All this was fine as long as they didn't ask for ID. Gil's driver's license had his picture on it, the picture of a seventy-plus-year-old man.

At the nightclubs, the bouncers wouldn't even let them in the door. The only place they could find to dance was a family restaurant and lounge that had a dance floor. Actually, the music was more to their liking. The noise that had poured out of the nightclubs was loud and frightening. The music here was lively: fox trots, tangos, and waltzes, along with some of the rock-n-roll and boogie-woogie hits from the past. The dance floor was theirs, as Gil and Delores "cut a rug" to a tune they hadn't danced to in over fifty years.

When the music stopped, people were standing around, clapping. One older woman put her hand on Delores's shoulder, and told her that she hadn't seen anyone dance like that since the forties. Delores had been a professional hoofer, in her younger years. She even danced with the Rockettes for a while, until she got pregnant. It was just like they were living the old days all over again. They never wanted the evening to end, but the place closed early and they were asked to leave.

Back on the street, Gil looked at his watch. "The bars are still open. Come on, Delores, I'll buy you a drink."

"Where are you going to find a place that will serve us?"

"We'll go to the Roustabout. Shorty knows me. I'll give him a wink; order the usual. He'll recognize me."

"Won't Shorty get in trouble serving you?"

"It's late, Delores, the place is dark, everybody's drunk, we'll sit in the corner, have one drink and leave. After this night I need a pick-me-up."

Gil was right about two things; the place was dark, and everybody was drunk, except Shorty. He refused to serve them and asked them to leave. Gil pulled out his driver's license and showed it to him.

"Look, Shorty, it's me, Gil McKinney."

Shorty took the license and held it up to the light. "I don't know how you know my name, kid, but this is Gil McKinney's driver's license. How did you get it?"

"Look at me, Shorty. It's me, Gil. Take a good look. I just look a little younger."

"Yeah, about fifty years younger. Now get out of here, punk, before I call the cops."

"Can I have my license back?" Gil asked.

"No way, punk! I said get out of here, now!"

Gil and Delores walked back to the parking lot in silence. Delores knew better than to say anything when Gil was in one of his moods. The ride home was equally as quiet, except for an occasional cuss word uttered under Gil's breath.

On Monday morning, Police Chief Walkins was handed a small envelope. "What is this, Delaney?" he asked the officer who had given it to him.

"One of the bartenders at the Roustabout brought it in this morning. I thought it might interest you, Chief."

Chief Walkins opened the envelope and held a drivers license close to his face. "Gilles McKinney. Yeah, I know Gil. We go back a long way. He was just like an uncle to me when I was a kid, him and his wife, Delores. We used to play ball after school in the lot next door to their house. They used to set there on the side steps and cheer us on. They made us lemonade and handed out Popsicles. Gil was a fireman, until he retired; one of the best. You've heard me talk about him before. See that he gets his license back."

"Yeah, but Chief," Delaney interrupted, "Shorty, the bartender that was working at the Roustabout on Saturday night, said that the guy he took this off of, claimed that he was Gil McKinney. He said the kid couldn't have been over sixteen."

"That's ridicules; the kid must have been on drugs. Gil has to be at least seventy."

"According to his license, he's seventy-five," Delaney offered.

"How did some young punk get Gil's driver's license? Maybe the two of us ought to go check this out, personally."

Gil woke up with another hangover. He went down stairs and into the living room for his usual morning bracer, but somehow, the thought didn't appeal to him. Instead, he went to the kitchen and retrieved a container of orange juice from the refrigerator. Delores was already up, making breakfast. She was humming to herself. Gil sat at the table and clamped his head between his hands. Delores's humming was about as welcome as his headache. There was a knock at the door.

"Can you get that, dear?" Delores asked. "I don't want these eggs to burn."

"Yeah, yeah, I'll get it." Gil got to his feet, rewrapped and retied his baggy bathrobe. He shuffled to the door, his floppy slippers nearly falling off twice on the way. He opened the door to a familiar face. "Hi, Chief," he said, nonchalantly, "what's up?"

The two officers were through the door and had him cuffed before he knew what was happening. Shorty was standing behind them, in the doorway.

"Is this the punk, Shorty?" Delaney asked.

"Yeah, that's him, alright," Shorty said, assuredly.

"OK, punk, where is Gil and who are you?" the Chief asked.

"Gil, ah, Gil and Delores went away."

"Away to where?" the Chief was walking around the living room looking everything over."

"They went to Europe," Gil said, nervously.

"And who are you that they would leave you in charge of the house?" The chief was pointing a finger in Gil's face.

"I'm his, ah, grandson."

"I've met Gil's grandson, he's over thirty."

"Did-did I say grandson," Gil stammered, "I meant great-grandson."

"And I suppose," the Chief said, looking at Delores who now stood in the doorway of the living room wiping her hands on a towel," that this is Gil's great granddaughter. I think you two had better go with us down to Juvenile Hall, until we can straighten this out."

"Can we at least eat breakfast?" Delores asked. "It's all ready."

"What do you have?" the Chief asked.

"Toast, scrambled eggs and bacon," Delores offered.

"Make yourselves a couple of sandwiches out of it," the Chief said, "you can eat them when we get to the station." He turned to Delaney, "Get a crew in here. Tear this place apart, if you have to. I want to find out what they did with the McKinneys."

"No!" Gil yelled, as they dragged him out the door. "That's not necessary!"

That day Gil and Delores sat in Juvenile Hall while the police poked holes in any wall that didn't sound hollow, took up part of the basement floor, where years ago Gil had removed an old cistern, dug up all of Delores's flower gardens, and any other place where the dirt had been disturbed. Even the once hallowed ground of Dolores's little dog, Peanut, had been desecrated. The box of elixir was confiscated, but once it proved to be nothing but water, it was returned.

Gil was taken in for questioning and given the "good cop/bad cop" routine. "What did you do with the bodies, punk?"

The bad cop was close to his face, his breath smelled of cigarettes and liquorish. Gil thought about how much he missed a good, strong cigar.

"I bet you think you're pretty clever, don't you, punk?"

The way the cop said "punk" sounded almost like "puke".

The bad cop grabbed Gil by the front of his shirt and threw him up against the wall. He had his hand on the back of Gil's head and was grinding his face into the wall.

This would be a good time for the good cop to jump in, Gil thought.

He took his sweet time. "Come on, Phil, he's a juvy," the good cop finally said. "You can't beat up on kids. They break easy, you know?"

The bad cop let loose, and Gil slid slowly down the wall to the floor. The good cop was there to help him up. He helped him back to the table and into a chair, brushing away at the back of his shirt.

"Y'know, kid, we still don't know what your name is. Right now, you're known officially as, John Doe. If you would just tell me your real name we could communicate on a more personal level. If not, then I'll just have to call you Johnny."

"I told you. My name is Gil." Gil was getting tired of this whole game; he just wanted to go home.

"OK, Johnny, have it your way. We know that your name isn't Gil. Gil McKinney never had a great grandson named Gil. The fact is he doesn't have a great grandson, only a great granddaughter named Patricia, who just turned twelve. Somehow, you don't look like a Patricia."

The bad cop was in his face, again. He grabbed Gil by the chin. "Maybe this one would like to be a girl. I know a guy they call "the Hulk" who has a room at the state prison. He could make you feel like a girl. We could make him your roommate."

"Phil, you're scaring the shit out of the poor kid. He's had a hard time and he's just a little confused."

"You're too easy on these punks, Frank. Let me take this sack of shit into the back room for about ten minutes. I'll get the information out of him." His eyes narrowed as he looked down at Gil. "No problem."

Gil didn't know how long he was there, but when he got back to Juvenile Hall, he found out that he had missed his supper. The only thing he had had to eat that day was his breakfast sandwich, a candy bar, and the two Cokes that the good cop had given him during his interrogation. He wondered what Delores was going through. He bet that whatever it was, it was similar. They would be trying to compare their two stories.

But what stories could they give them; that they drank some water and woke up the next day as teenagers? Gil knew that they would never believe that. He almost felt like confessing to the murder of Gil McKinney just so he could get some rest. The only thing that was keeping him going was that he knew that they would either have to charge them tomorrow, or let him go. He was sure that he remembered a law that said they could only hold someone for forty-eight hours or something to that effect. If they did charge them, the court would have to appoint them a lawyer.

A stiff drink and a good stogy would sure be good right now, he said to himself.

Delaney was excited when he flew into the Chief's office. "We got the report on the prints back for the FBI," he said. "They just came in on the fax. You're not going to believe this, Chief. They positively identified the boy."

"What boy?" the Chief asked, rubbing the sleep from his eyes. He was still on his first cup of coffee and not fully awake.

"The kid we brought in, last night, on the Gil McKinney case."

"Oh, yeah." The Chief took a sip of his coffee. "So what's the punk's name?"

"Gilles T. McKinney."

"Is this a joke, Delaney? Cause if it is, it ain't funny."

"No Chief, I had them check it out again. The prints belong to Gil McKinney, our Gil McKinney,"

The Chief was rubbing his face with both hands, now. "OK, Delaney, have the kid brought up to my office. I want to talk to him myself. We need to get to the bottom of this."

Gil had mixed emotions about being summoned again. He was bored, cooped up in that two by four cell. It seems that they don't put "juvenile killers" in with the general lockup, so there was nothing to do but sit on that hard bunk and stare at the walls. On the other hand, another day of interrogation didn't hold much appeal for him, either. This time; however, they didn't take him to the interrogation room, but to the Chief's office.

The Chief looked up from his paperwork and took a double take. "Did somebody beat you up, kid?" he asked.

"No," Gil said. He ran his hand over his face. There was stubble. "I just need a shave. Wait a minute!" He felt his face with both hands. "I never had to shave until I was nearly twenty."

Delaney was looking closely at Gil's face. "He does look older, Chief," Delaney said. "Now, he looks about twenty-one."

"Now will you believe me, Chief? I am Gil McKinney."

The Chief was holding his head in both hands. "None of this makes any sense; you're sixteen, you're twenty-one, you're seventy-something." He motioned for Delaney to come close, and then motioned for him to lean down so he could whisper in his ear. "What do we have on this kid, Delaney?"

"Well, Chief, he was trying to buy a drink at a bar, under age, and with a false ID."

"How old does he look to you, standing there, right now?"

"He looks about twenty-one, maybe twenty-two."

"So, it stands to reason, that if he is over twenty-one today, he must have been at least twenty-one yesterday, right Delaney?"

"Well, yeah, Chief, if you put it that way."

"And even if we don't think that he is the real Gil McKinney, the FBI says he is, right?"

"Yeah, Chief, that's what they say."

"Then I think you had better see to their release, personally, right now. With a good lawyer, these kids could sue the pants off of us."

"OK, Chief," Delaney said, starting out the door."

"Oh, and Delaney?"

"Yes Chief?"

"See if somebody out there has something stronger than aspirin."

Gil stabbed at the remote and his finger locked up again. He looked down at his wrinkled, liver-spotted hands and smiled. There was a knock at the door. "Dolores, will you get that. I hope it's not the Chief again, one more damn apology and I think I'll puke!"

"It's little Charley from next-door, Puddin' Puss," Dolores shouted back. "He wants to ask you something."

"Have him come in here." Gil set down the remote and took a swig of his double boilermaker.

"Hi, Mr. McKinney." Charley was about eight, a bit short for his age, and quite shy. "My mommy said that I had to come over here and ask you."

"Ask me what, Charley?"

"I was wondering if I could have that box in your trash."

"What for, Charley?"

"It's got stamps from Brazil on it and I collect stamps"

"I'll tell you what, Charley. You can have the stamps, but leave that box in the trash.

"OK, Mr. McKinney. Thanks," he said, over his shoulder as he dashed for the door."

"Wait a minute, Charley. Are the kids playing ball today, in the lot next door?"

"Yes, Mr. McKinney."

"Thanks, Charley. Enjoy your stamps." With a little effort, Gil pulled himself slowly up from his chair. "Honey Pumpkin!" he shouted to his wife, who was now in the kitchen. "Make up a pitcher of lemonade, and then grab your shawl. We've got a game to watch. I'm gonna grab a couple of cushions. My ass can't take those hard, concrete steps like it could when I was young."

THE EVIL THAT MEN DO

"Jesus pal, don't you think you've had enough?

"Screw you, Phil, you've been serving me this watered down swill you call whiskey for ten years and you still don't know my fucking name? Think a minute; it's right on the tip of your tongue, Ruben, Roderick, Richard; something like that."

"OK, Randal, you made your point, but a drunk by any other name, isn't he still a drunk? How about I call you a cab?"

Randal pulled his keys from his pocket and dangled them in front of the bartender. "Why do I need a cab when I have my own car?"

"Because you're drunk, and one of these days you are going to kill yourself."

"Ah, a consummation devoutly to be wished. You see I, too, can misquote Shakespeare."

"Suit yourself, Randal, but if you wrap your car around a tree and kill yourself, don't come crying back to me."

"Ah, yes, that unknown country from who's borne no traveler returns. What irony it would be, should I be the first to return, that I should seek out your sorry company? Alas, I have my keys, I've surely had one or two for the road, I see not one comely wench on whom I would bestow the sweet sonnets of love's true gist, and the pleasant lure of a dreamless sleep and drool-soaked pillow, doth beckon me from the sanctum of my humble abode. I bid thee farewell, loyal barkeep, for though I now see you faintly through blood-shot eyes, I will remember this moment, not, by morning's light."

Phil shook his head as Randal, with much difficulty, made his way out the door. Staggering around the parking lot, he finally found his car. He fumbled for several minutes trying to get the key into the lock before realizing that he had failed to lock the car door.

"Didn't I leave it unlocked at the fourth or fifth watering hole, also?" he muttered aloud. "What the hell is worth stealing, anyway? My cassette player hasn't worked in ten years, and the car has more dents and craters than the moon." He looked around the car. "The rear view mirror fell off three weeks ago. It doesn't matter. I don't want to see where the hell I've been, anyway."

After a few attempts, he managed to get the key into the ignition. The engine started with a roar, and the grinding sound finally reminded him that he had to let go of the key. It took every bit of concentration to maneuver the car out of the parking lot and onto the highway. Fortunately, the traffic was light, and the car that he pulled out in front of could, with horn blaring, easily avoid him.

"Sorry, asshole!"

He nearly lost control of the car, as he removed his hand from the steering wheel to extend his middle finger. He drove two blocks before he realized that he had forgotten to turn on his headlights. It started to rain. He, somehow, managed to turn on the wipers. The dirty, bug-smeared windshield suddenly looked like a brightly lit kaleidoscope. He leaned closer to the windshield to try to see where he was going. Up ahead, a light turned red and added still another color to the blurry pallet.

He cruised on through the red light, as another driver jammed on his brakes and skidded on the damp pavement. The car collided with the rear of Randal's car and sent it skidding sideways. Randal managed to straighten the car and kept on going.

"Lousy driver!" he muttered. "If I weren't so damn tired I'd stop and give him a piece of my mind."

The windshield cleared in time to allow Randal to see his turn onto highway 6. The rain was coming down harder, and the windows were beginning to steam up. He rolled down the driver's side window to let in some fresh air. The air conditioning no longer worked, and he was glad that this old car had side vents. The slapping sound of the wipers and the occasional rain blowing in through the open window had a bit of a sobering effect, enough to make him realize that he shouldn't be behind the wheel of a car.

He eased the car over to the outside lane and concentrated on keeping it well to the right of the centerline. He couldn't be sure if the blurry view was because of the rain-smeared windshield, his condition, or both. He thought of pulling off the road and sleeping it off.

"No, I can't do that. That will draw the cops. Another D.W.I on a revoked license. That would be just great, wouldn't it? Nah, I'll just take it real easy. Only a couple of more miles and then I'll be in bed sleeping this off."

As he made the turn onto First Street, he wiped out a row of trashcans, sending them rolling, noisily, down the center of the street, and causing him to swerve to try to avoid them. Lights suddenly came on in bedroom windows and he could see dark silhouettes, as curtains were draw aside. He sped up and nearly didn't make the turn onto East Park.

Not much longer and he would be home. He wondered what time it was. If it's too late, he might have to sleep on the couch. He didn't care; at this point he would gladly sleep on the floor, just as long as he didn't have to listen to his wife's incessant bitching.

"I thought you weren't going to drink anymore, Randal? Don't you care about your family? I never know when you're coming home, or if you're coming home at all. I half expect to see a cop knocking on the door to tell me that they found you dead in some alley, or the car wrapped around a tree."

"Always the nagging, always the bitching; no wonder I drink. That woman could drive anyone to drink."

"What the hell did she have to bitch about, anyway? He had a job; in fact he had a good job. The bills got paid. The mortgage got paid. What more did she want? He was a good accountant, and good accountants aren't that easy to come by. OK, so it was kind of a dead-end job with little chance of advancement, but with advancement comes more responsibility, and who the hell needed that? He liked everything just as it was. They left him alone and he did his job, and he did it well."

"So he got a little wasted on the weekends. Who did that hurt? A man needs some kind of recreation. A couple of drinks, a few laugh, maybe play some pool with the guys; is there anything wrong with that? The rest of the week he was home. A few cocktails, a little TV, and he would be in bed by ten. How more homey can one get?"

"Betty would even bitch about his cocktails. She doesn't realize that a person has to unwind after a hard day's work. She even bitched because he would let Junior have a couple of beers when they watched TV. It was only beer. He was drinking beer when he was Junior's age, and it never hurt him. Would she rather have him doing drugs, or have him going to one of those parties were everyone gets drunk or strung out on God knows what? Here he was, safe at home, tipping a few brewskis with the old man. Didn't she understand that this was the lesser evil? Betty just liked to hear herself bitch. Bitch . . . bitch . . . bitch."

The pressure of a full bladder now gave him incentive to speed up. A couple of more blocks and he could relieve himself in the comfort of his own bathroom. He began to move about in the seat, uneasily. Maybe he should have gone before he left the bar, or relieved himself in front of the car, in the parking lot. A cross street was coming up, but the stop sign was for traffic coming from the other way. He didn't bother to slow down.

The speeding car hit the front of his car and spun it around. His car hit the curb and flipped twice before coming to rest on its left side. Randal was wedged between the roof and the seat, his chest was crushed and his neck was broken. He had wet himself. His lungs were filling with blood, and he could feel the life leaving his body.

"I'm sorry, Betty. I'm so sorry," were the last words he ever spoke.

Corporal Stanton looked up from his notes. "I used to say that we ought to let all of the drunks out on the street for an hour or so, at the same time every night, and let them kill each other off, but seeing something like this just makes me realize that it just leaves another mess for someone else to clean up."

Sergeant Tooney watched as the body of a young boy was being removed from the wrecked Ford Escort. "The kid doesn't even look old enough to be out driving at night, let alone old enough to drink."

"He wasn't," Corporal Stanton said, holding up an ID card. "He only had a learner's permit. Some friend of his had to have bought the beer for him."

"Looks like they didn't do him any favors," the Sergeant shook his head. "What about the other guy?"

"Reeked of booze; like he took a bath in the stuff. By the looks of all the rusty dents, it was probably only a matter of time before he ended up getting into something more serious. Ironically, if he had been sober, and driving with a valid license, none of it would have been his fault."

"If the kid had to hit someone, better another drunk. Four-thirty in the morning is not a good time to have to wake someone up and tell them that their loved one won't be coming home. The Sergeant put out his hand. "Why don't I take one of those ID's and get at least one dastardly deed over with?"

Corporal Stanton held up the two ID's. "I don't think that will be necessary. They both have the same name and the same address, "Randal J. Westmont, and Randal J. Westmont, Jr. It looks like the father and son will be spending a lot more time together.

Sergeant Tooney shook his head, "Why does this shit always have to happen on my watch?"

THE WITNESS

The young boy was turned around in his seat and intently looking at Frank. Frank moved his hand so the boy could see the handcuffs. He made a gun with his free hand, pointed it at the boy, and pretended to pull the trigger. The boy disappeared and seconds later his mother appeared, glaring back at Frank. He flipped her "The bird". The mother and son got up and changed seats.

"Jesus, Frank," said Delaney, "he's just a kid."

"Yeah, so what's your point, Delaney?

"Weren't you ever a kid?"

"I had no time to be a kid, Delaney. In the neighborhood I lived in, it was all you could do to stay alive."

"We were all kids once, Frank, you, me, and even Tony Millano."

"I killed my first snitch when I was twelve, Delaney. Does that sound like a kid to you?" "You know, Frank, you have no soul. I'll bet you never had a dog or a cat when you were a kid, did you?"

"My old man didn't like them. I watched him beat a neighbor's dog to death with a two by four just for getting in our trash."

"Did you ever have a pet?"

"Yeah, in prison. I had me a rat I used to feed."

"What ever happened to it?"

"It bit me. I bashed its brains in with a shoe."

The train was moving, now, and the conductor came around to collect tickets. He looked at the two men, suspiciously, as Delany reached into his top, shirt pocket for the tickets. He punched the tickets and moved on.

"I don't need any problems from you, Constanso. I can sure as hell think of a lot of other places I would rather be than hauling your sorry ass all the way to Chicago; like home with my wife and kid."

"If we had taken the plane, we would have been there by now, and you could be home humpin' the old lady and beatin' the brat."

"You have such a way with words, Constanso; it's a wonder you never became a poet. They'd be watching the planes. The important thing isn't my comfort, but that you get to Chicago in time to testify against Millano."

"Do you really think that you're gonna get me there, alive. If I didn't hate cops so much, Delany, I could almost feel sorry for you, your future widow, and your fatherless kid. Millano has too many friends, Delany, and it's a long way to Chicago."

A man got up and made his way toward the front of the car. Delany watched him, carefully. He place his hand on the butt of his piece, hidden under his jacket.

"Take it easy, Delany; don't get your shorts in a knot. He's not one of them."

"How can you be so cock sure?"

"He looks too much like a gangster. The guy who nails me will look like an accountant, a lawyer, a priest or something. You'll never see it coming. It will be ping, ping, ping, ping and it'll be all over for both of us."

"Thanks, Frank, I feel so much better knowing that."

"Hey, how about the kid; he could be a midget, or the mother could be a fag in drag. Like I said, you'll never know where it's gonna come from."

"If you are so sure we're not gonna make it, why aren't you scared?"

Because I know that no matter what happens, you will be there to protect me. That's your job, ain't it, Delany, even if you have to take the bullet. I figure that will give me time enough to grab your piece and pump a few rounds into the SOB. In the confusion I could get your key, slip the cuffs, and get away."

"That's all good, Frank, but don't you think that there are other Marshals on this train?"

"Not the way I figure it. I figure that there is some poor sap moving with a lot more fanfare, disguised as me, while you and I slip away, unnoticed. Mallano is smarter than that. It won't be that easy. Besides, if you had a hundred feds it wouldn't matter. Mallano's guys would pick them out and neutralize them long before they came after the cheese."

"What makes you so fucking smart Frank?"

"I grew up with all of these rats, Delany, swam in the same sewers, and picked cheese from the same baited traps. You didn't grow up with a silver spoon in your mouth, either."

"Now, how do you know that?"

"The way you talk, the way you eat, and the way you pick your teeth. If you hadn't gone one way and I the other, we could have been alumni."

"Stop, Constanso, you're getting me all teary eyed."

Frank looked out the window. The landscape had changed from small towns and pine forests. Now they were passing small lakes and swamps. He figured they must be going through Georgia. The sun was setting, now, streaming through the window. The trees gave it a flashing effect like a thousand flashbulbs going off. He reached up to pulled down the shade.

Suddenly, there was a screeching sound, then a bump, and the cars jammed together. He lifted the shade. Why were we stopping way out here? He never got an answer. The car stopped abruptly and Delany and he were thrown against the back of the seat ahead. Then the car spun sideways and tipped to the right, throwing both of them against the window so hard that the glass shattered against Frank's shoulder. He got the sensation that they were falling.

Something hit the side of the car and the outside bulkhead gave way just in front of them. People were being thrown around the car like dolls in a shoebox. Frank grabbed the seat and hung on. Delany was trying to pull himself off of Frank. The impact had knocked the wind out of both of them.

Water was rushing in through the open gap in the side. The car rolled completely over on its left side. Delany tried to make it for the surface and pull Constanso with him. Frank swung as hard as he could. It wasn't easy, as he had to overcome the resistance of the water and use his left hand. The force caught Delany on the side of his head and his body went limp.

Frank used his feet to push out the rest of the window and crawled through. Using the handcuffs, he pulled Delany after him. The water was brown and cloudy and it was hard to see more than a foot or so. As he swam past the right side of the car, he could see people in the windows, some were struggling with the glass, and others were already dead.

He laid Delany's unconscious body on the track and fumbled in his jacket pocket for the key. He found it in an inside watch pocket. How predictable. He unlocked the handcuffs and dropped back into the water. He lowered himself to the right side of the car and began kicking in the windows. He reached down and pulled people through. He worked his way to the front of the car, and using all his strength he pulled the door open. He pulled bodies free of the door, leaving the obviously dead to float away.

He returned to the surface, gasped for air and dove again. Reaching back into the car he grabbed the mother and the little boy. The boy looked frightened. She looked dead. Never the less, he brought them both to the surface and went back down for others. He swam deeper and deeper into the car pulling more bodies from the tangled wreck. It wasn't long before he realized that there were no more left to save.

He walked along the track, away from the wreck. He needed to find some dry clothes, boost a car, and get the hell out of wherever he was. When he looked back the scene looked surreal. The engine and cars were scattered about like a tiny toy railroad, purposely derailed by a mischievous cat. He thought of the dead and dying and looked within himself for pity. He found none. He wondered why he had done what he had done. Suddenly he found himself thinking of the little boy and the dead mother. A passing thought put a tear in the corner of his eye. Not for that little boy, but for a little boy from so many years ago.

When Delany came to, someone was leaning over him.

"You OK, mister?"

Delany coughed up some swamp water and shook his head. He reached up and felt the side of his face. A left hook, he was sure. He looked around for the key to the cuffs. It was laying a couple of feet away. He removed the cuffs and rubbed his arm. There were marks where the cuffs had dug into the flesh. He felt inside his jacket. He still had his gun. "Yeah," he said, "I'm OK."

The man started to get up. Delany grabbed his arm. "I need to get to a phone. Can you tell me where I can find one?"

"There's a road down here about half a mile." The man pointed down the track. "About two hundred yards up the road is a gas station. There's a pay phone out front. Now, please, I have people who need help."

Delany got to his feet. He was feeling a little dizzy. Frank had gone this way, too; he knew it. Somehow he managed to make it to the road where he found a Deputy Sheriff.

"Names Mike Delany," he said, showing his badge. "I'm with the Federal Marshals. I was transporting a dangerous felon who got away in the confusion. I need to get to a phone, fast."

"Get in;" said the deputy, "I'll take you to the substation. Maybe we can find you some dry clothes, too."

Frank pulled to the side of the road as the engine coughed and sputtered and finally died. Steam poured out from under the hood and he knew that this car wasn't going another foot. He lifted the hood, not because he knew anything about cars, he didn't, but because it is the universal sign of distress. Sure enough, a few minutes later, a Good Samaritan pulled in behind him.

"Y'all havin' trouble, Mister?"

That, thought Frank, *should be quite obvious, even to a dump, country hick.* "Yeah," he said, trying to sound as "down home" as his city upbringing could allow. "I was drivin' along and it just quit. Do you know anything about cars? Maybe you could take a look."

The man stepped to the front of the car and peered under the hood. "Well, yer radiator's mighty hot. Could be a loose belt, or yer water pump."

Frank stepped in alongside and placed his hands on the front of the upraised hood. "You don't say." He looked around, and seeing no traffic, he brought the hood down hard on the man's head. He dragged him to the side of the road, behind the car, and rummaged through his pockets. He found forty-three dollars, some change, a gas card, and, in a sheath on his belt, a folding pocketknife. He threw the gas card back at the fallen man and kept the rest. He checked the guy out. He'd have a nasty gash on his head and a headache for a while, but he would be OK.

As he drove off in the man's car, he checked the gas gage. It had a full tank. How *thoughtful*, he thought. The main road wouldn't be safe for him so he took to the secondary roads. When it got dark, he found a car on the back street of some small town and swapped plates. Ten minutes later he crossed the state line into Tennessee.

Just south of Nashville he stopped at a small all-night diner to get something to eat and studied the map he had found in the glove box. He was in no big hurry. He would take the scenic route and avoid the main roads as much as possible. By the time he hit Decatur it was still dark. He pulled into a used car lot and mounted the plates on a late model Ford. He only went a few miles before he was forced to find a gas station. Car dealers are never too generous with their gas.

Sergeant Nichols was just enjoying his first cup of coffee when a big guy in a flannel shirt and ill-fitting dungarees came in to his precinct. He did; however, recognize the shoes, standard prison-issued oxfords. He laid his hand on his pistol and motioned for back up. "And what can I do for you?" he asked.

"You need to get hold of Michael Delany with the US Marshall's office and tell him that you have Frank Constanso in custody."

"And why would I want to do that?"

"Because I'm a very big fish, and if you have any intention of drawing a pension, you had better not let this one go. I need a clean cell without a window, where I can get a few hours sleep. I've been on the road for twelve hours and haven't slept in over twenty-four."

"Hell, why not. Welcome to the Ritz, Mr. Constanso. That's Michael Delany, you say?"

Delany had just gotten out of the shower when the phone rang.

"Get down here, Delany." It was Donnally, the Chicago DA. "Constanso's turned himself in."

"Frank Constanso? Why the hell would he do that?"

"That's what I want you to find out. Get down to the Fourteenth Precinct. Take ten agents and an armored car if you have to, but get him to the courthouse safe and sound. He's do to testify in three hour."

As Delany got dressed, he wondered what the hell Constanso was up to. He had pulled him out of the flooded train. But then, at that point, he didn't have too many options. It was either pull him out, or cut off his arm. But the gun? Why didn't he take the gun? A guy, like Constanso, must feel naked without one. And why the hell would he turn himself in? Did he hit his head, or something?"

An hour later he put the same questions to Frank Constanso.

"You don't get it do you, Delany? All those guys I did, that was business. I didn't hate those guys, hell, half of them I didn't even know until I did them. They were just a mark and when I took them out I got well paid. I always prided myself in doing a clean job, and I like to think that none of those marks ever knew what hit them."

"Now, Tony Mallano and I go way back. Back when we were kids rolling drunks, doin' numbers, and later a little muscle work. We were like family. We took care of one another. I never had no real family. My father used to chase skirts and beat my old lady when he got drunk. One day she did him in with one of his own gulf clubs. While she was doing time, I went from one foster home to another. Finally, I ended up in juvy, and when I got out Tony gave me a job. A big mouth DA, named Baleeno was shooting his mouth off about how he was going to put Tony away. Tony wanted him silenced. I took him out at his kid's birthday party from a big oak across the street. He was lying down in a chaise lounge. I used a small caliber rifle. The bullet bounced around inside his head and never exited. No one even knew that he was dead until an hour later, and by then I was back in Chicago hearing about it on the radio."

"Like I said, Tony and I were like family. I took care of him and he took care of me. About two years ago, in Miami, I was hoofing it back to the hotel, trying to work off a fine New York strip, when I got the feeling I was being followed. I turned a corner and ducked into an alleyway. Who do I find following me but Big Al McCarthy. He worked for Tony, occasionally, doing odd jobs and a few hits now and then. He was an amateur; sloppy, messy, and careless. I jabbed a shiv into his back, and before his big legs stopped moving, I dumped his sorry ass over a four-foot fence and into a vacant lot. I could never stand that fucking mick."

"I knew he was after me, and I knew why. The week before, I heard that Benny Serrano had gotten it in Chicago. At the time, the Feds were closing in on Tony; and me and Benny had one thing in common; we knew too much. I didn't want to think that Tony could stoop that low, but when I saw McCarthy, I knew that I was next on the list. Like I told you before, this business isn't like it used to be. You never know where the hit is coming from. It could be a priest with a Bible, a lawyer type, or even a broad. Now days, it's easy money for college kids, Real Estate salesmen, and school teachers."

"I was sure you were never going to get me to Chicago, but when the train derailed, I knew that it was no accident."

Delany looked skeptical, "Do you think that Tony would put hundreds of lives in jeopardy just to save his own skin?"

"In a heartbeat. He would take out a whole city if he thought it would save his own sorry ass."

"So, Frank, you think that there was one of Tony's men on the train?"

"No, not on the train. Not if they knew that it was going to be wrecked. Someone would have been waiting and watching."

"So how did you get away without them seeing you? Delany asked.

"After I did McCarthy, Tony would have known better than to send someone I would know; therefore, whoever he sent wouldn't know me. They would have been looking for a Federal Marshal with a prisoner in tow. When I passed them I was just one of the victims, limping away."

"Lucky for you we found you when we did."

Frank lay back in the chair and chuckled to himself. "An anonymous call, Frank Constanso, in room 201, in a Miami hotel. You Feds couldn't find your asses with radar."

"You turned yourself in? Why?"

"When Millano found out about McCarthy, he would just send someone else. I thought I would stand a better chance with the Feds."

"So, are you going to testify against Millano?"

"You may not think much of me, Delany. I've done a lot of bad things and I've killed a lot of people. Some of those people were good people, and some of them were shit. I don't judge. I do know, when this is all over, my life ain't worth a shit. A month, two months, six months, sooner or later they're gonna find me with a sharpened toothbrush jammed into my chest. That is inevitable. It all works out as jailhouse justice. No one is going to weep. No one is going to care. I gave you my word. There are only two things that have ever mattered to me: my integrity, and my family. Since my family has turned against me, all I have left is my integrity. I'll testify. I'll make sure that Millano gets what he has coming. I ask but one favor."

"What's that, Frank?"

"I sent five grand to an undertaker in Genoa. I spent some time there, and I liked the place. Just make sure that I get a decent burial."

Delany put the flowers on the casket. The only other people there were the undertaker and the grounds keeper; the undertaker kept looking at his watch. At least it was a nice day. Constanso had been right about just about everything. The punk that got him, three months after he was sent upstate, was a lifer with nothing to lose; however, the weapon of choice was a sharpened spoon handle. Millano was convicted, but with some finagling from his lawyers and good behavior, he might get out in eight to ten years. The headstone was nice. Delany picked it out. It had the usual shit: date of birth, date of death, full name, but there was room for something else. The old, "Rest in Peace" just didn't seem to cut it. Franks tortured soul may never find peace. He thought what he had picked out Frank would have liked. There was a simple scroll at the top and below was, "Francis Michael Constanso, 1914 to 1956," and below that it read, "A man of his word."

THE GREAT GEORGIA
WORM CAPER

As I recollect, it was over forty years ago when the whole thing finally came to a head. That would have made it around the summer of '69. Bill Burton just got his barn painted and old Fox Neeley finally got the county to put some lime rock in that big, old pothole in front of his driveway. My youngest daughter was off to college, learning "animal husbandry", of all things, and my third grandchild, Billy Ray Talbert III, blatted out his very first rebel yell, shortly after midnight, on August 6th. So, as y'all can see, I remember that year very well. Now, old Issy Stovert was said to be the man behind the whole thing, although there was certainly enough blame to cover a whole parcel of folks, old Judge Klampert, and Doc Bedford notwithstanding.

The Stovert farm is only a couple miles down the road from here, just past the big dip in the road that always fills in with water whenever it rains. Their old, Ford-Ferguson, steel-wheeled tractor can still be seen, rusting away in the north field, where it coughed its final breath, about the same week President Kennedy was assassinated. Issy's mother, Clare Stovert, had died the year before of heart failure, and everyone who knew her was surely sorry to see her go. She was a fine woman and the sole reason the Stovert farm didn't end up on the auction block, years before. Stoat Stovert was never much of a farmer. Nothing he planted ever did well, except maybe the year he planted a whole field of corn and ended up with a bumper crop of corn smut. Some Spanish-speaking feller came around and bought the whole smear. He could hardly speak a word of English; just kept rubbing his belly and making yum-yum sounds like you could actually eat the damn stuff. He brought in his own crew, and within two days every bit of that puffy, black, cancerous-looking stuff was bagged up and hauled away.

I was sure glad when Stoat burnt what was left of the corn and plowed the ashes under. It was about the first crop he had ever made a profit on, and he had real plans on what he was going to do with the money. He planned to plant the whole farm with peanuts so's the crop would be ready when the pickers came down from Sodus that year. I didn't have the heart to tell him that it was already too late in the season for peanuts.

Fortunately, Clare had another use for the money. She had Stoat build her a chicken coop out near the big sinkhole. She had him clear the sinkhole of all the palmettos, scrub oak, and brier that had been growing there since Jesus had cut his first tooth; not an easy job, indeed. She had this idea that all the manure from the chicken house could be thrown right into that sinkhole. This would save them the bother of hauling it away. She bought 1000 White Leghorn chicks, and by the first year was selling all the eggs she could produce through Biff Williams, down at the Feed-n-Food store in Prescott.

Now Issy was always a sickly boy, with arms not much bigger that a pencil stem. As the story goes, his old hound, General Lee, saved his life one day by grabbing the seat of his britches, when a big old dust devil nearly blew him away. He couldn't work in the fields, because after about twenty minutes in the sun you would find him collapsed beneath some shady water oak, panting and soaking up water like some floundered carp. Clare put him to work, tending the chickens, gathering the eggs, and throwing the straw and chicken droppings, out the windows and down into that sinkhole. But it wasn't until after the first batch of chickens stopped producing eggs that Clare's real enterprise began. She started cooking up those chickens in a huge pot her mom had given her, right after her and Stoat were married, for the initial purpose of boiling the laundry. This pot, however, produced some of the finest chicken soup that ever titillated a Southern taste bud. People came from miles around to buy a quart Mason jar of Clare's fine product. Clare offered to give back the dime deposit on the jar whenever people brought the empty back. No one ever took her up on it though, because they would just turn it in for another bottle of delicious chicken soup. There was always someone sitting on the front porch just waiting for the lids to "pop."

It wasn't long; however, before some snooty woman from the County Health Department came around and told her that she couldn't make her soup in the same kitchen she used to cook for her family. This all seemed mighty silly to me, seeing that Clare's kitchen floors were probably much cleaner than some of the plates you might find in some of those fancy, big city restaurants. Under penalty of heavy fines; nevertheless, Clare decided to look for another alternative. Now, there was an old carriage house out back that had been a catchall for anything that Stoat figured might someday be useful. Clare looked it over with a calculating eye, and Stoat knew that he was, again, in for a lot of hard work.

She had him move out all that old horse-drawn farm machinery, whiffletrees, yokes, harnesses, saddles, and other useless paraphernalia that had adorned the floor, walls, and ceiling for the last 20 years, for no other purpose than for the fact that Stoat never wanted to throw anything away. She had him load it onto the big wagon and haul it up to the family landfill, up near Pearson Creek; hopeful she would never have to see it again. Even Stoat's rusty, old, beloved "48 Ford two-door, upon whose rear seat young Issy's beginnings were first implanted, found a new home out behind the barn. Within two months, the old carriage house was transformed into a gleaming, new, chicken soup factory, with tile floors, shiny paneled walls, acoustic ceilings, and a stainless steel counter that reverberated the harsh glare of the new fluorescent lighting system. There was even a brand-new, six burner gas stove. Stoat would have gagged if he had seen the total bill, but since everything was purchased with Clare's "egg money", that privilege was irrefutably denied him.

Issy, unable to keep up, as his mother increased the number of chickens in the ever expanding chicken coop, was given more help in the form of two local high school boys who would help out on weekends and after school. Issy put more and more of the real work onto the young boys and learned to cope nicely, as he assumed the role of the benevolent dictator. More pots were purchased and production increased. The production of eggs had now become a bothersome nuisance and the once proud rooster became part of the stock and broth as a new breed of chicken took over the coop. The soup was still sold in quart mason jars, but now it had store bought labels that spoke of calories and daily requirements; as if any of her customers cared about such things.

Clare died two years later. Issy was the one who found her, headfirst and parboiled in her final batch of home-cooked, succulent nosh. Some folks say it was the best batch she ever made, although, knowing the circumstances of her death, I never tried it, myself. Stoat always blamed this increased production for the death of his beloved wife and, maybe, rightly so.

After Clare died, Stoat and Issy tried to keep the kitchen going. They had the family recipe, but without Clare's astute ability to taste the developing brew and add just a dash of this and a pinch of that, making each batch the exact, mouth watering perfection of the ones before, customers began to dwindle. Besides, neither Stoat nor Issy could really comprehend the subtle difference between a "teaspoon" and a "tablespoon". The flood of ten-cent deposits, paid out for the returning jars, depleted much of the money that Clare had managed to put away. Also, because neither Stoat nor Issy were known to take up broom or mop with much enthusiasm, the premises began to take on a very unpleasant, funky odor. It wasn't long before the snooty, county lady came out, taped a notice to the door, and the chicken soup factory closed its doors forever.

Stoat, his loving wife snatched from his midst, his income cut short, and his farm failing around him, took to the bottle. It wasn't long before this once husky man became a frail, lifeless ghost, whose diminishing hulk could have been easily hidden within Issy's shadow.

The two boys, in lieu of wages due, beat their former lord dictator until he could barely walk, and after loading up several crates of chickens, drove off, running over poor General Lee on the way out. They say Issy took General Lee's death harder than his mother's. He cried for three days, even though each sob caused his ribs to ache as if they were being ripped from his chest. The chickens quickly disappeared into the cook pot, for ready cash, for the payment of various sundries, and to fend off the power company. Issy was making a lot of trips into Crooksville with the old Ford pickup, and it wasn't long before the chicken coop fell silent.

One night, as Issy sat out behind the old chicken coop, sipping Jack Daniels, dipping, and spitting into the old sinkhole, he reached into this brown paper bag he had brought back from Crooksville and fished out a sugar cube. As he was about to pop it into his mouth it slipped from his fingers and rolled down the bank into the pile of straw and chicken manure. He jumped down into the hole to retrieve this sweet treasure, but try as he might, he couldn't find it in the fading light. He started to the house to fetch a flashlight, but passed out somewhere between the '48 Ford and his mother's old rose garden. Six hours later he awoke and retraced his path to the old sinkhole, as the sun was coming up and he no longer had a need for the flashlight. When he returned to the sinkhole he discovered that his boot had smashed the cube when he had jumped into the hole, and the sugar had filtered down into the straw. Pulling the straw aside, Issy saw an amazing sight. Hundreds of Georgia red worms were gathered at the spot and were all having a "bad trip." They were jumping and wiggling around as if they were dancing on an electrical wire. You see, the cube had been laced with LSD.

Issy gathered up the worms, put them into a bucket and rushed them to the house to show his Pa. But by the time he reached the house, all but a few of the worms were dead. His Pa was in no condition to appreciate the situation, anyway. Issy found him in the living room, slouched in his favorite chair, holding a mixture of warm Coke and lamp oil. It was at that very moment, looking into his father's bloodshot eyes, the morning sun streaming into the filthy room, his head buzzing from lack of sleep and strong whiskey, that the greatest idea of his useless existence occurred to him.

If the fishermen could see these "dancing worms" he knew that he could sell all that he could dig up. There was at least four feet of chicken manure in that old sinkhole, and millions and millions of healthy red worms. All he had to do was figure how to get the worms to dance at the right time and a way to keep them alive until they did. He knew he had to be straight and sober to tackle a problem of this magnitude. Snatching up his father's glass, he replaced it with his half-empty bottle of Jack Daniels and, dumping the contents of the glass into the woodstove as he passed; he mounted the stairs to his bedroom.

That evening he went back to Crooksville and spent the last of the chicken money on LSD and two bottles of cheap whiskey for his dad. He swore off everything until he could figure out a way to make this thing work. He experimented with different doses. He found that a little went a long way. After all, worms don't have very large brains, and it doesn't take much to get them high. He discovered that he didn't even have to feed it to them. He had to but merely dilute the sugar cubes in water, and mist them with the resulting solution using one of his mother's old perfume atomizers. It took a few minutes for the LSD to take effect, and once they did their little dance, they would die in about half an hour. Sure, he could mist the worms before they were sold, but if the fisherman didn't use them before half an hour was up, they would be dead. No one would come back to buy more dead worms, even if they could do the Tarantella. He still had to devise a way to keep them alive for a longer time. There was no way he was about to divulge his "secret ingredient" to anyone.

He discovered the secret by accident. One night, while working late, he had just misted a fresh batch of worms when he remembered that he had put the last two TV Dinners into the oven. He rushed back to the house to rescue them, forgetting about the worms until the next day. During the night the temperature dropped down into the thirties. When he finally went to the barn to continue his experiments, he found the worms still setting where he had left them. Thinking that they would have frozen to death, he dumped them out on the floor and began counting out another batch. Meanwhile the worms thawed out and started crawling around. As Issy watched, to his amazement, they went into their little dance one by one. They continued to dance for about one half hour, and then one by one they died. This was the answer! By keeping them cool until you were ready to use them, they would be alive and ready to do their little dance. All he needed to do was to keep them in Styrofoam containers with a little ice.

Issy filled a couple of containers with misted worms, took them to the house, and put them in the refrigerator. He had to know just how long they would stay alive if you kept them cool. After three days he brought the first container outside and dumped them on the ground. Shortly, they began to move around and they did their little dance. Again, a half hour later, they died. Issy was happier than he was the day he found out that he was 4-F. He iced up a Styrofoam cooler, filled it with three-dozen containers of worms, and hauled them down to Biff Williams' Feed-n-Food store. When he showed Biff how the worms danced, Biff's eyes lit up like a lizard at a bug convention. Biff could see that these worms had potential. He unloaded the soda from one of his coolers and immediately ordered another 10 dozen.

After a couple of months Issy realized that he would have to continually replenish his worm bed if he wanted to keep the operation going. Issy started hauling' in chicken manure from other local farms. People said it was the hardest they had ever seen him work, man or boy. It was even more surprising to see Issy starting to develop some muscles. Even young Cora Davis started to take notice, and that itself is something to be said. Folks say her family has a direct line to former Confederate President Jefferson Davis, himself, and hereabouts you don't get much closer than that to being real southern royalty.

Mrs. Davis; however, didn't take kindly to the way her daughter fell all over young Issy whenever he came around to scrape the sweet essence of life from the floor of the Davis family chicken coop, and she didn't spare much effort to hide it. Cora didn't care. She would give young Issy goo-goo eyes, whenever she thought her mother wasn't looking and even when she thought she was.

Business was a boom for Issy and the trips to Williams store went from once a week to once a day. Also, Issy didn't have to drive all the way to Crooksville any more. A young man from Crooksville delivered the "secret ingredient" right to Issy's door, once a month. Jack Daniels was now a permanent guest in the Stovert home, and Stoat was now waking up with a better grade of hangover. They even had a woman that came in once a week to clean. At first, she turned down the job when she saw the condition of the house. She told them that they might want to think about wiping their feet before they left the house to keep from tracking all that filth outside. Issy offered to keep her husband in free fishing worms as long as his wife worked for them. The woman was back the next day.

One day, old Doc Bedford called and ordered 200 of Issy's finest worms. He was going out of town on a fishing trip and said that he would pick them up on the way by. Issy misted up a couple of containers and placed them in the refrigerator. About an hour later Stoat dragged himself out of bed. It was one of those rare mornings when he was actually hungry. He looked into the refrigerator and thinking one of the containers contained some of Clare's spaghetti with her delicious homemade sauce, dumped it into a frying pan with a half a stick of butter and fried it up. When Doc Bedford arrived, Issy came in to retrieve the two containers of worms. When he could only find one, he looked over on the counter and saw the empty container.

"What er ya eatin', Pa?" he asked.

"Skeddy," Stoat replied, not even looking up.

"Pa," Issy said, "we ain't had no skeddy in this house since Ma died. Now, they just gotta be my worms you're eatin'."

Stoat looked down at his half-empty plate. "Damn!" he said. "These just got ta be the best damn worms I ever et. Truth is, I think they might be the only worms I ever et. Least not whilst I was sober."

Now, Doc Bedford, wondering just what was taking so long, stuck his head through the door.

"Doc. Pa just et half a container of fishin' worms." Issy looked worried. "Is he gonna be alright?"

The Doc laughed. "Don't worry about your Pa, Issy. Worms can't hurt you. Why people have been exploring the possibility of using worms for a food source for years."

With this Stoat went back to eating his breakfast.

"Pa! What the hell, ya doin'?"

"Sorry, Son, but these are just so good, I hate to waste em." He held out the fork. "Try em."

Issy put his hand against the fork, stepped back, and made a face. "I ain't eatin' no damn worms."

"Oh, come on, ya lily liver, taste it. If y'all don't like it, spit it out."

Issy put the fork to his mouth and took a little nibble. He rolled his eyes a little, and then took another taste. Thereafter, he took a whole mouthful. "Wow! This here's good." He scooped up another forkful and turned to Doc Bedford. Y'all got ta try this, Doc!"

Doc looked long and hard at the fork and stroked his whiskers.

"Come on, Doc," Issy urged, "you're the one what said that it was good for ya."

Doc Bedford squinted his eyes and took a small bite. Suddenly his eyes opened wide. "God! This is delicious!" he exclaimed. "Tastes just like a bit of Southern heaven. You could have something here, Issy. Why with the proper marketing, <u>we</u> could have this in every store in America, maybe even the world!"

"We?" Issy picked up on that very quickly.

"Why yes, we're partners in this, aren't we? After all, you will need my medical expertise." He turned to Stoat. "You didn't do anything special to these worms, did you?"

"Special?" Stoat scratched his head. "Don't think so. I just fried em up in some butter, same way I always cook up left over skeddy. I were thinking of putting in a little Jack Daniels, but I don't rightly remember doin' so."

Doc turned to Issy. "We need to fry up a few more batches, just to make sure they all taste the same."

Issy opened the second container and handed it to Stoat. The other two men watched as Stoat added the butter, and fried them up to a crispy, golden brown. They each grabbed a plate and dug in, wolfing down the new batch in record time.

"Good's the first one," Stoat remarked, washing the last mouthful down with good belt of Jack Daniels.

"He's right, you know, Issy," Doc added. "This was every bit as good as the first batch. Why don't we make up another batch, so we have some to show to Judge Klampert."

"Whoa! Wait a minute!" Issy was not too happy with this new thought. "What do you mean 'Judge Klampert'?"

"Look, Issy," Doc began to explain. "Since the main ingredient is worm, we have to be really sure that we're not violating any federal laws, here."

"But you and I both know that old Judge Klampert is the crookest judge in Clinch County, and maybe the whole damn state of Georgia!"

"And that," argued Doc, "is precisely why we need him. If anyone can figure out how to get around the law, it's the Judge."

"And I suppose," Issy said, "he will want an equal share."

"One quarter," Doc said, "just like the rest of us."

"And what will he do for his share, besides figuring out how to get around the law?"

"We're all equal partners. We will all have to share the workload."

"You too?"

"Yes, me too," the Doc assured him, putting his hands on his hips. "I can work just as hard as any man here!"

"What do you think, Pa?"

Stoat had just finished off the bottle of Jack Daniels and was beyond thought.

Old Judge Klampert did figure out a way around the worm thing. He suggested that they only put the words "chicken byproducts" and "all natural ingredients" on the label. After all, the worms were raised in chicken manure which is a "chicken byproduct", and Georgia red worms, raised in pure chicken manure are about as "natural" as you can get. The Doc proposed that they call the new snack *Anne Lida's, High*

Protein, All Natural, Power Snacks. Annelida, he explained, being the scientific name for worms. Issy wanted to call it "Issy's Snacks". Issy, however, was voted down three to one.

The first batch went on the shelves in July of that first year. It was an instant success. Soon, big brand names were offering to buy them out with offers in the hundreds of thousands of dollars. The group steadfastly held out, not caving in to pressure from the big companies. They felt that someday, they too, could be one of the biggies. They were still working out of Cora's old chicken soup plant; although now, much enlarged and improved. Moreover, plans were in the works for a much larger facility.

Now, Thomas William Biglow was the Regional Director of the Food and Drug Administration, at this time. Rumor has it that he had great ambitions for running for Governor. However, there was one obstacle standing fully in his way. No one had ever heard of Thomas William Biglow. This, Biglow had decided, was all about to change. It seems he had come into some important information concerning a certain food product presently being sold on the market under the name of *Anne Lida's, High Protein, All Natural, Power Snacks.* His informant had told him that the product was laced with a controlled substance, and that if he had it tested he might be very surprised. (It appears that Issy had found a cheaper supplier for his secret ingredient and this didn't hold too well with his former supplier)

Biglow did just that, and when he got the results back from the lab, they showed that this product, that had become one of the most popular after-school snacks in the country, contained traces of LSD. He knew, if he played his cards right, this could be the plum that would get him into good stead in the public eye. Who could be a bigger hero than the man who captured and prosecuted the baddies who were putting mind-altering drugs into the mouths of unsuspecting babes? He set up a huge clandestine raid on the factory for the eleventh of January and planned on taking personal charge of the whole operation.

On the fateful morning of January 11th, Stoat had just put up the last batch, himself. Issy had left him to go off to see Cora Lee Davis, now that he was allowed to visit the family homestead as pretty much an equal. You see, in Mrs. Davis' eyes, he was no longer "trash", but was now a man of means. Issy had lugged up a batch of fresh worms and instructed his Pa to be sure to process them within the hour, as they would surely spoil. He donned his Sunday best, and sped off to Cora Lee's in his brand new one-seater sports car.

Stoat, already on his second bottle of Jack Daniels, lost track of time. By the time he got around to processing the new patch of worms they were all dead. Not wanting to put anything into the ovens that were spoiled, and not wanting his son to know that he hadn't done what was expected of him, he climbed down into the sinkhole and dug up a fresh batch. He dumped the old worms out behind the barn. He put the worms into the special oven and, since no one else was around, he added a half bottle of Jack Daniels just to ensure freshness.

It was shortly after that that the Feds arrived. They handcuffed Stoat and confiscated the last batch of *Anne Lida's, High Protein, All Natural, Power Snack* as evidence. Stoat was escorted off to jail, as a dragnet was sent out for other cohorts. Meanwhile, the sight of men in suits in town on a non-Sunday inquiring as to the location of the here afore mentioned factory, attracted a lot of attention.

One person in particular, the young son of Biff Williams, a boy everyone called, "Squirt", realized that something was "coming down", an expression I know he didn't learn from watching Andy Griffith. Calling out to the Davis place, he hoped to tell Issy that the "gig was up" and that he need to "split", now. The thing was, young Squirt's call had arrived too late, as Issy and Cora Lee had already departed for points unknown, about an hour before.

It didn't take long for the Feds to round up the rest of the "mob", and at least three of the "dope peddlers" were paraded before the press with the promise that justice would be served. Meanwhile, the evidence was taken into custody, placed under the scrutiny of the lab boys, and every test imaginable was invoked upon the suspected egregiousness. I hear that when the official report was handed to Biglow he nearly pooped his pants.

"What do you mean there's no LSD?" Biglow was reported to have shouted, "The other samples were loaded with it."

"Yes sir," said the technician, "but we could find nothing in this batch but traces of what appears to be Jack Daniels Whiskey."

"Well, isn't alcohol a controlled substance? Aren't you required to pay a tax on any alcohol? Don't we have them for tax evasion? They still can't feed this to our children and get away with it!"

"Well, no, sir. You see, when they cooked the product, they boiled off all of the alcohol. As I said, there were only traces of Jack Daniels, not any alcohol."

The three partners were released from jail and, needless to say, Thomas William Biglow never was nominated for Governor. Issy and Cora were never seen again, nor was the $6,540,436.68 that had previously been in the account of the *Anne Lida's, High Protein, Snacks, Inc.* Without Issy and the secret ingredient, which the threesome was informed would have them all doing hard time if it ever materialized in their product again, the company was doomed. Doc Bedford went back to his practice. Judge Klampert successfully ran for Governor that next year. Stoat, they say, still receives a shipment of fine whiskey from Europe, every week, which he immediately trades with Bert Loften at the liquor store, for Jack Daniels.

The only other thing I would like to mention is to make a small note of a peculiar item my daughter brought back from her trip to England last year. It was a package of something called *Issy's Snacks*. They are being sold all over Europe, and I hear they are quite popular. Now, I'm quite sure that they bear no resemblance to the *Anne Lida's* product afore mentioned in my narrative; although it does bears some resemblance as to texture and taste; the label clearly states that this product . . . and let me adjust my glasses for the print is fine . . . is "Made from pure beef byproducts and all natural ingredients." As you can clearly see there is no mention of chicken, whatsoever.

SUPPLY AND DEMAND

Just to the right in the southern sky, slightly above the moon and just to the east of the Crab Nebula, there is a small star. On some nights you will be able to see it without the aid of a telescope. This, of course, is if the moon isn't too bright and the sky is clear. This star doesn't have a name, only a number, and if you were to ask me what that number is I would only tell you that I had forgotten. Numbers, like names, slip through my mind like rain through a screen door. Besides, here on earth this star is not considered to have any real significant value. It isn't part of some well known constellation, or of great substantial use to navigation. To the individuals who live on three of the twelve planets that orbit this distant star; however, its significant value is fairly obvious.

Blados, the largest of the three, is also known as *the mother planet*. The creatures, spawned from her womb, bear little physical resemblance to us here on Earth; although, in practice, there would seem to be a universal mold for behavior. Attributes, both good and bad, abound on this planet just as surely as if they were mirror images of our own. Sparked many, many years before our own civilization, theirs was yet nurtured from the same cosmic dust and universal elements that first felt the sun and tasted the virgin waters of our very own planet so many eons ago. For as the diversity of life, on our own planet, displays a sameness in mood, reaction and temperament, it should not be surprising to learn that the inhabitance of this planet and the two outer planets, Telmon and Forsenar, also bear a remarkable singularity.

Blados, now stripped of most of it raw materials, has only one natural resource left: it's huge, destitute, desperate, and ever-growing population. Telmon was first colonized nearly one hundred years ago. For nearly forty years its raw materials were hauled back to Blados to feed the hungry industrial machines. Resentment grew between the two planets until a war started that was to last for the next sixty years.

Meanwhile, a rich industrialist, grown fat from the sale of munitions, decided that Forsenar would be a safer place from which to run his business. There were a few small settlements on that planet at the time, and Dellus Galoun, the owner and Chairman of the Board bought them out with goods and the promise of shares in the new corporation. In fact, the whole planet was set up as a corporation with each resident receiving a share of the profits proportionate to his or her usefulness.

Forsenar was rich in raw materials, and it wasn't long before it became a rich and powerful planet. Dellus, no longer bound by any sense of loyalty, was supplying both Blados and Telmon as they continued to pursue their ceaseless annihilation of one another. With their own resources now nearly diminished, the fighting was reduced to sporadic encounters that for the most part were ineffective. Each planet plotted to pool its remaining reserves into one final effort to obtain complete victory over the enemy who had plagued them for so long.

Dellus Galoun was seated at his desk enjoying his morning cup of hot gruto, when his young assistant, Hiole Brutiea stuck his head through the door.

"Major General Vegaleen to see you sir."

"Send him right in, Brutiea, and have my secretary fetch us a couple of fresh cups of gruto." He got to his feet as the General came through the door. "So happy to see you again, General," he said. They clasped hands, locking their seventh fingers in the traditional gesture. "What can I do for you?"

The General waited until the door closed behind the young assistant. "I must be assured that what I have to say will not leave this room."

"Why that goes without saying, General," Galoun said, as he placed his arm around the General's shoulder and guided him to a large, comfortable chair, in front of his desk. "What kind of a businessman would I be if I couldn't keep a secret? You know that anything you have to say here in my office is safe with me."

The General looked around. He seemed satisfied as he set his briefcase on the floor. "Very well, Galoun. Your word is good enough for me. I have always known you as a man of integrity." He moved closer to the desk. "We are planning an all out assault on Telmon in six months. We will need to amass a fleet of warships such as no one has ever seen before. We will annihilate the Telmonians, and Blados . . . he placed his hand on his chest . . . will emerge victorious. We have found new sources of rare metals, and are willing to dig to the very core to find more, if necessary." He set his briefcase on his lap. Popping it open, he removed a handful of papers and laid them on the desk. "This is what we will require."

Galoun picked up the papers, rocked back in his huge chair, and looked them over carefully. "This will require . . ." he paused as the secretary entered the room with the two cups of hot gruto and set them on the desk.

"Will there be anything else," she asked, smiling.

"No, Balena. That is all that is required," Galoun said. "Thank you."

The General followed her with his eyes as she left the room. "Nice togerts," he said.

"Yes," agreed Galoun. Although, did you notice, the fourth one doesn't seem to match the rest."

"Still," the General said, winking, "I wouldn't slap her out of my slizgog."

Galoun laughed. "Why do you think she's my secretary? But back to what I was saying. This will require a sizeable deposit. Do you feel that your people are willing to sacrifice this much for victory?

"I have aboard my ship six gilvits of zorbidine, worth over 100,000,000 draggits. This I will give you in good faith. When the goods are delivered, we will be able to pay whatever is reasonable. The question is, will you be able to deliver the weapons within the allotted time?"

"I don't see that as a problem, General. We can have everything ready for you in three months."

"That is amazing, Galoun." The General got to his feet and again reached out his hand. "In three months then, "he said. He gathered up his briefcase and left the room.

Brutiea was leaning on Balena's desk when Galoun summoned him to his office. "The General has some zorbidine for us; six gilvits to be exact. I want you to see that they are safely secured. Then I need you to come back here. There are a few things we have to go over."

Galoun lay back in his huge chair and removed a doobler from the top drawer of his desk. These he kept for special occasions. He placed it in his mouth and lit it. Brown smoke circled his head as the strong scent of blenend, and fine imported talewood, permeated the room. *One of the few things that Blados still has to offer,* he thought, as he removed the doobler from his mouth and studied it momentarily. He smiled to himself. If all went right he would no longer be buying dooblers off the black market at 10 draggits apiece. After all, in an "open society" the price would drop dramatically.

Brutiea returned shortly and took a seat in the same chair the General had just vacated. "I secured the zobidine, sir," he said, adjusting himself in the seat. "I placed it in a locker in the armory and placed an armed guard in front of the door. May I say, sir that it looked like quality stuff."

"Good, very good. We'll transport it over to the treasury tomorrow." He handed the General's list to Brutiea. "Here is the list of weapons I have promised will be delivered to Blados within the next three months."

Brutiea looked the list over carefully. "Eight battle cruisers, twelve fleet destroyers, two hundred virulent fighters, various armored vehicles, mortar, cannons, and various small arms."

"Will there be a problem?"

"No, sir. We may have to reopen some of our older facilities in order to make the production date, but we have done this before. What sort of armament do you want installed, sir?"

"Disintegrators and anti-personnel weapons, only; we don't want space littered with debris, do we?"

"No, sir, we certainly don't."

"Now, what I would like you to do is to see to it that all our old facilities are reopened. See if you can put on a second shift in all the factories."

"But, sir, we will be able to handle this easily without putting on all that added expense."

"Of course we can, Brutiea, but what about the next orders?"

"The next orders, sir?"

"Yes, Brutiea." Galoun took a deep drag on his doobler. "What do you think is going to happen when the Telmonians find out about this huge arms build-up by the Bladosites?"

"But how are they going to find out, sir?"

"You are going to see that the news is leaked, of course."

"Me, sir?"

"We can't exactly blare it out, you know. It will have to be done discretely. If a few of those still loyal to Telmon were to accidentally come into contact with the order forms, through no fault of our own and without our knowledge, and the information got back to Telmon; could we really be held responsible? This is a big operation and it is going to be very hard to keep a lid on it. Don't you agree?"

"Wholeheartedly, sir, why the spies, here on Forsenar, are too numerous to even imagine. Something this big is bound to leak out, despite our best efforts."

"Good man, Brutiea. Get on this immediately. Time is the factor here. Three months. I gave my word and I am a man of integrity."

It was only a week before General Deeba Woker, the leader of the Telmon Planetary Defense League, was in Galoun's office. He sat in the tall chair before Galoun's desk, sipping his gruto and nervously clicking his mouthparts.

"To what do I owe the honor of this visit?" asked Galoun."

"You know perfectly well why I'm here, Galoun," General Woker said angrily. There is a rumor the Bladosites are planning an all-out attack on Telmon! Do you deny it?"

"General Woker, my friend, you know that I am bound by honor and am not allowed to comment on any rumors you may have heard. I'm a businessman. I have an obligation to my customers."

"So! What you are saying is that the Bladosites are your customers. This can only mean that they are building up their armament. You are a shrewd one, Galoun; a slimy ruk that would suck the fluids from his own mother's throat!"

"General Woker, please, I hold you only in the highest esteem. You must see my position. If I were to divulge any information of my dealings with, say, General Vegaleen . . . ."

"Vegaleen!" General Woker was on his feet now. "Of course, if Vegaleen is involved it could be nothing but a full-scale invasion. I didn't come all the way here to see you gloat. What can you tell me?"

"Well." Galoun rocked back in his chair. There was a thin smile on his face. "Now, if you were one of my customers, there is no reason that I couldn't advise you on what weapons you might want to order; for your own defenses, of course, and just in case there was a threat of an invasion by persons unknown."

"I see. And these, of course, would be rather expensive weapons."

"Well. There is a time factor to consider here. This would, of course, drive up the cost of production, which I would have to pass onto you."

"Damn it, Galoun! You were a Telmonian once, yourself. Don't you have any loyalties?"

"Only to my customers, General. Only to my customers."

Months passed, and the factories on Forsenar were running at full capacity. Ever male, female, and child old enough to work was employed at top wages. Labor was being smuggled in from Blados and Telmon. People were willing to work alongside former enemies for the privileges of decent wages, good working conditions, and full stomachs. The only thing the wars had ever provided for the masses was unemployment and the promise of a quick and merciful death. Here, they found less crowded conditions; better sanitation, freedom, and the veil of impending doom had been lifted.

Vegaleen and Woker kept insisting on increasing their arms as each side feared the other would have the advantage. As the final days drew near, the factories ground to a halt as raw materials and spare parts could no longer keep up with production. Vegaleen and Woker both insisted that they needed more battle cruisers and fleet destroyers. For the first time in his life, Galoun was at a loss. Here he had a seller's market . . . the one thing that all good businessmen dream about . . . and he had nothing left to sell. He retired to his office, ordered a whole pot of gruto, and pondered his next move.

If only he could find some cruisers and destroyers somewhere. Even if they were used, he could get three of four times the price for them, but only if he had them now. Then an idea hit him. Forsenar had over fifty battle cruisers and some one hundred and thirty odd destroyers. Surely they could spare a few. After all, they had been setting dormant for over forty years. Most of them were old. Why replace something you never use? Who was there to fight with; the Bladosites and the Telmonians were too busy fighting with each other? Besides, the expense of traveling this distance to fight a war with the Forsenars would be astronomical. It would be a war they could never win.

The plan was a good one. The Forsenars could get rid of all of their older cruisers and destroyers at an exaggerated price, and then replace them with more modern ships at a later time. When the Bladosites and the Telmonians had depleted all of their resources and had pounded each other into weak and pathetic planets, the Forsenarians could swoop in and easily defeat them in their weakened state, and declare peace for all the planets. Galoun would be a hero, the wars would be over, and he would declare for himself some sizable holdings on each planet. All he had to do was convince the Board.

Convincing the Board proved to be harder than he thought. Some of the board members were not too happy with the thought of reducing the size of the fleet. Dellus Galoun had to use all his tact to persuade them, but persuade them he did. He convinced them that the huge profits and the ultimate chance of ending the wars far outweighed any possible danger. Even by reducing their fleet by fifty ships, they would still be a force to contend with, as neither Blados nor Telmon would have as large a fleet as Forenar. Besides, it was about time to replace their old ships with more modern ones, a point that none of the board members could disagree with.

The old ships were refitted and added to the growing arsenal. Vegaleen and Woker were not too happy with the idea of paying exorbitant prices for used ships, but when it was explained to them that the alternative would be no ships at all, they became more receptive to the idea. Their resources exhausted, the two warring planets had to content themselves with what they had accumulated. In the end, they had come away with exactly the same number of similar weaponry of all dimensions.

This was no accident. Galoun had seen to it that each apposing army would be of equal strength. He wanted the war to drag on to the point of mutual annihilation. When each planet had exhausted all of their fighting ability, he would invade with fresh troops and superior weaponry and force them into submission. After, he would isolate and destroy any pockets of resistance and declare himself the supreme ruler. The idea was both simple and foolproof.

Everyone would benefit. First of all, the dreaded wars would be over. With the combined resources of the three planets, there would be work for everyone. Factories now devoted to producing items of war, would be converted to peacetime use. Battlefields would, again, become farmland. Fortifications would be torn down and habitats constructed in their stead. He would be a hero to all except the warring factions and, of course, these would be quickly eliminated. All Galoun needed to do was sit back and wait. In a few short months everything would be over.

As anticipated, word came back to Forsenar that Blados was preparing for a mass invasion. Telmon, apparently aware of the eminent danger, was amassing its own massive fighting force. Ganoun waited patiently for word of the first encounter. By midday he was informed that the two opposing forces were closing in on one another.

Ganoun went to the executive lounge where he had instructed that a huge viewing screen be erected. He sat between Brutiea and Balena, as the ships came within firing range. Several media vessels from Forsenar sat just out of range to document the impending battle. Smiling to himself, Ganoun handed Brutiea a doobler. The two men sat back and awaited for the first round of action. Nothing happened! They watched as the two fleets turned, changed direction, and then took out one of the media vessels.

"Holy Femstray!" Ganoun shouted. "What was all that about?"

No one could answer him. All the executives just shook their heads and shrugged their shoulders.

"Somebody get me a line to General Vegaleen!" he yelled, quickly making his way back to his office. "There has to be a good explanation for this. Attacking unarmed media vessels is an open act of war! Don't they realize that?"

"Generals Vegaleen and Woker are on line one," Balena informed him.

Ganoun was thunderstruck. "Both of them?" he asked.

"Yes, sir," Balena said.

"Hello," Ganoun said, pushing the button on his communicator. "What is the meaning of this?"

"Haven't you figured it out yet, Ganoun?," came the voice of General Vegaleen.

"It's simple, Ganoun," General Woker explained. "The invasion has started."

"Invasion? Invasion of whom?" Ganoun asked.

"Why the invasion of Forsenar, of course," General Vegaleen informed him.

"You can't attack us," Ganoun insisted. "Our defenses are far more superior."

"Superior to whom?" Woker asked, laughing. "Our informants tell us that you have reduced your fleet by fifty ships. This means that the combined forces of Blados and Telmon outnumber your fleet one and a half times. Within the hour we shall have Forsenar surrounded. We have already sent an emissary with our surrender terms to your Board of Directors."

"Why?"

"All these year we have been fighting," Woker continued. "All these years Blados and Telmon have been exhaust their resources, while Forsenar sat back and got fat off of us. Eight months ago we signed a peace accord. It was at that time that we realized who the real enemy was. It was you, Ganoun, you and your greed."

Just then, armed guards stormed into Ganoun's office and pulled him up from his chair. "What is happening here!" he shouted into the communicator.

"Your Board has decided to accept our generous terms," General Vegaleen informed him. "We are putting you into protective custody, as we feel you are in danger on your own planet, and are far too valuable to be left to die."

"At least, we agree on one thing," Ganoun said. "I can still be of great service to the people. What position did you have in mind for me?"

"The first ten years," General Vegaleen explained, "you will work in the crystal mines of Cardovilla. The next ten years you will be gathering fletog guano on the isle of Zimplasket. After that, if we feel your work ethics have improved, we may move you up to a janitorial position, perhaps as head latrine cleaner."

Ganoun said nothing as the guards escorted him past Balena's smiling face and down the corridor that led to the transporter room. She seemed happy, even if her fourth togert didn't match the rest.

THE CLOCK TOWER

Nestled in the golden hills of Austria, in the Bavarian Alps, near the border of Germany, lies the little village of Drefenstein. As the village awakens to meet another dawn, a light breeze has filtered down from the mountains rustling the trees along the road young Hans Clauson must take to school each morning. He loves the fall with its bright colors, the cool air that nips at his cheeks, and the smell of burning oak emitting from the village fireplaces. What he hates, on this day and every other day, is having to walk the same streets on his way to school. He knows that they will be waiting for him; the village boys. Oh not all of them of course, just two, the Stout brothers, the village bullies that relished in the sport of teasing Hans because of his impediment, for Hans cannot hear; he is stone deaf.

The boys taunt him and throw rocks to make him angry. He shouts at them and calls them names, but the words never come out right. It's hard to pronounce words, properly, when you have never heard them. They find humor in this, and it only makes them taunt him more. Even when school is out, they will find him and tease him no matter how hard he tries to get away from them. There is; however, one place where he can find solace, one place where no one would think of looking for him. It is his secret place, and he takes all precautions to make sure that no one ever sees him go there.

The crowning glory of Drefenstein is its beautiful clock tower. Towering five stories above the village, its hand-cut stonewalls topped with a hand-carved frieze, and ornate soffits, make it one of the finest clock towers in the country. Its huge clock face glistens in the morning light, its ornamental hands and gilded numbers showing like glowing embers of the sun itself. Built and dedicated by a wealthy patriarch, its bells have serenaded Drefenstein and the surrounding hills, for nearly eight decades.

It is the bells that Hans loves the most. At noon each day they will ring out a familiar melody, followed by twelve soundings of its huge brass bell. Hans's favorite spot is a small loft just above the clock face where a small window gives him a birds-eye view of the whole town. He always tries to be there at noon when the bells begin to ring. There is a small window in the back of the building that is always left open slightly, for ventilation. This is how Hans obtains entry into the building.

On school days, he rushes the two blocks from the school, down an alley, across a back yard, to be in position in time for the chorus to begin. On weekends and when school is not in session, he will sit for hours in front of the little window and watch the traffic far below as it scurries by silently on the busy street. When the bells begin to chime, Hans can feel the vibration through his entire body. It's the closest thing to hearing that Hans has ever experienced.

After school, Hans has to hurry home to fix supper for his grandfather. He never knew his father, and his mother had died when he was very young. He went to live with his grandparents. His grandfather worked in a small saw mill, just outside of town. His grandmother died last year, when he was eleven. There is just him and his grandfather, now, and he doesn't know what he would do if he were to lose him too. He has no other family and no real friends.

The Stout brothers will wait for him, to chase him home and call him names. He knows the names, even though he can't hear them, he can see the words formed by their lips. "Dummes huhn," they will shout (stupid chicken), or "depp" (idiot). He never could understand why they would want to torment him; after all, he had never done anything to them. He can dodge most of their stones, and he is use to their insults. He only wonders how much longer he must endure this abuse. He is twelve, and this has been going on for the last three years. They tease him and push him around at school. He longs for revenge, but how?

Grandpapa has told him that they will go on bullying him until he stands up to them. There is no pleasure in picking on someone who fights back. But Hans has never quiet mustered up the courage it takes to fight back. It is much easier, for now, just to run away. He's a fast runner. He can easily outdistance the fat Stout brothers. It is only at school, when they corner him in the hall or in the bathroom, that they are able punch him and kick him. The sounds he makes could hardly be recognized as cries for help.

On this day, just before lunch, the Stout brothers had caught up with him in the hall. They pushed him back and forth between them until Walther Stout, the older brother, grabbed him from behind. He held Hans tightly while his younger brother Fritz punched him in the stomach several times. Hans pushed backward, forcing Walther against the wall. Picking up his feet, he kicked Fritz in the chest. Fritz stumbled backward until he collapsed against the far wall, gasping for breath. Hans swung his right foot back and kicked Walther sharply in the shin. He let go of Hans as he grabbed his shin in pain.

Hans sprinted from the school, across the school grounds, and down the street with the two brothers in close pursuit. He cut first down one street, and then another, until he was sure he had lost them. Then he cut through the alley and across the backyard behind the clock tower. It was then that he saw the brothers rounding the corner. He was hoping that they hadn't seen him as he squeezed through the window on the ground floor of the tower. When he was inside, he looked back to see them coming. He was now trapped, and the only way to go was up.

He climbed the circular staircase to the belfry, two steps at a time. He climbed the ladder to the clockworks room, and then a shorter ladder to a trapdoor that opened into the small loft above. He closed the trapdoor and waited, knowing that they must be able hear his heart beating! He hid in the corner of the small loft; the small window illuminating the room as the noonday sun streamed in. For the first time he wished the window were not there. The roof was above him; there was no place left to run.

The trapdoor pushed open, and Walther pulled himself into the loft, his brother right behind him.

"Well, dummes huhn," he said, "cozy little place you've got here."

"Yes, dummkopf," Fritz added. "This will be a good place to teach you a good lesson." He was rubbing his chest with one hand and making a fist with the other. He waved his fist under Hans' nose. "You're going to pay for kicking me, depp!"

"And just to make sure you don't go anywhere until we're through, Walther said, "I'm going to secure this hatch." With this he took a broom from the corner and, with great effort, jammed it between the roof and the handle of the trapdoor. "There," he said, seemingly pleased with his work, "it would take more than a wimp like you to pull that away."

They came at him, both at the same time. Hans knew that this time he would have to put up a fight. After all, he had nothing to lose. They would beat him anyway, if he fought back or not. Walther came at him first and Hans hit him as hard as he could in the face. Walther stepped back putting his hand to his mouth; it came away bloody. He seemed surprised. Fritz jumped in and grabbed Hans' right hand. Hans hit him with his left and Fritz stepped back. Grandpapa was right. The brothers couldn't take it as well as they dished it out. The two were crying, now, Walther holding his mouth, and Fritz with his hand over his right eye.

"Come on!" Hans shouted. "If you want me, come and get me!" His words were not clear, but they understood them perfectly.

Just then the bells began to play their sweet melody. To Hans it was as he imagined the sweet voices of a choir: first the sopranos, then the tenors, and lastly the huge bass voices would join in. He felt the floor shaking as the huge bell began to strike the hour. Looking over at the brothers, he saw that the brothers were holding their ears. There was blood running down the inside of their wrists.

Christmas in nearly here, and little has changed in this sleepy, little village. One thing has changed, however. Hans no longer has to dodge stones and insults. The fact is, he now enjoys his walk to school with his two new companions; his two, new, deaf companions. He's teaching the Stout brothers how to hear with their eyes, their noses, and their fingertips. Each day at noon, the three companions climb to the loft above the clock and listen, with their bodies, to the beautiful chorus of the bells.

THE PIANO MAN

The Rococo Lounge is a fanciful, cozy little nightspot that lies just off Lexington Avenue, on East 36th Street, in Manhattan. The premises has not always been fanciful, nor has it long been known as the Rococo Lounge. Before Jacqueline Everhart purchased the place it had been known simply as the "East Manhattan Bar and Grill. A mysterious kitchen fire had left the walls blackened, and the whole building with a bad smell. This, and the long list of code violations, was all that was needed to convince the owners to grab the insurance check, accept Jacqueline's generous offer, and vacate the premises with not even a backward glance.

Her friends, upon seeing the place, thought that Jacqueline had taken leave of her senses and could not, for the life of them, understand what she planned on doing with this "rat infested, smelly, hell hole". The place hadn't been remodeled since prohibition was appealed, and the cracked plaster walls; sagging and yellow stained ceiling; grooved and warped hardwood flooring; abundant mouse holes; and bold, parading roaches, should have been evident to even the most casual observer, seeing-eye dog notwithstanding.

What had caught Jacqueline's eye was the bar. It was massive and oval, constructed of contoured oak and rich, dark veneers. The rail was of pure brass, embossed with the name of the manufacture on every bracket, stemming from an era when people still took pride in their workmanship. The countertop was inlaid in black polished marble that, aside from a few scratches and minor chips, was still In good shape. In fact the whole bar was in remarkable condition, crying out only to be cleaned, refinished, and cherished. Jacqueline knew that this was a remarkable find. A bar of this kind, in restorable condition, was indeed a rare and invaluable asset. To construct such a bar, at today's prices, would be exorbitant.

There were other things, too, that had caught Jacqueline's eye. The antique, brass sconces needed only to be buffed and rewired. Ceiling fans were still in good shape, as were the two chandeliers that hung between them. The building was well constructed and solid. There were apartments upstairs, and a small antique shop next door. If, at some future date, she might want to expand, she could vacate the shop, and with the help of some support pillars, remove the common wall.

The building was in need of repairs; she knew that already. She had been to the city and had gotten a complete list of all the code violations before she even considered buying the place. The real estate people had also informed her of the violations and structural problems, as they were required to do. They did omit a few minor things, and Jacqueline was quick to point them out. She was no stranger to real estate, having served in that profession for the last twenty years. Her father was a builder, her uncle was an architect, and she had drawn on their expertise in her fledgling years whenever necessary. She was her own person, now, and well respected; with an eye to spot things that others might overlook.

Contractors were brought in. The whole building was rewired, the walls stripped and refurbished, and the ceiling replaced. The hardwood flooring was beyond refinishing, so she had it removed and replaced with new. The kitchen was remodeled: the counters were replaced as well as the appliances, the exhaust fans, and the plumbing. A new grill and deep fryer replaced the old iron stove, and the old cracked linoleum flooring was replaced with imported, quarry tile. Jacqueline had a hand in the decorating, and with the draperies, tapestries, carved frieze, and the nude paintings, she had added, the place began to take on the air of a nineteenth century English brothel.

The centerpiece of the Rococo was a used, full concert, grand piano she had picked up at an auction at an excellent price. She already had a piano player in mind; a pianist, actually, who could pound out a piano concerto from memory, or a Gershwin tune with equal ease. His name was William Lorusso, and his soft, low tenor voice was smooth and soothing. She had met him at a party the year before. He was the entertainment. He worked at a small lounge off Fifth Avenue. She had gone there to listen to him on several occasions. When she had seen the piano at the auction and decided to buy it, she knew that he would have to be the one to play it. She went after him with a vengeance. She plied him away with a delicious salary and a free-rent apartment in a building she owned just four blocks away. When he saw the apartment he couldn't refuse. It came fully furnished, with a large living room, a spacious kitchen, a master bedroom, a guest room, two baths, and a king-size, soft-side waterbed. It was an apartment to kill for.

It was twenty after five, that Saturday, when William Lorusso came through the door of the Rococo. He was a tall, thin man in his late thirties with piercing blue eyes that were tinted with more than a touch of pink. He wore a heavy gray trench coat and dark, knitted gloves, but no hat. A gust of wind brought with it the white, puffy snow that followed him as he came through the door, and settled on the red carpet of the foyer. Snow had nestled on the hair that encircled his balding head, forming a white halo that he brushed at vigorously with both hands.

Noleen, the cocktail waitress, was filling salt and sugar containers and trying, in her altered state, not to get the two confused. She was young and pretty, twenty-three, with dark brown hair and light blue eyes, set in a smooth, delicate face, the color of lightened tea. She had a slight Jamaican accent, inherited from her parents, as Noleen had never even seen Jamaica.

"Is you crazy, Bill?" she asked. "Has you got a death wish, mon. You walked all that way with no hat, in this shit? Damn, Bill, you a fool. With all the testin' the government's doin', messin' with the ozone and all. They blame it on the Freon, but it's really them neutron bombs, chemtrails, and all that stuff they has been playin' around with, all these years. You ain't got no idea what kind of shit is fallin' out of that sky! And you with no hat? You just got to be crazy!" She wiped up some spilled sugar, picked up the salt and the sugar bags, and walked off toward the kitchen.

"Nice to see you again, too, Noleen!" Bill yelled after her.

She freed one hand and flipped him the "bird" over her shoulder.

Bill took off his coat, shook the snow from it, and folded it over his arm.

"One of these days you two will have to kiss and make up," John said, as Bill made his way to the bar.

Bill slid onto one of the barstools and laid the coat on the seat next to him. Removing a handkerchief from his pocket, he wiped the melted snow from his forehead. "Ah, she doesn't mean anything by it. It's just her way of saying hello."

John was tall and muscular, with long blond hair that he wore tied in a ponytail. His eyes were light blue, almost gray, and when he smiled, as he did often, his teeth shown straight and true. It was a tribute to the skill of his dentist, as well as John's willingness to endure long, painful, expensive procedures to achieve any goals he set for himself. He was meticulous about his clothes as well. He wore a white, ruffled dress shirt, blue pants that were sharply creased, a red vest, patent leather shoes, and a black bow tie. He looked more like a soldier in the service of the Queen, than a bartender from Manhattan. He made Bill's usual, without being asked, and placed it on a coaster before him.

"Looks like it's gotten worse since I came in," he commented.

"There's about two or three inches out there, now, and it's still coming down. You don't think that will affect the crowd, tonight, do you?"

"Nah." John smiled. "Not this bunch. They'll be in if they have to come in on dog sleds."

The day bartender was still working, but being here before his shift started was not unusual for John. He would come in early, weed out the empty liquor bottles, empty the trash, and begin wiping glasses, while the day man would restock the cooler with fresh beer and ice. John took his job seriously, and with a certain amount of pride. Clean glasses were a big part of that pride. He had once told Bill that serving someone out of a dirty glass was like expecting them to drink out of a toilet. John was probably the best bartender in Manhattan, if not in the whole damn city. He could make almost any drink from memory. There weren't too many people who had ever stumped him, and even then, never more than once.

But it was his whole demeanor that made him such a good, all around bartender. He lit their cigarettes, kept their glasses full, was a good listener, and never gave advice unless he was damn sure that he knew what he was talking about. He was very intelligent, well read, and could converse on nearly any subject. He seemed to be far more mature than his twenty-six years. He put up with the drunks night after night with poise and discretion. They were his customers. He felt that if he offended them, they might not come back. He did his best to keep them happy.

John didn't drink. In the three years he had tended bar at the Rococo no one had ever seen him drink anything stronger than Coke. Bill would liken it to a chef that had never tasted his own food. Yet night after night, he continually produced a quality product. There were few complaints, and those were always quickly remedied. He was his own bouncer, although it seldom got to the point of violence. Obviously, because of his size, he intimidated people. John worked out at a gym every day. Only a fool would challenge him. To do so would be a little like taunting a bear.

It had been the money that had attracted him to bartending. He had learned the necessary skills in Bartender's School, and perfected them with his own inexorable attention to detail. John knew if a certain drink required a twist of lemon, a slice of orange, an olive, a flag or a paper umbrella. However, if a customer requested a twist of lemon, a slice of orange, a paper flag or the entire Constitution, he would receive it with a smile. The job did pay quite well. Nobody knew just how much John did make, except John and the IRS. With the tips he received from his appreciative customers, he had to be doing pretty well. Of course this all depended on keeping the "lounge lizards" happy and coming back week after week.

A large part of that responsibility also fell on Bill's shoulders. He was the nightly entertainment. Even when people weren't listening to his music and it became nothing more than the background for loud conversation, it was still part of the atmosphere and the drinks still flowed his way. John saw to that. The tip jar would go hungry on such nights, and Bill would quickly get stewed. No one seemed to notice or even care when he began to play badly.

Even on his worst nights; however, Bill played better than most piano players. All of those years of practice, lessons, college, schools, always focused on one goal, how could he be less than polished? Bill wanted, more than anything, to be a concert pianist. His wife, Elizabeth, had been the driving force behind him. She wanted him to succeed; and she made him feel as though he really could.

He had almost made it, too. If a drunken driver hadn't killed his beautiful wife of three years, things might have been different. His world crumbled around him after Bess died. He went to pieces. He did a short stint in a clinic. He was sure that it had helped him. But when he got out, he wasn't so sure anymore. He no longer knew what he wanted to do with his life. His dreams had been shattered. What had once been so important to him, no longer held any meaning.

He found solace in the bottle; it's comforting warmth eased the pain, and the tears seemed to flow less often. Without Bess to guide him, he lost track of his goal. It soon became a forgotten dream. He had started playing in bars and lounges about eight years ago. The Rococo was his third job. He had been here nearly three years. Long enough so that the Rococo seemed like home. It was a great job. Where else could he work and get blitzed at the same time, night after night? By two o'clock every night most everyone was either high or drunk, except for John and possibly Carl, the manager. Jacqueline Everhart, the owner, would wander in some evenings, unannounced. Most of the time she was high. It was as if they were one big, high, drunken family, and Bill was the choreographer.

Saturday night; however, was the best night of the week. This was when the "good crowd" came in. They were the regulars and whomever they happened to bring with them. They were ready to party, and they would gather around the piano bribing Bill with cold beer and cash as the wide mouthed jar atop the piano seemed to smile, its gluttonous appetite finally appeased. They would challenge his memory as he searched his mental reserves for long forgotten favorites and show tunes. Amid the "oohs" and "ahs", his skillful fingers would strum out a tune on the soft, stringed cords of the piano. This would set fingers and toes tapping as he directed a chorus of unharmonious voices through the long forgotten words of an old favorite. Bill knew them all. Occasionally, Bill would catch a tear forming in the corner of a wrinkled eye, as a vivid memory would pass swiftly through an unshielded brain. Tonight, Bill hoped, would be such a night. He sucked the last remnant from his glass, and set it back on the bar.

"Want another?" John asked.

Bill looked at his watch. It was nearly six. "Nah, he said, "make it a beer. I need to be sharp for when the crowd comes in. So what's the latest joke?"

John laid his towel on the bar and leaned toward Bill. "Well," he said, "there's this old farmer, named Silas, standing at the pass-through window of the local chicken franchise, talking to the owner. He looks over at the parking lot as a pickup truck pulls up and a young boy gets out. 'That's that good for nothin', Billy Bob,' Silas says. 'Why, he ain't nothin' but a god damned, lazy, no good, chicken fucker!' With this, he storms off toward his own pickup on the other side of the parking lot.

"Billy Bob comes to the window and says, 'I know Silas was sayin' somethin' bad about me. He ain't never liked me ever since he caught me in the hay barn with his daughter. Tell me what he said, Virgil, so's I can go whomp the shit out of him, right proper!'"

"Now, Virgil looks at Billy Bob and says, 'I'm a God fearin', Christian man, and what Silas said is both vulgar and unconscionable. It would be contrary to my moral upbringing, as well as my religious convictions, to repeat his words.' Billy Bob looks at Virgil and says, 'I would never ask a man to go against his religious convictions, so's I won't ask ya to repeat what Silas said.' Virgil smiles and says, 'Good, now that that's settled, what can I get you today?' Billy Bob studies the menu for a moment and says, 'I think I'll have the three piece, fried chicken dinner.' 'Ok,' says Virgil, 'now, will that be to go, or will you fuck it here?'"

It wasn't one of John's best, but it did get a good laugh out of Bill. It was six o'clock, now, and Bill sat down at the big piano and warmed up with a few show tunes. There were few people here this early, but that didn't seem to bother him. After all, he got paid by the hour, not by the customer. He sang a song from "The Music Man", as he looked around the lounge. There were only six customers. There was a small, but distinguished looking, older gentleman seated at the bar, his eyes were fixed on a young man and woman seated at one of the tables against the wall. He seemed to be intently watching their every movement as if he were contemplating what they would do next. Bill had never seen him in here before.

Professor Elwin Holman had just come to New York from the Los Angeles area, where, until three years ago, he had been an English professor at the prestigious, Pepperdine University, in Malibu. He recently took a job with the University of New York, here in Manhattan. An incident in California had forced him to resign his position at Pepperdine, an incident that was never mentioned on his recent application to The University of New York. You see Dr. Holman is a Peeping Tom, a voyeur.

He doesn't enjoy having sex with women, but rather, he enjoys watching other men do it. When in California, he had a neat little arrangement with a two prostitutes. They would bring men to an apartment, and have sex with them. Dr. Holman would pay them to let him watch from the apartment next door. The mirror above the dresser was replaced with a two-way mirror, and there was a large patch of wallboard missing behind it. Professor Holman rented both apartments under a fictitious name. He would occupy the one apartment on the weekends, and watch as a long line of "Johns" filed in and out of the apartment next door.

One day, one of the prostitutes confided in the wrong person, and the word spread quickly on the street. The vice cops caught wind of it, and quickly set up a sting operation, raiding both apartments at the same time. The forty-eight year old professor was literally caught with his pants down. He was arrested, along with the prostitutes, and charged with "lewd and lascivious behavior". He was taken to the local police station where two detectives gave him the "good cop-bad cop" routine until he finally told them what they wanted to hear.

He posted bond and was out on the street within the hour on his own recognizance. He returned to court a week later. He had a good lawyer, and he got the charges reduced to soliciting. The good Professor pleaded guilty, and was released after paying a modest fine. This; however, was only the beginning of his troubles. The story hit the papers, and because of his position, the story received much more publicity than it actually should have deserved.

He retired to the university parking lot one evening, to find that his precious Ferrari sports car had been desecrated. The headlights had been adorned with, what looked like, false eyelashes, the grill had been surrounded with blood red paint made to look like lipstick while crisscrossed lines, resembling net stockings, where drawn down both sides of the trunk and fenders with black marker. On the windshield were duct taped two large, pink pillows, adorned, in the center with two brown paper plates, and centered within them were two bright red, paper cups. Across the back window was a pink sheet, taped to the body, and folded to look much like women's panties. Professor Holman was devastated! It was his expensive pride and joy. If he had been married, he would have rather that they had raped his wife, and now in retrospect, perhaps even his seventy-two-year old mother. Since the university was founded on religious and moral principles, the good professor was asked to resign his position, which he did. He sat home and moped for months. His Ferrari was repossessed a year later. Without a job he was unable to keep up the payments.

Six months ago he had moved to New York. Because of his credentials, he was never asked too many questions, or at least not the right ones. He merely told them that he had resigned his position in California and moved to New York because he felt that New York had so much more to offer. It was a point he didn't need to argue with New Yorkers. They accepted his explanation, unchallenged. Three weeks later he was schlepping English to a bunch of students with strange accents, and walking the halls of a university buried deep within the bowels of this strange congested city. He convinced himself, that here a car wasn't necessary, not even a Ferrari. He still missed his car. It was like the passing of a forlorn lover.

He had; however, learned a valuable lesson. He would never again solicit another prostitute. He was still unable to give up his voyeur ways, and he scouted the city until he found just the right apartment. It was a high-rise, just across the street from a battery of other apartments. He purchased a powerful telescope and a set of binoculars. He would busy himself, each night, scanning the nearby glut of brightly lit windows from his own darkened apartment. It wasn't always fruitful, but it was still exciting and a whole lot safer.

He now noticed that the piano player was looking at him. He had been staring at the couple across the bar. He swung around in his seat and picked up his glass. He took a long drink of the martini, and set it back down. The couple had caught his interest because the girl had looked a lot like one of the prostitutes in California, and the boy, with his dark-rimmed glasses and protruding ears, reminded him of himself, when he was young.

He felt a little embarrass and thought again why he was here. The weather was bad, the windows were foggy, and the snow was heavy at times. It just wasn't a good day for observing. He had gone for a walk to experience the snow, felt a chill, and had found this cozy little nightclub. This place really wasn't bad. He had never been here before, but the piano player was good. Tonight, he just didn't want to be alone. He took another quick look at the girl. If it weren't for the fact that she was too young, he would swear that it was the same big mouthed, fucking whore that had gotten him into trouble in California. He downed the rest of his drink. He was playing with the glass when the bartender came around.

"Would you like another, Sir?" John asked.

"Yes, thank you."

"Martini, right?" John knew what the man was drinking, but he asked anyway, in case the man wanted to switch his drink.

"Yes," said the Professor. "A little less vermouth this time."

John made a gesture with his thumb. "Gotcha," he said. John made the drink a little stronger and charged him accordingly, taking the money from the bills and change still on the bar left from the twenty he had broken for the first drink.

The Professor paid no attention. "The man plays a nice piano," he said.

"This ain't nothing," said John. "You should hear him play the 'long haired' stuff. Bill studied to be a concert pianist."

"Do tell," the Professor said, showing some interest."

"Do you like that kind of music?"

"Indeed I do." The professor smiled broadly. "Very much."

John tilted his head toward the piano player. "Slip a couple of bucks into his jar and ask him to play you something. It's early yet. He'd probably be glad to do it."

"What should I ask him to play?" the professor asked shyly.

"Whatever you want. He knows them all."

The Professor got up from the bar, snatched up the change and started toward the piano. He stopped abruptly, and went back and retrieved his drink.

Bill looked up as the man approached, and smiled. "Can I help you?"

"Do you know 'Petit Chien'?" the professor asked, hopefully.

"Chopin. Yeah, I know that one. It just happens to be a personal favorite of mine. It goes something like this, I believe." Bill's fingers began to fly over the keys as he strummed out the haunting melody.

The Professor stood there, transfixed, his face flushed red. He put his hands to his mouth as tears began to form in the corners of his eyes. Old memories returned to him, as he thought of his tortured youth. Even as a boy, he was short and dumpy, and boys and girls alike made fun of his thick glasses. The classics had been his only love, from an early age, both in music and in literature. He removed a ten-dollar bill from his billfold, placed it in the jar, and retreated toward the men's room, handkerchief in hand.

Bill finished playing and looked over at John. "Was it something I said?"

John leaned out over the bar to see if the man was out of sight. "Funny little guy, ain't he? I think he liked your playing, though."

Bill looked at the jar. "A ten dollar bill! I guess he did."

The professor returned, and as he passed the piano, Bill held up a glass. "You forgot your drink," he said.

"Thank you," the Professor said, politely. "That was an excellent rendition. I should know. I have listened to some of the best. Why, may I ask, are you wasting your time here?"

Bill smiled. "I like it here," he said, piercingly.

The professor realized that he had overstepped the boundaries of good taste, and retreated to the bar. He ordered another drink and wondered if he were really ready to be with other people. His thoughts were interrupted, as a men slid into the seat next to him. The man nodded his way and waved to the bartender.

"A Rum and Coke, John," he ordered, "and hurry, I think my blood/alcohol level is dropping below 1.6." He turned to the Professor. "Anti-freeze," he explained, "getting nasty out there. My name is David Wheat," he said, extending his hand. "Haven't seen you in here before."

The two men shook hands. "Elwin Holman." He thought of adding 'Professor' to that, but decided it might sound a bit pompous. "No, I've never been in here before. I'm new to New York. I really don't get out much."

David smiled. "Well ya picked one hell of a night for your comin' out, Pal. It's nasty out there. It's the worst I've seen it in all the time I've been in New York."

"I've always enjoyed the snow," the Professor confessed, "although I never had to live in it, before."

David took a drink of his freshly delivered Rum and Coke. "Where ya from, if ya don't mind me askin'."

"LA," the Professor replied. He felt that being more specific would only prove to be confusing, especially to someone not familiar with California.

"Oh, no wonder." David was laughing. "Ya don't get no snow out there, right?"

"In the mountains," the Professor explained. "mostly in the mountains, although they do get snow in northern California."

"I'm from Nebraska myself," David explained. "We get lots of snow out there. Ever heard of Valentine?"

"No," admitted the Professor, "I can't say as I have."

"Well, not many people have. Actually, I lived about ten miles north of there, almost to the South Dakota border. That's all Indian country, up there. My ex-wife is Indian. She still lives there. She remarried. Got three or four kids, now. I still run into her, whenever I go up there. It's not hard to run into people you know, when ya come from a place where ya know everybody. My Pop just retired about two years ago. I think he's kind of proud of the fact that I've stayed with the Navy for eighteen years. The way I used to raise hell, when I was young, I think he figured I'd either be a bum or be doing time. My marriage only lasted four months. I guess she just wasn't willing to put up with my drinking and running around. I can't blame her. The main reason I left and joined the Navy was to get away from her and her constant nagging. She filed for the divorce the week after I left. You married?"

"No." The Professor smiled sheepishly. He was wondering if David was ever going to come up for air. "I guess you might say that I'm a confirmed bachelor."

David put his hand on the Professor's shoulder. "Hey Pal, you're in good company. The first time I saw the sea and her many moods, I fell in love with the bitch. I've been courtin' her ever since." David smiled to himself as he thought fondly of his time at sea. He loved the way the sea would cradle him in her calm, gentle arms, and dazzle him with her beautiful sunsets. He loved the wind, the rain, and even her violent upheavals. Riding high above the sea, the blue-black sky churning menacingly above, the dark sea topped with foaming whitecaps, rushing upward to grip the ship in a bone shaking grasp, gave him a rush, the kind of which could be found in no known drugs. He had served ten years on Destroyers, and he loved every minute of it.

". . . in the Navy?"

David realized that he had been lost in thought and hadn't been listening to what Elwin had been saying. "I'm sorry," he said, "I was thinking. I didn't catch what you said."

"What do you do in the Navy?" the professor repeated.

"I'm an ET," David offered.

"An extra-terrestrial?"

"No, I'm an Electronic Technician."

"That sounds exciting."

"Only if you cross the wrong circuit, or fry your brains with microwaves. Most of it is just boring, tedious detective work; finding a bad part, a short, broken wire, or a bad solder job. Sometimes it's easy, like a bad fuse or a fried part that's easy to spot, but most of the time it's testing panels and circuit boards. That can get boring. Right now, though, I'm TAD.

"What is TAD?" the Professor asked.

"Temporary Assigned Duty. Right now, I'm on shore duty. You see, when you're a lifer, like me, you do so much sea duty and the Navy lets you do so much shore duty. To tell the truth, I'd rather be out to sea. I'd like to get transferred to your neck of the woods. Maybe San Francisco or even Hawaii. Hell, I've seen most of the east coast. I've been to Europe, most of the islands and most of South America. What I'd like to do, now, is spend some time on the west coast. Maybe even go to Japan."

"It sounds exciting," the Professor admitted. "I was never in the service, myself. Medical problems kept me out of the active duty. I often feel that I missed a lot."

So what do you do, Elwin?"

"I teach English Literature."

"You're a school teacher?"

The Professor smiled. "Well, actually, I teach at the University."

Whoa! That means that you're one of those Professors. A doctor, right? Jesus! You must think that I'm a awful idiot, rattling on, the way I've been doing'."

"On the contrary, David. I'll bet you are good at what you do. I find it fascinating. I can't even program a VCR."

David leaned over and put his hand to his mouth. "To tell the truth, Doc, neither can I."

An old man, on the other side of the bar, looked up from his drink to see where the laughter was coming from. The Bartender was standing before him.

"Want a refill," John asked.

The old man looked at his glass. Even the ice cubes were gone. "Yes, thank you."

"Gin and Tonic, right?"

"Yes, thank you," the old man repeated. His eyes were sad, as he listened to the familiar tune the piano player was now playing. The bartender set his drink before him and the old man set a ten-dollar bill on the bar. John scooped it up, made change, and laid it before him neatly, with the bills on the bottom and the coins stacked systematically on top. The old man took a long sip of his drink and tried to forget about the pain in his body. 'Cancer' they had said. Five months, maybe six. What did they know? What did it matter anymore? He was alone again. Cora, his wife of fifty-three years, had died two years ago. The kids were scattered, so far away. And now, Mona, too, was gone. She had left him two days ago, sometime during the night. Now he was alone, completely alone.

He was trying to think of a tune. It was the tune that he and Cora had dance to on their first date. He used to know it well. He used to hum it all the time, when he was young. Why couldn't he remember it? How beautiful she was on that first night. How handsome he looked, all decked out in his Army drab. They danced well into the night. He could still see her; her white gown flowing behind her, her soft blue eyes sparkling, her mouth formed into the silly smile that had melted his heart into chocolate pudding. With the war, the separation, the kids, the struggling, and all the pains and sorrows they had been through together, not once had he lost track of that silly smile.

He grabbed his drink and a dollar from the stack, spreading the change across the bar. He left the rest of the money, and walked to the piano. He sat on the corner of the piano bench, his legs, suddenly, not feeling very steady.

"Could you play me a song, Son?" he asked.

"Sure," said Bill, downing the last of a now warm beer. "What song would you like to hear?"

"Well," said the old man, "that's the problem. I don't know the name, and I'm not even sure how it goes. All I can remember is that it was soft and sweet and rather sad."

Bill looked over at the old man, surveying him for a moment. The ice cubes were rattling against the sides of the old man's glass, his hand was shaking so badly; and it looked as if he had been crying. Bill spread his fingers across the keyboard and began to play "Reverie". The old man's eyes lit up with recognition as a smile came to his lips, "I believe that's it!" the old man shouted. "How did you know?"

Of course Bill didn't know. He only knew what kind of song the old man wanted to hear. Memories can play tricks on you. One song might sound much like another. The old man listened intently, humming to himself as he sipped his gin and tonic. When Bill finished playing, the old man pulled himself to his feet, placed a dollar in the jar and left.

Finding his bar stool again, the old man mounted it with some effort. He closed his eyes and hummed the tune over and over in his head. He had forgotten about his pain. His mind wandered back to the war, and the beachhead at Normandy. He had been there on June 6th, 1944 at a place they called Omaha Beach. The nightmare! All the things he had tried so long to forget came streaming back to him now in vivid memory. He was standing in the belly of the landing craft, so young and so frightened. The bow was down and bullets were hitting the craft inside and out, ricocheting off the inside and hitting the men from all sides. Orders were being screamed, and men were tripping over the bodies of their comrades. Men fell into the water, as machine gun fire ripped through their bodies, their heavy equipment dragging them down. He sidestepped and jumped. His pants were wet long before he ever hit the sea. He went to the bottom, and there he had to cut himself loose from his gear to keep from drowning. Surfacing again, he pushed his way through the chest-high water, as bullets splattered nearby. Everything seemed to be in slow motion. Try as he might, he could go no faster. Machine gun and mortar fire were bursting around him, and the ships off shore were giving the Germans hell. The air was filled with choking dust and smoke, as he finally made the beach.

There were bodies everywhere, in the water, and on the beach. People were now reduced to unrecognizable litter! There were headless torsos, other were missing legs and arms. Many were mercifully dead while others wrenched and screamed with pain. He dragged himself face first onto the sand, and dug in like a rutting sea turtle. He waited for orders that never came; there was no one left to give them. He could hear the bullets screaming close by, and the sounds of those dyeing around him. Somehow he managed to make it to the seawall. There were many men crouching there, many of them wounded. Bullets rained down on them from the bluffs above. He remembered thinking that no one could live through this. He sat with his back to the wall and shook with fear, as the fire from above rained havoc on the next wave of soldiers.

He had been wounded in the leg and foot. He hadn't even realized it until it was all over. He was taken to a first-aid station, and finally evacuated back to England, where he had spent the next three months in a hospital. He never rejoined his outfit, the bones had been shattered in his left foot and he would have a permanent limp. He spent the rest of the war in England, with a desk job. They gave him the Purple Heart. It only made him feel even more guilty for being alive while so many of his comrades had died. He couldn't keep it. He threw it in the trash. He was safe in England, but three quarters of his company had died that day. He never talked about the war. He was too ashamed.

He put his hands on his forehead as the tears rolled shamelessly down his cheeks. He thought again of Mona. "Where could she have gone? Why did she leave him?"

Bill hadn't noticed that Rowena had wandered in. She stood behind him and placed her hands on his shoulders. Bill looked up into her face.

"How are you doin', Bill?" she asked, her sparkling, dark brown eyes in direct contrast with her white skin. Her soft mouth, donned with some sort of shimmering lipstick, twisted up on the sides as she smiled.

He could see the light filtering through her soft brown hair. She bent to kiss his lips, exposing to him her soft, full cleavage. He brought his lips to hers and savored the pleasure of the all-too-brief encounter. The sweet scent of her hair filled his nostrils, and the taste of her stayed with him long after their lips had parted. "Well as can be expected," he replied. "And you?"

"I just got back from Vegas," she said, now rubbing his shoulders. "A one week sojourn. Mary knew these two guys who were going out there to have some fun. They wanted a foursome. She thought of me. Hell, I needed a vacation. I made it a working vacation. All expenses paid. It wasn't bad. I had fun." She winked. "I took plane fare, just in case."

"We missed you here."

"Bullshit! she said. "I'll bet Carl was happy. It left one more stool for a paying customer."

He smiled up at her. "You know better that that. You are the ray of sunshine around here."

She looked down into his face. "Jesus, Bill! You look like shit. Are you eating right?"

"Three squares a day," he lied. "I eat like a pig."

"You're full of shit, Bill." She got a serious look on her face. "What you need is a good woman to look after you."

Bill diverted his eyes back to the keyboard. He knew just who he would like that woman to be.

She kissed him softly on the back of his head. Do my song for me, will ya, Hon?"

She smiled as he began to sing the haunting words of "Piano Man". Bill watched Rowena retreat to the bar and take her usual place at the stool closest to the door. She was beautiful and seductive, reminding him of a patient, black widow awaiting the arrival of some unsuspecting prey. She didn't have to wait long. A well-dressed man, in his mid-fifties, came through the door, and without much hesitation slid into the seat next to her. Bill could see her smile, as the man said something to her. He could imagine the conversation; he had seen this same scene so many times before. Small talk would be exchanged, he would buy her a drink, eventually money would be discussed, and they would leave together.

An hour or two later, she would return. Her make-up would be fresh, her hair fixed differently and she would be wearing a different dress, something elegant, but sexy. You would never see Rowena in anything tasteless. She left no doubt that she was a bill of goods, to be purchased for the right price. Just the fact that a gorgeous creature like her would be sitting alone, was proof enough for most men. She never flaunted her wares. She would expose just enough cleavage to show her large breasts, and enough leg to suggest a shapely thigh. However, she would never think of wearing her dresses above the knee. That would be flaunting. Rowena was a professional, not a streetwalker.

Bill watched jealously as the man ordered Rowena a drink. He began to play "Never on Sunday", and Rowena sent him a coy smile.

Paul Decker slid into the seat next to David Wheat. Paul was in Real Estate. He was a handsome man, if a bit chunky, with reddish-brown hair, hazel eyes and a real gift for gab. Besides his Real Estate business he had also written quite a few novels. Nothing anybody would want to make into a movie, but sappy, romance novels, the kind that women sop up like vintage wine. It put food on the table and paid his bar tab. That's all he cared about. He never wanted to be the next Hemmingway. It did pay him well enough so he could live without the Real Estate, but it was the Real Estate that filled a large void in his life. He never married. He claimed that he never had the time. In the Real Estate business he got to deal with a lot of other people's wives. You would be surprised, he would explain, how many husbands would send their wives to deal with the Real Estate people. Quite often Paul got to try out a waterbed or a sauna, long before the husband ever got to dip his toes. The nice thing about married women; they never tell tales, and they don't expect flowers.

"How ya doin' Chief?" Paul said, slapping his friend on the shoulder.

"Pleasantly sober," David answered. "How about you?"

"Suffering from the same malady, but I know what to do about that." He raised his hand. "Hey John, over here! What are ya drinking? Run and Coke, right? Why the hell do I need to ask?"

"Oh no ya don't." David reached into his pocket and pulled out a roll of bills. Pealing a twenty off the top, he threw it onto the bar. "You bought the last round, pal."

"Who, the fuck, keeps track of shit like that?" Paul asked.

"I do," replied David. "I never forget important things."

John brought Paul's drink, and David motioned to his own and the Professor's drinks. "Freshen us up, will ya, John." He turned to Paul. "I'd like you to meet Professor, Elwin Holman," he said pointing at the man seated next to him. "Professor, this is my friend, Paul Decker."

The two shook hands behind David.

"Professor," Paul commented. "I hope you don't mind me asking. Professor of what"

"English Literature," the Professor replied. "I teach English Literature at the University, or should I say I try?"

"Paul here is a writer, you know," David interjected.

"Oh." The Professor looked interested. "What have you written?"

"Oh," replied Paul, "nothing you'd want to read. I write under the pseudonym: 'Susanna Bullet'. Romance novels. Women like to think women write all of those books. I guess it gives them more of a feeling of intimacy."

"Oh yes," the professor smiled broadly, "I've seen your books around campus. The girls like to underline the passages, and pass them back and forth. I confiscated one of your books one day, and read the underlined passages out loud. I did it merely to embarrass the girls. Halfway through I realized that what I was reading was more than just provocative, it was profound and humorous. It held the class spellbound. Now, if only I could get them to listen to Shakespeare in the same manner."

"You flatter me, Professor."

"No, I mean it. You have real talent."

Bill looked around the lounge. The place was getting busy. He looked at his watch. Nine-fifteen; it was still early. A small group was now gathered around the piano; and Bill was leading them in a medley of old songs. Noleen was keeping them supplied with drinks, as the top of the piano became a bar unto itself. Bill certainly didn't mind, for the wide-mouthed jar had taken on a greener hue.

At a corner booth, in the back of the bar, sat three men in business suits. It was one of those old-fashioned booths, shaped like a horseshoe and upholstered in lavender and buff colored, tufted and pleated vinyl. It was always sticky and made lewd noises when you moved. This didn't seem to bother the threesome, whose loud conversation was in direct conflict with the off-keyed singers gathered around the piano.

Noleen looked down at her pad. "OK, that's one Old Fashion, one Heineken and a glass of Port, right?"

"Bring us some pretzels and some potato chips, too, Sweetheart, while you're at it," Harold added. Harold Freed was a man in his late forties. He was tall, with thick black hair that had already receded almost to the middle of his head. He was wearing a gray, tweed suit. He looked up at Noleen through dark rimmed glasses. He liked what he saw. He wasn't really into black women, but this one was different. She was young, shapely, had nice tits, a well-formed ass, long legs, soft features, long black hair, and she was light-skinned. *Must be some white blood coursing through those veins,* he thought.

"How many?" she asked.

"How many what, Honey?" Harold countered.

"How many bags of chips and pretzels does ya want, Sir?"

"How about a couple a bags of each, Sweet Thing." He was leaning out of the booth and staring at her butt. "Did anybody ever tell you that you have nice . . . eyes?" he asked.

Yeah, she thought to herself, *and I has great tits, too, but they ain't on the menu.*

She smiled, "Well, thank you, sir." She looked around the table. "Will there be anything else?" They shook their heads. She turned and left. As she walked across the floor she placed her hand on her hip, and wiggled her ass. *Eat your heart out, Dickhead!* she said to herself.

Harold whistled. "Now that's one sweet, piece of ass! She could wrap those long legs around me anytime."

"Jesus, Harry." Jesse was shaking his head. "You know, sometimes you can embarrass the shit out of me. She's young enough to be your daughter, for Christ sakes! Besides, one day you're talking about how disgusting inter-racial marriages are, and now you want to have sex with a black girl?"

"Fuck you, Jesse! I just said that she would be a nice fuck; I didn't say I wanted to marry the bitch. Besides, the color doesn't rub off, you know?"

"You don't have any respect for women at all. Do you Harry?"

"Sure I do, Jesse, if they fuckin' deserve it!"

"Do you think this girl doesn't deserve it because she's black, or because she's a working girl?"

"Actually, I paid her a complement."

"Saying that she would be a nice fuck is a compliment, Harry? What would you have done if someone had said that about your wife."

"I'd punch out their fucking running lights!"

"So, it's only a compliment if you say it, right Harry?"

"Oh bullshit, Jesse! She didn't hear me."

"Not if she's almost completely deaf, she didn't. Jesus, Harry, the whole bar heard you!"

Simon threw up his hands. "Will you two knock it off? Listen to yourselves. With all the cussing, it sounds like a truck driver's convention, over here! Here come our drinks. Can you two stifle yourselves at least until the young lady leaves?"

Noleen set down the tray of drinks and handed them out. They were all quiet and smiling. "That will be $9.13," she said, looking around the table."

Harold handed her a ten-dollar bill. "Keep the change, you pretty little thing, you."

"Thank you, Sir." She turned and left. "Eighty-seven cents. I think I'll go buy me a new yacht," she mumbled under her breath.

"See what I mean, Harry?" Jesse Warner was in his late thirties. His face was round and almost childlike. His deep, blue eyes were large and full, giving you the impression that he might be unable to blink. A small mouth seemed to set high beneath his pug nose, and protruding cheeks made him look as if, at some early stage of his development, he had been left lying on his face, and it had never popped back into place. His face was always white and smooth, lending easily to the myth that he never had to shave.

"See what? What, the fuck are you talking about, Jesse?

"Did you have to say, 'you pretty little thing, you'?"

"Hey, Jesse, women eat that shit up. They love it. Believe me!"

"Somehow I don't think so, Harry." Jesse took a sip of his drink, and set the glass back down. She probably just takes it in her stride. I'm sure she gets it all the time. Jesus, Harry! That's sexual harassment!"

"Because I told her she had nice eyes, and I called her a 'pretty little thing'? I don't think so, Jesse."

"I don't recall you ever talking to the other waitress that way, Harry. The one that quit."

"Glades," said Simon, "her name was Glades."

"Yeah, Glades," repeated Jesse.

"Jesus, Jesse, she was forty-five, at least, ugly as sin, and talked like a sailor. If I had told her that she had nice tits, she would have thought I was flirting. You have to watch what you say around a woman like that."

"And if she's young, has a nice body, and is maybe black, you can say anything you want?"

"I didn't say that, Jesse."

"What if some woman came up and patted your ass, Harry. Would you like that?"

"Sure, Jesse, if she was pretty."

"What if she wasn't? What if she were fat and ugly, and well over seventy. Would you like it then?"

"No, maybe not, Jesse, but I didn't pat her on the ass; I just said that she had nice eyes."

"But that wasn't what you were thinking, Harry. You were looking at her ass when you said it. What if this same woman came up to you and said, 'Hey, big boy, I like that lump in your pants?'"

I'd probably just laugh."

Simon was just sitting there, shaking his head, sipping his drink, and chuckling to himself, as the two men countered each other.

"What if it were another man?"

Harry sat up in his seat. "I'd deck the mother fucker!" he said loudly.

A broad smile came across Jesse's face. "I must have hit a nerve. You know why this shouldn't happen? Because you have rights, that's why; so does that girl, and you're stepping all over her rights. I'll tell you another thing, Harry. You do this shit in the office, and you'll be treading on thin ice."

"I ain't stupid. I know with whom I can kid with, and with whom I can't. I've been with this company for over twenty-six years. Fuck, Jesse, you haven't even been dipping your wicket that long. But you're talking company policies, now; right? Fuck rights! We don't have any fuckin' rights!"

"What do you mean, we don't have any rights? It's all right there in the Constitution."

In the mist of this free-for-all, Simon caught Noleen's attention and ordered another round of drinks, using only hand movements.

"So what you're trying to tell me, Jesse, is that you and I have the same rights as everybody else, right?"

"Yes! Of course!"

"That's all bullshit, Jesse! Only the privileged have real rights. They could throw us in prison for no reason at all. If they wanted to, they could take that precious Porsche you've got stashed in your parent's garage, up in Schenectady, and there's not a fucking thing that you could do about it!"

"Now, that's bullshit, Harry. The government can't do that. It doesn't matter who you are. We all have rights!"

Harold laughed. "The government doesn't care about you or me. They can cram you into the cogs of hypocrisy, and crush you like a grape."

Noleen brought the drinks and the table went suddenly quite. Simon gave her an extra five dollars. She gave him a warm smile. "Thank you," she said.

Simon leaned across the table, nearly spilling his fresh drink. "Keep them coming," he said, almost at a whisper. He turned to Harold. "Don't you mean 'bureaucracy', Harry?"

"Shit! I don't know. I can't even remember what the fuck we were talking about." Harold's eyes were following Noleen. He thought about how much he missed his wife.

Simon was a stocky man, five foot eight, with a head full of thick, salt and pepper hair that was so curly, it almost looked like a wig. At sixty-three he was the oldest of the group and had been with the company for over thirty years. "Well, Harry," Simon offered. "The way I see it, you were offering a socialistic point of view, and Jesse was defending our democratic form of government." Simon was just beginning to feel the wine.

Harold took a long sip of his drink. "That's right, or at least it's close. The government runs us. We don't run the government. It's politics, just politics, and politics is perhaps the only dirty word that's still socially acceptable to utter in mixed company!"

"Now that's bullshit, Harry, and you know it!" Jesse tried to get to his feet. He realized that he couldn't while seated in the booth, so he sat back down. "What about the Bill of Rights and the Constitution? Are you going to tell me that they are nothing but ass wiping paper?"

"Crumbs!" Harry had spilled some of his drink, and was now mopping it up with a paper napkin. "They are just little dog bones that the governments hands out to keep us from whimpering. Try to exercise those rights and the government will bury you in paper work, or slam it so hard up your ass, they'll leave you bleeding for weeks! It's just a facade. If we all tested it, it would all come crashing down, like a deck of cards."

"How can you sit here and say that, Harry? What are you, some kind of fuckin' Commie?" Jesse was obviously getting upset.

"Come on, Jesse," Simon pleaded. "We were just supposed to have a few drinks, share a few laughs, and have a friendly discussion. Now you guys are getting personal!"

"Commie?" Harold repeated. "That kind of thinking went out with the McCarthy era."

"You talk about the government as if it was an entity," Jesse said. "In reality it is made up of people. There are working people just like us, and people with power who try to run things. They all have different agendas, policies, reasons, and goals. There are deals and compromises made every day. The whole system has been around for over two hundred years and has kept this country going through wars and depressions. It is a system of checks and balances that has kept pace with the changing times of a crazy world. No, it's not perfect, but it's still the best we have."

Harold shook his head, "Jesus, Jesse, you sound like the poster boy for the Conservative Party. What will you do next, stand up and sing 'God Bless America'?

Jesse leaned across the table. "If I could stand up I would," he said, smiling.

"What about Ruby Ridge, Jesse? Here is a good example of the government gone awry."

"I'll give you that one, Harold. Ruby Ridge was a little extreme, but the fact that we heard about it proves something. If something like this happened in a lot of countries, you just wouldn't hear about it. Americans have the right to know what is going on, and even when the government fucks up."

Harold downed the last of his drink. "Yeah! Well, I'll bet there is a lot going on that we never hear about."

Noleen delivered a fresh round of drinks and Jesse handed her fifteen dollars. "Keep the change," he said trying to mimic Harold.

"Gee, thanks, mister," she said.

Harry didn't even seem to notice. "Let's ask this pretty lady what she thinks," he said. "Tell us, Sweetheart, do you really think that the Government really cares about us little people?"

"You askin' the wrong person, Mister," Noleen said, starting to walk away.

Harold reached out and touched her arm. "We really do want to hear your opinion, Honey."

"The government ain't never done nothin' but crap all over me," she said.

"How can you say that," Jesse chimed in.

"That's a long story." Noleen started to turn and walk away, again.

Harold held up a ten-dollar bill, and snapped it between his fingers. "This sounds like a story I'd like to hear, Honey. How much persuasion would it take?"

Noleen snatched the bill from his hand. "That'll do it," she said, smiling. "Not much to tell. I were married when I was sixteen. He were twenty. At first, things wasn't too bad, but then, after my baby is born, Vance starts runnin' 'round on me. We breaks up for a while, but then I takes him back. That be my worst mistake. He gets me hooked on drugs then he leaves me again for some young bitch. I were havin' trouble makin' it on my own, so I gos for welfare. The caseworker finds out about my drug problem, an the bitch turns me over to Family Services. They takes my baby girl away from me, an tells me that I ain't gonna see her again, till I get myself straight. They order me to sign up for rehab, but I ain't got no kind of money to do that. I don't do nothin' like I used to, but they still won't let me have my baby back! I gets to see her once a week, on Saturday, for two hours. Believe me, that shits! Now, you tell me how they can just take away my baby, like that?" There were tears forming in her eyes.

Jesse took her hand. "Honey, they're only trying to protect your little girl. All you need to do is get yourself straight, and I'm sure that you'll get her back."

She pulled her hand away. "You think it's all that easy? You don't know nothin' 'bout nothin'!" She turned and walked away.

"Jesus, Jesse!" Harold said. "You had to piss her off, didn't you? Now, she'll probably be spitting in our drinks. You know what those people are like."

Jesse never got a chance to reply.

"Those people!" Simon's voice was angry. "One of 'those people'? I'm one of 'those people', Harry. I'm a damn Jew!"

"I didn't mean you, Simon." Harold was looking around, grasping for words. "These people have a whole different culture." The words were no sooner out of his mouth than he realized that that was the wrong thing to say.

"And, of course, we Jews don't."

"What I mean, Simon, is that they have an entirely different up-bringing. You know, with the drugs, the music, even the way they walk, and the way they talk."

"So, what you're saying Harry, is that there are no decent black families, who bring up their children to fear God, obey the laws, and respect other people?"

"No, Simon, that's not what I meant at all."

"You're such a bigot, Harry, but I guess I can't blame you. Somewhere, in your upbringing you were spoon-fed all that bull shit. Your parents were probably bigots, and as you grew up, you began to believe that what they told you was the truth. Maybe it's because I'm a Jew, but I fail to see how the amount of melanin in a person's skin, or the way they talk or walk could have any bearing on who they are. As long as there are people on both sides who think the way that you do, the situation will never get any better. If you really want to know what's wrong with society, Harry, put a finger on that pulse!"

"The truth is, if you were lying here on the floor, your life draining from your body, you wouldn't care if the person breathing life into you was black, or the paramedic jump starting your heart was flaming homosexual. At that instant, these things would have no meaning. As long as 'those people' aren't messing with you, why should these things matter at all?"

Jesse was silent through the whole thing. He, too, was one of 'those people'. He had discovered his true self when in his early twenties. In reality, this was when he finally admitted it to himself. He had known that he was "different" his entire life. He had dated many girls, through the years, but he had never known real love, not until he met Martin. Martin was tall, athletic, and very handsome. They met at a party on the west side and hit it off from the very beginning. It was destined for disaster from the start. Martin was flamboyant with his homosexuality, while Jesse was a "closet queer", who was always afraid that someone would find out. At first, their clandestine sojourns to the Catskills and Canada were a source of amusement for Martin, and he went along with them, but soon he tired of sneaking around, and left Jesse for a younger man with whom he played tennis.

Jesse felt that he had good reason not to be open. He had a good job, a great apartment, not to mention his Porsche in Schenectady he was still making payments on. That was another thing. The reason his Porsche was in Schenectady was because he was afraid to drive in New York.

He had so much to lose. None of the people he worked with knew, none of his friends; not even his own parents. It was his best-kept secret, and he wanted to keep it that way. Martin just didn't understand. Jesse didn't want to be known as the "fag that works in finance". He hated that kind of label.

"Jesus, Simon," Harold was saying, "you don't jump into the parley very often, but when you do, you come armed for bear." Harold made a sound like a wounded puppy. "Pull in your claws, boy. Sometimes Jesse and I get a little off track, but we mean no harm." He extended his hand. "Can we shake and start over again?"

Simon took Harry's hand in his. "You know I love you, Harry. You're an asshole, but you're one of the nicest assholes I know. You're good company, even though sometimes I think that your mouth should have its own septic system. And you, Jesse, you let Harry get to you. He likes to say things to get you going. Half the time he doesn't even believe what he's saying. Harry loves this country. They're still pulling shrapnel out of his leg from Nom. Which reminds me. Millie and I are making plans for our annual soiree, in June. You guys are coming, right?"

"Jesus, Simon, this is February," Harold said. "That's four months away."

"You know Millie, Harry. She likes to plan things well in advance, right down to the last hors d'oeuvre. All we need to know is if you guys are coming, and if you're bringing anyone. How about you, Jesse, are you still going with that little dish you brought last time?"

Jesse's face turned beet-red. The girl he had taken to Simon's last party was Martin's sister. He had every intention of bringing Martin, but at the last minute, he chickened out. Lena offered to be his last-minute replacement. Martin stayed home and stewed. This was the beginning of the end for their relationship. He had often wondered what would have happened if he had shown up with Martin. Perhaps he would still have his lover, but everything else would have surely come crashing down around him like the walls of Jericho. He was sure.

"No," he said, "we broke up months ago." Of course, he was really referring to Martin and himself.

Simon touched Jesse's shoulder. He could see the hurt in Jesse's eyes. "Sorry, I didn't mean to open any old wounds. Too bad, you made such a nice couple. How about you, Harry? Are you coming tandem?"

"Yeah, Simon. I'm sure I can find some slut that enjoys free food and bad company. If not, I'll just hire an escort." He looked over at Rowena, at the bar. "I wonder what our resident whore gets for a one-night stand?"

Jesse looked over toward the bar. She was already wearing a different dress. This meant that she had taken care of business at least once this night. "No telling," he said. "She might just charge by the pound."

All three picked up on the unintended pun at the same time.

The sound of laud laughter caught the attention of the old man at the end of the bar. He wondered how anyone could be so happy while he was so miserable. He was beginning to feel the effects of his drinks, and melancholia was affecting his every thought. *Why did Mona have to leave him?* He dried his tears on his sleeve as he drained the last remnant from his glass. *Damn you, Mona. Why did you leave me, now?* he whispered.

John's usual vigilance had been distracted, and he didn't notice the old man's empty glass. Noleen was sitting at the bar, her face as pale as her tea-colored complexion would allow. There were beads of sweat on her forehead, and she trembled as she tried to light her cigarette with a match. The match went out, and in frustration, she threw the cigarette on the bar. John was there, now, holding a lit lighter. She retrieved her cigarette, and took a long drag. It didn't help.

"Ya got anything, John?" she asked.

"Like what?" John asked, coyly.

"You know what the fuck I mean! I need a fix! I paid for my daughter's ballet lessons, and it left me short this week. My supplier won't extend me no more credit. I'm gonna lose my apartment. My life is shit, John! I needs somethin'!"

John filled a water glass half-full of Vodka, and passed it over to Noleen. "Drink this quickly," he said. "Don't let Carl see you. He's been looking for a good reason to get rid of you. It's the best I can do for you."

Noleen took the glass and got down behind the bar. She downed the whiskey quickly. Suppressing the urge to gag, she held her breath, and grabbed John's hand. After a few seconds, she took a few deep breaths.

"Better?" John asked.

"Yeah, thanks." She closed her eyes, as she let the warmth course through her body. "It ain't the same, but it's better'n nothin'."

"So, where are you going to stay, if you lose your apartment?"

"I don't know. I might just have to come up with a job that pays better."

"John looked into her soft brown eyes. "You mean prostitution?" he asked.

"If that's what I has to do," she answered.

"That sucks, Noleen! You're a decent, young woman who has just been dealt a bad hand. I can't stand to see you lower yourself like that."

"Lower myself? John, get in touch with reality. I'm an addict! I ain't no Princess Di. When I crash, there will be no one to blame, but me."

"Why don't you move in with me? I've got a big apartment. I'd love to have you."

Noleen looked at John for the longest time. "John, you is got to be the most beautiful white man I has ever met. You must have dozens of gorgeous white women just fightin' for a chance to slide into a warm bed with you. What use could you possibly have for a used-up, doped-up, nigger bitch, like me? What could I possibly be to you, and what would you be to me?"

"I'd be anything you wanted me to be, Noleen." John's face had a serious look. "I'd be your friend, if you'd let me. That would be up to you."

"If I thought you was serious, John, I'd take you up on that offer."

"I'm a serious as a heart attack, Noleen. Have I ever been anything but honest with you? Just tell me what you want to do with your life."

There were tears in Noleen's eyes, now. "I wants to kick this habit, get my daughter back, and become a beautician. I went to school for that, years ago, I just ain't never had the guts ta try."

"Move in with me, and I'll get you into rehab. When you get out, I'll get the best lawyer I can find, and we'll get your daughter back. Then, maybe we'll get the hell out of this town. We'll go to California. I'd like to get into movies, and you could open your own beauty shop."

"It's a beautiful dream, John, but how is all this gonna happen? Where is all this money gonna come from?"

"I've been saving for years, Noleen. I have over $80,000 in the bank. I've always had the means; I just never had the courage. With you at my side, I think I could do it. I've loved you from the first day I met you, I just never had the guts to tell you. Not until now. Please say yes."

Noleen climbed up on the barstool, put her arms around John's neck and kissed him softly. "I think you a damn fool, John, and I think you has lost your mind."

Carl saw Noleen sitting at the bar. He watched as she kissed John. It looked like more than just a friendly peck. He came over to the bar as Noleen was leaving. "She hasn't been drinking, has she?" he asked.

John grabbed Noleen's glass from the bar and rinsed it in the sink. "No," he said, "just some soda. She was thirsty, so I poured a glass for her."

Carl watched as she made her way back toward the booth where the three men in business suits were sitting. She didn't look like she was drunk. She had a smile on her face that he hadn't seen in years, and a spring in her step that was never there before. He looked toward the back of the bar and saw an elderly man with his face down on the counter top. "We can't have that," he said to John. "We need to get him out of here. If you have to, get him a cup of coffee, sober him up a little, and get him a cab."

John went around the outside of the bar and gently shook the old man by the shoulders. He didn't wake up. He shook him a little harder. Still there was no response. He put his hand on the old man's neck, and felt for a pulse. There seemed to be none. He called Carl over. "I think he's dead, Carl," he said softly.

"What do you mean, you think he's dead?" Carl said, much louder than he should have. Then more softly he asked, "Are you sure?"

"Yeah, I'm pretty sure. I can't feel any pulse. John touched the old man's cheek. "Feel him," he said, "He's cold as ice."

Carl put his hand on the old man's cheek. "Oh, Jesus, Jesus, Jesus!" he said.

"Do you want me to call 911?" John asked, reaching over the bar for the phone.

Carl grabbed his wrist. "No! Don't do that! Jesus! We don't need our customers seeing bodies being dragged out of here. Not tonight of all nights. Why does this shit have to happen on a Saturday; the best night of the week?"

"Yeah! He was such an inconsiderate bastard, wasn't he?"

Carl ignored John's sarcastic comment. "Here," he grabbed one of the old man's arms, "help me carry him into the back."

"You want me to help you carry him into the kitchen?"

"If someone notices they'll think that he's drunk, and we're taking him back to feed him some coffee. That's all."

John and Carl lifted the old man by his arms and carried him into the kitchen. The kitchen was empty, the cook having left at 8 o'clock, the witching hour for most barroom kitchens. If someone required a sandwich, or an order of fries, it was Carl's job, as manager, to see that the order was filled. They propped him up in a chair next to the door, while Carl tried to decide what to do next.

"OK." Carl unlocked the back door and pulled it open. There was a wall of snow about six inches deep. A gust of wind blew a quantity of the white stuff across the kitchen floor. "We'll put him out here in the alley. Then I'll call 911 and say that we found a dead bum in the alley."

"Have you lost your senses, Carl? Look at it. It's freezing out there."

"So what's your point, John? Are you afraid he's going to freeze to death?"

"Have you no respect for the dead?"

"It's not like he was my long lost uncle, John. I don't know this guy from Adam."

"He was a customer, Carl. We have a duty to look out for the well being of our constituents."

"You're not a priest, John! This is a bar, not a church. This guy is just another lounge lizard. A dead lounge lizard!"

"But he was my lounge lizard, and I feel responsible for him." John started rummaging through the old man's pockets."

"Now what the fuck are you doing?"

"I'm trying to find out where he lives."

"What good is that going to do? You gonna call up the old man's wife? I can see it now, 'Hello, Mrs. So-n-so? Could you please come and pick up your husband. He's dead!'"

John found an ID card in the old man's wallet. "Here it is. His name is Albert Milner. He lives about six blocks from here, in the old neighborhood. I know about where it is."

"That's nice to know," Carl said, "I'll send flowers. Now, do you want to help me move Albert out to the alley, or do I have to drag him myself?"

John stepped forward and closed the door. "Let's call a cab."

"What?" Carl was kneeling beside the old man, Albert's lifeless arm around his shoulder and was about to lift him from the chair.

"We can call a cab and take him home."

"Take him home! We just call a cab, load Albert in it and take him home?"

"That's it, Carl. It's as simple as that."

"What's the cab driver going to think?"

"He'll just think that he's drunk. After all, this is a bar."

"What if he has a wife, and she asks why we dragged him home if we knew he was dead?"

"We'll feign ignorance. We'll say that he must have died on the way. It's still better than finding him here, right?"

Carl threw up his hands. "OK! OK! I'll go call a cab. You go back to the bar. I'll let you know when he's coming. Go talk to Bill. See if he can cover for you while we're gone."

John found Bill on one of his breaks. "I'll have to leave in a little while. Something has come up. Do you think that you can cover for me for about a half-hour or so?"

Bill look around the bar. It was busy, but it was mostly the regular crowd. He knew that if he told them that John was off on an errand, they would take any inconvenience in stride. Besides, Rowena was back. What better opportunity would he have to stare into those soft brown eyes?

Carl returned and pulled John aside. "The cab companies are shutting their fleets down. They say the weather's too bad. I found an independent that will come, but he said he wants double."

"So?"

"Well, I think you ought to pay for half the fare. After all, it was your idea."

"Fine!" John started to grab his coat from under the bar.

"Might as well wait. He's got to come cross-town. With the weather the way it is it might take him forty-five minutes to an hour."

"What about Albert? Do you think that he will stay seated in the chair for an hour?"

"I propped him up with a push broom."

The cab arrived in fifty minutes. John and Carl managed, with some difficulty, to slide Albert into the back seat.

"What's with your pal?" the cabby asked.

"A bit too much good cheer, I'm afraid," Carl offered. "Today was his birthday. He just turned eighty."

The cabby was looking into the over-sized rearview mirror. "You'd better check his pulse. He looks more dead than alive," he laughed.

The two men in the back each managed a nervous chuckle.

"Where will it be, gents?"

John pulled the card from his pocket and read the address. "Do you know where it is?" he asked.

"Hey. I've been a cabby in this town for thirty-two years. There ain't too many places I can't find. Sit back and enjoy the ride. It's a madhouse out there; all the idiots that think they can drive in this shit are on the road! I think that I'm the only one that was smart enough to put chains on."

Normally it would have taken them ten minutes to get to their destination, but tonight it took twenty. The cabby was having no problem with the snow; it was the other drivers that were causing all of the delays. Stoplights were the worst traps, with cars unable to get moving again once they had stopped. Three times their cabby pulled up on the sidewalk to get around them. Finally he pulled up in front of a row of run-down tenant houses.

"This is as close as I can get. I think it's the second one down. Do you want me to wait?"

"Yes, please," John said, anxiously.

The two men managed to get Albert out of the cab, and with much difficulty, they dragged him along the sidewalk to the door of the apartment house. The sidewalk was slippery, and they were both having trouble keeping their footing.

"I wish the hell I had worn rubbers," Carl said.

John tried the door. "It's locked," he announced.

"Shit!" Carl shifted the old man's weight. "Check his pockets on that side," he said. "See if he's got a key."

John found a key ring in the coat pocket. He tried the first key and it worked. The door banged against the wall as it swung open and the two dragged Albert inside.

"Here's his mail box," Carl said, squinting at the row of boxes along the wall in the dimly lit hallway. "Albert P. Milner, 4-D."

"Jesus, Carl! That's on the fourth floor!"

Carl looked over at John. "It was your idea."

John hoisted Albert up in order to get a better grip. "OK," he said. "Let's do it."

The two men started for the stairs.

"The stairs are too narrow, Carl said, angrily. We'll never get him up this way. Let me grab his shoulders, you grab his feet. We'll have to go up single-file."

The two men struggle to get Albert up the stairs, sweating and groaning, as the rickety stairway creaked and moaned under the weight of their heavy footfalls. At last, they reached 4-D.

Carl knocked on the door. They waited a couple of minutes. He knocked again. "I don't think there's anyone home," he said. "Try the keys."

John tried three keys before he found the right one. The door opened easily, and the two men dragged Albert inside and laid him on the floor. John found the light switch as Carl turned to close the door behind them. A small, calico cat scooted through the closing door and hid under a small table.

"OK," said Carl. "He's home. Let's go."

"We can't just leave him here." John walked through the cluttered living room, and opened the first door on the right. "Bathroom," he said. He tried the next door. "Yeah, here it is, this is the bedroom. Let's bring him in here."

"Jesus, John! What if his wife comes home?"

"Carl," John looked around the messy apartment, "does this look like it has a woman's touch?"

"I guess not," Carl admitted.

They carried Albert to the bedroom and lay him on the bed.

"Good enough," Carl was looking at his watch. "Let's go, the meter's running!"

John knelt by the bed. "Let's at least take his shoes off."

"Then we could read him a bed-time story! Jesus, John! Let's get the hell out of here!"

Just then, the cat jumped up on the bed, and started licking Albert's face. The two men stood, mouths agape, as the old man's eyes opened wide.

"Mona! Mona," Albert cried, "you came back!"

Carl didn't even remember touching the stairs or the front door. When he got to the cab, John was already there, instructing the cabby to 'step on it'. "I thought you said he was dead," he said softly.

"Hey, what do I look like, a fuckin' doctor?"

On the way back, the cabby etched the two men's likenesses into his mind. He knew he would be called upon to identify these two "perps". He was sure they were up to no good.

"I wonder who those men were?" Albert asked, as he stroked the soft head of his furry femme fatale. She purred softly in his lap, as he kissed the top of her head. "It doesn't matter. All that matters is that you're home again, you naughty little girl."

When John and Carl got back to the Rococo, Paul Decker was tending bar, and Bill was back at the piano. The drinks were a little stronger than normal, and there were no olives, umbrellas, or orange slices, but no one was complaining. Their limit of tolerance having been reached, the regulars had stormed the sanctity of the inner bar. They had hoisted Bill bodily upon their shoulders, and after having placed Bill at his rightful place behind the piano, they by unanimous decision, anointed Paul with a goodly amount of Beefeater's Gin, and appointed him "Keeper of the Bar". Paul accepted the position with solemn, though slightly dampened, dignity, and with the help of his friends and fellow patrons, managed to keep the booze flowing.

A workable pricelist notwithstanding, Paul charged everyone two dollars, regardless of the type of drink they ordered. The Rococo had not realized any great profit during John and Carl's absence, but the two-dollar charge, when Paul had remembered to collect it, did keep the losses to a minimum. Carl was just glad to be back, and that Jacqueline Everhart had not arrived in his absence. If she had witnessed this financial carnage, his job would have been referred to in the past tense.

Carl retreated to the kitchen amid an onslaught of back orders, while John busied himself with the job of cleaning and reorganizing his desecrated bar. Things had discreetly returned to normal when Jacqueline Everhart finally arrived, fashionably, at 11:20 pm.

"John," she said, removing her gloves as she passed the bar, "the usual."

John raised his hand to indicate that he understood.

Jacqueline walked to the kitchen and confronted Carl. "What's the take, tonight?" she asked, as she removed her coat.

"I've been really busy, and haven't had a chance to check the till," Carl confessed.

She folded her coat and laid it on Albert's recently vacated chair. "Jesus! Do I have to do everything myself?" She went back to the bar and ducked under the walk-through. Opening the register, she removed the tray and scooped up the bills beneath. "Don't let this thing get this full, John. Put it in the box." She knelt down, opened a small safe below the register, and removed a box of money.

"Sorry, Jacqueline. We've been busy as hell."

"I'm glad to hear that you're busy, John, but I don't like to leave this much money in the register. Take time to put it in the safe." She closed the safe, and turned to walk away.

"Your drink, Jacqueline," John said, as she passed.

She turned to take the drink, then pausing; she looked down at John's shoes. "Why are your shoes so wet?" she asked.

"I spilled a bottle of club soda," he lied.

"It's not like you to be so clumsy, John. You're not on any drugs, are you?"

"You know me, Jacqueline. I don't even drink."

"Either do a lot of dopers." She took his head in her hands and studied his face. "Your eyes look clear. You're not coming down with something, are you?"

"I may be coming down with a cold."

"Well, that explains it," she said. "Your face is as red as a beet. You need to take care of yourself. I can't afford to lose you."

This was typically Jacqueline, relating to others in terms of her own needs. She left the bar in the same manner, locking herself in the office in the back. She dumped the money on the desk and counted it. Not bad, considering the weather and all. She looked out of the little, office window at the crowd. There was a large group gathered around the piano. She watched Bill as he sat tall behind the piano, his fingers flying delicately over the keys. She imagined him as a lover. He was tall, not bad looking, intelligent, and he had an air of elegance about him. He was a lush, but with the right help he'd "clean up" fine. With his talent, and her money, he could be something.

What? Are you crazy? She said to herself. *He's my meal ticket. Without him this place would be just another hole-in-the-wall bar. By yourself another vibrator, Jacqueline girl, and leave him right where he is!*

She thought of Dudley, her ex-husband. *I wonder who he's fucking, now. He's probably slept with every woman in Manhattan, by now. The bastard! Why did I have to fall for a guy that couldn't keep his pants zipped?* She grabbed up her drink. *To you, dear Dudley. I hope some irate husband comes home, finds you in bed with his wife, and blows your brains out!* Tears started to form in the corners of her eyes. She buried her face in her hand. *Oh, God! How much I miss you. You bastard! You fucking bastard!*

The sound of happy singing now streamed into her inter-sanctum. Bill was pounding out the tune to 'Zippity-du-da'. *How can they be so happy,* she wondered, *when I'm so fucking miserable?* She removed a plastic bag from her purse and dumped some of the white powder on the corner of her desk. She shaped it into a line with the side of a credit card. Rolling up a ten-dollar bill, she sucked the residue, first into her left nostril, then into her right. For a moment her eyes teared, again, this time not from pain, but from pleasure. *Fuck them all!* she said, smiling to herself. *Men are pigs!*

Rowena shook a cigarette from her pack, and put it to her lips. A hand appeared from her left with a lit lighter. She took the hand and guided it to her cigarette. The cover was beautifully carved, imported jade. She followed the arm back to a tall, handsome man in his early thirties.

"Is this seat taken?" he asked.

"No," she said, smiling up at him. "Help yourself."

He sat down and extended his hand, "Leonard Jones," he offered.

"Rowena Page" she countered, offering her own hand.

She was surprised that instead of shaking her hand, he held it firmly and kissed the back of her brocaded glove.

"A gentleman," she said, smiling broadly. "How rare these days."

"Not as rare as a beautiful flower, such as you, among all these weeds."

"Flattery will get you everywhere," she laughed.

"One can hope. May I freshen your drink?"

"Sure." She pushed her glass forward. "A Shirley Temple."

"You're kidding?"

"A girl has to keep a clear head."

"So be it. A Shirley Temple and a Scotch on the rocks," he shouted over the din. "Is it always this noisy?"

"Only on Saturday," she informed him. "By midnight the whole place goes wild."

He leaned closer to her face, "Is there some place we can go where it's not quite as noisy, and maybe a little less crowded?"

"That depends," she answered, coyly.

"Oh, Oh. This is where we talk about money, isn't it?"

"First," she said, smiling, "You have to answer one question."

"Hung like a bull," he offered.

She punched his arm, gently. "That's not the question. I need to know if you're a cop."

"If I were, would I have to tell you?"

"If I ask."

"Well, the answer is no. Do I look like a cop?"

"You are better looking than my usual . . ."

"John?"

"Yeah."

"Let's just say that I'm from out of town, and I don't want to be alone tonight. Fair enough?"

Rowena took a sip of her drink and grabbed her pocketbook. "Your place or mine?" she asked.

"Yours," he answered, simply.

"Should we call a cab, then?"

"No need. I have my own car."

"It's pretty bad out there. How good of a driver are you?"

"I'm from upstate, sweetheart. Up there, we don't even consider it snow, until we get two or three feet of it."

She smiled and took his arm.

Bill watch Rowena leave. This was the second time tonight. He was hoping she would call it a day. He just loved being near her, having her hanging around the piano. She had such a beautiful voice, and she knew all the old show tunes. What a ray of sunshine she was.

He didn't like seeing her leave with this latest John. He couldn't put his finger on it, but there was something about him that made the hair stand up on his neck. He wanted so much to run from the bar, grab her arm and tell her to stay. She could stay with him forever, he didn't mind.

He had fallen in love with her from the first day she wandered into the bar. What a beauty she was. He loved her soft brown eyes, her long flowing hair, her deep voice, her quick wit, and the way she walked. Hell, he loved everything about her, except her occupation. How he would love to pursue a career as a concert pianist. He would sweep her off her feet and take her away from all this.

What a fool! To think that they could be anything more than friends, was pure fantasy. What did he have to offer someone like her? She was so beautiful, so graceful, so elegant, so . . . so . . . everything. He was a piano player with a drinking problem, in a dead-end job, playing to a bunch of lounge lizards! What a catch! He played for drinks, tips and sustenance, the emphases being on the drinks. He couldn't even remember the last time he ate a square meal.

Jesse was returning from the men's room, when he heard a familiar voice. He turned to see his ex-lover Martin Fraser standing by the bar.

"You look well, Jesse," he said.

Jesse could hardly believe his eyes. Martin was thinner, paler, stooped. "I wish I could say as much for you, Martin. Have you been ill?"

"You might say that, Jesse," he feigned a smile. "I've got AIDS."

"Jesus!" Jesse felt his knees begin to buckle. "I need to sit," he said. They worked their way to an empty table in the corner that was stacked with glasses and empty bottles. They sat down and Jesse cleared a spot between them, reached across the table, and took Martin's hands. "I didn't know."

"How could you have? I haven't seen you in over six months."

"How?"

"After we split, I was less than monogamous. Jeremy was into multiple players. I thought I loved him. I fell in line to make him happy."

"Where is Jeremy, now?" Jesse asked. "He left me right after I got sick. I can't blame him."

"The guys a jerk, Martin! What are you doing for yourself?"

"I'm taking medication, I'm into therapy. I don't know how much longer I can work, though, and when I quit, my insurance will stop."

"Can't you get some kind of disability from the government?"

"I applied for it, but that kind of stuff takes years. I've only got months. With treatment I could maybe last for six to eight months. Without it, who knows?" Martin's tears were flowing freely, now. "I'm a dead man, Jesse, any way you look at it. It's only a matter of time. If only I had stayed with you, Jesse. I was a fool to leave you. I loved you. I still do."

"It was my fault, Martin. If only I hadn't been such a fucking jerk!"

Tears were flowing steadily at table three. Noleen did an about face. The mess could wait until later. She made her way back to the bar and caught John's attention.

"Need something?" he asked.

"Support and courage," she said, "and a good stiff belt of something couldn't hurt."

John poured her a double shot of Rum. Noleen looked at it.

"Ain't you got nothin' stronger?" she asked.

"There is nothing stronger, Noleen. That's 150 proof."

She drank it slowly. "I'm takin' you up on your offer, John. I want ya ta take me to rehab, first thing Monday morning. You got ta promise me."

"You can count on me, Noleen."

She reached into her pocked and handed him some keys. "Go to my apartment, after, and get me some clothes, and my daughter's picture. They can burn the rest for all I care, but ya got ta help me, John. There ain't no way I can do this thing alone."

"You go home with me tonight. I'll see that you're in rehab when the doors open on Monday." He handed her a bag. "Here," he said, "put these in your pocket."

"What are they?"

"Samplers. I get them from the suppliers. It will get you through the night."

She slipped them into her apron. "Thanks, John, I'll never forget this."

"You better not." He blew her a kiss. "Now, go! I'm busy."

Rowena was having second thoughts about Mr. Jones's driving abilities. Sure they had reached her apartment in something like record time, considering the weather, but on several occasions he had frightened her nearly out of her wits. She opened the door and shook the snow from her coat. She stepped inside and hung it on the coat tree. Leonard took off his coat and threw it over a chair, the snow melting into the carpet.

What an asshole, she thought. *At least, he could have hung it up with mine.* Would you like a drink," she asked.

"You got any scotch?"

She walked over to a small bar in the back of the living room, and picked up a bottle. "Looks like there's just enough for a couple of drinks. Do you want some on the rocks?"

"No," he said, rather sharply, "I haven't got the time. Just bring me the bottle. Is the bedroom this way?" he asked, starting down the short hallway.

"Yes."

He downed the Scotch and set the bottle on an end table. "Well let's get at it then, shall we?" He waved her on, and as she passed, he followed. He removed his shirt and tie, and throwing them onto the bed, he began to remove his pants.

"Do you want me to turn the bed down?" she asked.

"That won't be necessary," he informed her, throwing his pants on top of his shirt and tie. "We won't be using it."

She wondered what he meant. She was folding her dress when he came up behind her. He grabbed her bra and ripped it from her. He groped her breasts, as he forced her up against the dresser. She turned to protest, and he struck her hard on the left side of her face with a closed fist. She fell to the floor, stunned. He was on top of her, ripping away her panties and brutally penetrating her, anally. She tried to scream, but he grabbed her by the hair, and forced her face into the carpet. Her screams merely became muffled cries. She found herself struggling for breath. She reached back to claw at him with her long nails. He hit her again. As he sodomized her, she kept drifting in and out of consciousness.

One of her eyes had swollen shut, and when he had finished, she watched him through her good eye, as he dressed. He stood over her, opened his wallet, and threw a ten-dollar bill onto the floor.

"I'm leaving you a ten because I'm feeling generous," he said. "I've had better for less. Your too old, bitch. Your tits are too soft, and your ass is as big as a blimp. You should have paid me to fuck you. I'll be coming through town in three more months. Tighten your ass and tits up, and I might give you a twenty next time."

She lay on the floor until she heard the apartment door close, cursing him under her breath. Slowly she pulled herself onto the bed. She looked into the mirror. The side of her face was badly bruised, and her eye was black and blue and swollen shut. She could see finger marks on her left breast and scratch marks on her arms and shoulders. She looked down at the ten on the floor, and spat at it. It wasn't the first time she'd been beaten, raped or even sodomized. This incident only tended to bring back memories of Syracuse and her stepfather.

Looking carefully at her reflection in the mirror, she realized that one thing Leonard had said was true; she was getting older. She pulled herself up from the bed, went to her pocketbook, and retrieved a pearl-handled switchblade. She kept it there for protection. A lot of good it did her this night. She rested it on her left wrist and thought how easy it would be just to drag it across. She thought about it for a very long time.

She thought of Bill, and how she had fallen in love with him from the first day she had met him. How her heart ached for him. How badly she wanted to care for him, and help him with his drinking. But she was a whore. She wasn't good enough for him and she knew it. All they could ever be was friends; she knew that, too. There was no sense trying to kid herself.

She looked at her reflection in the mirror. "You're a loser, Row! That's all you've ever been! That's all you ever will be!" Suddenly she pulled herself to her feet. She thrust her face toward the mirror. "No!" she screamed. "I won't except that! I can find a job, and honest job, even if I have to clean toilets or sling hash. I'll make myself clean, and then I'll go after Bill with a vengeance. "Thank you, Leonard Jones, or who ever you are," she said, wiping a tear from her good eye, "I owe you a lot for making me realize what a loser I've been," she slammed the point of the switchblade into the top of the dresser, "but if I ever see you again, I swear I'll kill you!"

She dragged herself to the bathroom and showered. She used plenty of soap, and scrubbed her whole body, vigorously. She wanted to scrub away all that she had been; all that she had become. She thought of it as a baptismal, the rebirth of the new Rowena, and the death of the old. She showered for over an hour.

By 1:00 am the crowd had thinned considerably. A lot of people had to go to church in the morning. Beside the snow hadn't let up, and the lounge lizards had to seriously think about how they were going to get home. Noleen had had a busy night, but now that things were slow she was beginning to wish that she had something stronger than the little bottles of booze John had given her. The bald guy, from the back booth was watching her as she cleaned up the tables. She pretended not to see him as he came toward her.

"You don't look so well," he said.

"I got a little cold," she lied. "It'll go away."

"I think you got something worse than a cold. I think you need something."

"So," she said, starting to move away, "what's it ta you."

"Maybe I can help." He reached into his pocket and pulled out container of pills. "Morphine," he explained. "This is good stuff. A few of these and you'll be right back on top again."

"What makes you think I need them?"

"I've been watching you. Believe me, it's obvious."

"Where'd ya get those?" she asked.

"There mine. Prescription drugs. The best kind."

"How much you want?"

"I don't want money, if that's what you mean."

"Then what?"

"Sex."

Noleen turned away from him. "I don't do that shit! How desperate do ya think I is?"

"I don't know. You tell me. How about a blow job, then?"

"In your wildest dreams!"

"A hand job?"

"Is that all you wants, a hand job?" She could see he was getting aroused.

He reached over and touched her breast. "I'd like to spend a little time with these, too."

She pulled his hand away. "OK. But not in the middle of the lounge."

"Where can we go?"

Noleen looked over at the bar. Carl was enjoying a drink and talking to Jacqueline. "Meet me in the storeroom in back of the kitchen in five minutes. Don't let nobody see you. I'll finish clearing the tables, and meet you there."

Jacqueline was being pleasant. Carl figured that she must be high on something.

"The weather is really shit, out there, Carl," she was saying. "It's been coming down all night. I'm not sure I even want to go out in this."

"There is a sofa in the office. Why don't you sleep there?"

"I love this place, but I don't want to live here. There are a few hotels within walking distance. I thought I'd stay at one of them. What are you going to do?"

"I don't know. I haven't decided, yet."

"We could split the cost," she offered.

Carl smiled. He was never sure if she was serious or not. Jacqueline was still a pretty woman at forty-two. She must have been a real knockout when she was young. She wore too much makeup these days, and her clothes fit a little tighter, but, all and all she was still a fine figure of a woman. The thought of bedding down with her had its appeal. Especially since his own marriage wasn't doing so very well.

Oh, Mariann and he were still cordial toward one another, but the strong love they once shared was no longer there. Sex seemed more like some kind of drill, or duty, not the passionate experience they used to enjoy. Everything changed when the second baby died. He tried to explain to her that miscarriages happen a lot of times, and she might have gone along with that if it had not happened twice. The doctor explained that there was nothing wrong with her, that it was just one of those things. She didn't want to hear what the odds were of it happening again. As far as she was concerned, any odds were too high. She just didn't want to take the chance, again.

Now, when they kissed, their lips would barely touch. When he tried to touch her, she would shrink away. The last time they made love was nearly eight months ago. At that time he felt like he had raped her. He found more enjoyment making love to his hand. At least then, he didn't have to deal with rejection.

Now, an older, experienced, certainly not unattractive woman was offering to share her bed with him. There would be no commitment, just good healthy sex. All he would have to do is call Mariann, and tell her that he was staying in town tonight. This was the opportunity of a lifetime. The weather was bad. Few cabs were running. Why should he try to fight the weather to get home when there were good hotels only blocks away? Snuggling up with a nice warm body, on a cold winter's night, why not? Who would be the wiser?

Noleen found Harold in the back of the storage room. One part of her was hoping that he wouldn't be there, while the addict in her was glad he was. She turned on the light, pulled the door closed, and pushed a mop bucket against it. At least the sound of the bucket would give them a warning if someone came. She didn't want to be caught in the back of this storage room with a white man.

"Let me see those pill again," she said. He handed them to her and she shook them out of the bottle. "There must be almost thirty."

"Yeah, it's a full bottle. I just got them today."

"What are they for?" she asked.

"I've got this . . . a . . . condition.

"It must be one hell of a condition if you is takin' pills that strong."

"Hey! I'd rather not talk about it. Are we going to do this thing or not."

Noleen knew when to keep her mouth shut. "What do you want to do first?" she asked.

"I want to touch your bosom."

Noleen started to unbutton the top of her dress. "Ya can call them tits. I ain't gonna faint away like some, fuckin', prima donna."

She was wearing a thin, white bra, and her dark nipples showed through the material. She pulled the sleeves over her shoulders and let the top of the dress fall about her waist. Harold watched with fervid anticipation, as Noleen reached around and unfastened her bra. Her breasts were small, but firm, standing straight and proud as if gravity no longer existed. While Noleen freed the straps from her arms, Harold slid his hands beneath them, slowly, as if a sudden movement might frighten them away.

"Magnificent!" he said, loudly.

"Will you be quiet? I ain't anxious to share this Kodak moment with everyone."

"May I kiss them?" he asked.

She grabbed the front of his pants, pulling him toward her. She started working on his zipper. "No," she said, "get your damn pecker out here so I can get this over with. If I don't get my ass back out there pretty soon, they're gonna start wonderin' what's happened to me."

First Harold had trouble getting his penis out of his bikini briefs, and then it got caught sideways and refused to come out through his zipper. "Perhaps if I take my pants off," he said.

"We ain't got no time," Noleen insisted. She reached through his zipper, grabbed the very end of his penis and yanked it out.

"Ouch! Jesus! Careful!" Harold shouted.

"Be quiet," Noleen cautioned. "Is this as big as it gets?"

"It lost its enthusiasm when you grabbed a hold of it with those long fingernails!"

"Well, make it hard again, so we can get on with it," Noleen insisted.

"I can't just will it hard, sweetheart, it needs encouragement."

Noleen pushed up on her breasts. "Do this help?" She toyed with her nipples. "How about this?"

"No, it doesn't," Harold said. "I just seem to have lost the moment."

"What?" Noleen couldn't believe her ears. "That's a woman's line! Men get it hard lookin' at a lady's lingerie ad, or a Betty Boop cartoon! If ya think you're gonna talk me into getting' down and suckin' on it, you crazy. It's plan 'A', sucker, or nothin'!"

"I just can't do it this way."

"Ain't you the one that kept lookin' at my ass and tellin' me what nice eyes I had? Ain't you the one that kept callin' me 'Honey', an 'Sweetheart', and 'you pretty little thing'? Didn't you tell your friends that I was a sweet piece of ass?"

"You heard that?"

"Didn't everyone? I need those pills! Get that thing up, and let's get it over with."

"I'm sorry. I just can't any more. Call it a touch of conscience," he said. "My wife died two years ago." Harold wiped the tears from his eyes. "If I did this thing I would be shaming myself, and disgracing her memory."

Noleen ran her hands through her long, brown hair. Beads of perspiration were running down her face, now, and her hands were shaking.

"I'm sorry," Harold said. "Please forgive me!" He took her hand and pressed the bottle of pills into it.

"Why?" she asked.

"Because I was such an asshole. I tried to take advantage of someone who was hurting. Please try to forgive me. I don't think I'm going to forget this lesson for a while, at least not until I heal."

Noleen kissed him on the cheek, slid the mop pail out of the way, opened the door, and left.

She stopped by the sink, popped two of the pills, and rinsed them down with a glass of water.

Harold painfully tucked his pride into his pants, and carefully zipped up his fly. *Next time I think of trying something like this,* he said to himself, *I'll get my head examined.*

Jacqueline bumped into Harold as she jumped up from the bar. "What about you, asshole!" she said. She opened up her coat. "Would you pass up a good piece of ass, like this?" She wrapped the coat back around her and walked quickly toward the door. "Oh, never mind!" she shouted over her shoulder. "All men are pigs!"

Harold went back to the booth and picked up his coat. Jesse was gone, and Simon was sitting alone. "I'm going home, Simon," he said, as he began to button up his coat. "By the way, your little soiree, I'll definitely be coming solo. I'm swearing off women for good. They're all fucking crazy!" He pulled up his collar and walked toward the door.

As he reached the entrance to the foyer, Noleen ran up to him.

"Here," she said, and pressed the bottle of bills in his hand.

"What's this for?"

"I ain't gonna need them all," she informed him. "First chance, I'm putting myself in rehab.

"Good for you, Honey." He put his arm around her and kissed her on the cheek. "I wish you luck."

"I kept a few just to get me through. I figure you must need them, or you wouldn't have them. Are you gonna tell me what there for?"

"I've got cancer," he said. "Sometimes it gets a little rough."

She watched as he made his way to the door, forcing it open against the wind and snow.

"Oh sweet Jesus," she said. "That poor man!"

Jesse appeared at the booth, just as Harold was leaving. He was holding hands with another young man. "Harry's leaving?" he asked.

"He mumbled something about swearing off women," Simon informed him. "I think he's gone off the deep end."

"I wanted him to meet Martin."

"Hi Martin," Simon offered his hand. "Any friend of Jesse's is a friend of mine."

"He's not my friend, Simon, he's my lover."

"Oh."

"You don't look surprised."

"Should I be?"

"You've known?"

"How long have we known each other, Jesse?"

"Five and a half, six years?"

"About that long."

Jesse shook his head in disbelief. "But you never said anything."

Simon grabbed his coat off the back of the seat and worked his way out of the booth. "What was I going to say, Jesse. 'Hey! You're gay!' It just didn't seem that important to me."

Martin and Jesse sat down at the booth, across from each other. "Do you think Harry knows?" Jesse asked.

"No." Simon put on his heavy coat, and leaned on the counter. "Harry's not as shallow as he appears. He has a lot of respect for you."

"What makes you think that?"

"He wouldn't argue with anyone he didn't respect, or consider his equal. What would be the use? Whether he could handle knowing that you're gay, is another thing. Harry has some deep-seated feelings about things like that. Then again, who knows? Harry could surprise all of us. He has that quality." Simon fastened his coat and waved. "See you, Jesse. Nice to have met you, Martin. Take care of that cold; you look like shit."

Simon decided to walk the six blocks to his apartment. He wished that he had thought to wear his boots,

"Bill looked at his watch. It was nearly closing time. John had already called for last rounds. He had watched all night for Rowena to return. When she didn't, he began to worry a little. It had been a good crowd. He removed the bills from the jar and placed them in his billfold. He didn't bother to count them. What did it matter? He wasn't going to get rich. He poured the coins into his hand and put them into his right pocket. They felt heavy there, so he put some of them in the left pocket. There was a large, ceramic piggy bank at his apartment for the change. He had no idea what he would do with it when it was full.

There were two young men seated in one of the booths. One of them had been sitting with two other business types, earlier. The other young man wore a warm-up jacket, and Bill had seen him wander in about an hour or so ago. He was thin and pale, and Bill had notice a couple of lesions on his neck. He looked like the poster boy for AIDS. They looked like a couple of lovers trying to catch up on lost time. He felt a kind of kindred spirit. Perhaps time was running out for them, like it was running out for him. How long could he go on pickling his brain, night after night?

He had been playing a medley of tunes from "South Pacific", but no one was listening. Loud conversation was emitting from the hanger-oners. He pounded the keys with revulsion. Why don't they go home? But then what did it matter? His apartment, or here, things do not get any better. Here he was becoming angry with the very people who made his way of life possible? How could he hate the very people who made it possible for him to maintain an almost perpetual state of inebriation? What would he do if he didn't have this job? Sober up, and become a concert pianist? Fat chance of that!

Bill took a sip of his beer. It was warm, but he was used to drinking warm beer. At least, there were no ice cubes to water it down. Once in a while he would drink a shot or two, but Carl would get upset if he got really blitzed. Beer allowed Bill to maintain a certain level of intoxication, somewhere between mellow and puke-faced drunk. He could tell by his psychological pain when he wasn't drunk enough, and by the buzzing in his head when he was too drunk. He strove to keep a middle road.

His nightly routine was always the same. He would walk the four blocks to his apartment, shower and change into his bedclothes, sit down with a bottle of the best whiskey he could afford at the time, drink until he got blotto, then pass out . . . sometimes on the bed . . . until sometime in the afternoon. The degree of his hangover was usually in direct proportion to the quality and quantity of the poison he had quaffed the night before.

The next day he would make his way to the local liquor store, spending much time perusing the shelves. Bill was not a grab-n-run shopper. He selected his booze as carefully as a runner might select his footwear. There were many things to take into consideration. Pedigree, of course, was important. Then there were things like, proof, price, and color. Bill didn't like watery looking spirits. He loved the dark amber look of fine whiskey. He would leave for others the essence of rotten potatoes, and the bitter juniper berries, plucked from evergreens. Grain was his passion.

If nothing else, Bill was dependable. Perhaps the word "predictable" would be more appropriate. He had never taken a vacation. There were no trips to Niagara Falls, The Grand Canyon, or even the Bronx Zoo. Bill was not the tourist type. From what would he take a vacation, playing the piano and drinking? He might as well give up breathing.

The only ray of sunshine in his life was Rowena. Rowena Page wandered into his life about three years ago. She had come from Long Island, somewhere near North Haven and Sag Harbor, where she was perhaps a little too well known. Bill noticed her the first day, and so did a lot of other people. Rowena and Bill struck up a relationship almost immediately, and Bill was happy when she decided to make the Rococo her sort of home base. They were friends, although Bill knew almost nothing about her. He knew that she had come, originally, from some little farm community upstate, somewhere near Syracuse. She had gone to college, there, for a couple years, but dropped out of college when her father died, and moved back home. Her mother remarried, and Rowena disliked her stepfather very much. She never talked about it, but Bill got the idea that he had done something bad to her. She moved to the city when she was twenty-one, and had lived in the area ever since. This was all Bill was able to get from her in three years.

The crowd was breaking up, and John began cleaning up. Carl took the money from the till, and the small safe, and put it up in the big safe in the office. He saw the white residue on the corner of the desk, and immediately understood why Jacqueline had acted the way she did. She got that way when she was stoned. Either that, or she would become a complete bitch, in which case few would have noticed.

It was a well-known fact that Jacqueline had little use for men, unless of course they served some useful purpose. Judges, politicians, and people of influence were high on her list. Despite this fact, she hated to be alone. This is why she extended the invitation to Carl to spend the night at the hotel. She couldn't bear the thought of spending the night in a strange hotel room, alone. At least at home she would be with her two dogs and her live-in housekeeper, Mary. Mary had been the fifth in eight months, indicating that perhaps her low opinion of men extended also to domestic help.

Carl looked out the barred window in the back of the office. Everything looked white outside. There was snow piled six inches high on the sill, and Jack Frost had preformed his dazzling artwork on the panes. He scraped a small hole in the frost with a letter opener. Despite the efforts of the City to keep the streets clear, he could see that there were still three or four inches of accumulated snow. He began to wonder how he was going to get home, or if indeed he was. Jacqueline had booked a room at the Sheraton Hotel, a few blocks away. He began to wonder if he would be so lucky. There was a studio couch in the office. It didn't look very comfortable, but it might have to do.

The bellboy closed the curtains and set the key on the nightstand. "Will there be anything else, Ma'am," he asked.

Jacqueline looked him over as she reached into her pocketbook for a tip. He was pimply-faced young, maybe even too young for her. But, what the hell, any port in a storm. She smiled, "What are you doing after work, Honey?"

He smiled back. "Going home to my wife and son, Ma'am," he replied.

She handed him the tip. *I wonder why I have to tip the little bastard when I don't have any luggage?* she thought to herself. "Well, good luck. The weather is really bad out there, you know."

"Yes, Maam, I know." He was still smiling. *It would have to be all the way up to your wrinkled, old pussy, before I'd sleep with you, bitch,* he said to himself. He looked at the two-dollar tip, and amended his thought to . . . *you old cheap bitch.*

Jacqueline laid her coat upon the bed and looked around the empty room. A sudden chill came over her. *Alone, in a strange hotel, what's wrong with this picture?* she thought. She gathered up her purse and headed for the elevator. *There's got to be a stiff dick in this hotel, somewhere,* she thought to herself. *There's no way that I'm sleeping alone.*

When she exited the elevator, she did a quick survey. There was a tall man, about forty, in a business suit crossing the lobby. She had to do a quickstep to catch him. "Excuse me, sir," she said, smiling up at him, "could you please direct me to the lounge."

"Of course," he said, looking her over. "I was going there, myself. If you would like to join me, I believe it is this way."

"Why thank you, sir," she said, her voice dripping with sweetness, "I would be honored." She offered her hand and he guided her toward the lounge. "You're quite tall," she commented.

"Six foot six," he replied.

"Oh, my," she said, smiling back at him, "that is tall." A thought raced through her head. *Tall men, big dicks? I wonder if it's true? I'll find out tonight if I have to drag him up to the room and rape him.* Out of the corner of her eye, she noticed him admiring her cleavage. She pressed her breast against his arm. *I think he'll come willingly.*

Paul Decker and David Wheat decided to share a cab, since they were both going in the same direction. When it pulled up front, they ran from the door and jumped into the back seat.

"I don't remember it ever being this bad," David said. "How about you?"

"Never this bad," Paul confessed. "Although, I do remember a couple of times when the city almost shut down completely."

"Hey Cabby," David yelled, "you having any trouble getting around?"

"Nah," the Cabby said, confidently, "no problem."

"How's the bridge?"

"Still open, as far as I know."

"I live just off of Henry."

"Yeah, That ain't no problem."

"My pal, here, lives the other side of Prospect Park."

"Now, Prospect Park I don't know about. That could be a problem."

David turned to Paul, "You could stay with me. I've got one of those pullout couches. It's not the most comfortable bed in the world, but it's got to be better than a slab in the morgue."

Paul smiled. "Good point."

Noleen sat down at the bar as John put the last of the night's receipts in the safe. "Still going to your place?" she asked.

"If you're game." He looked at her face. "You're looking much better," he said. "What's up?"

She reached into her pocket and produced a small handful of pills. "I've took a few of these."

John grabbed her hand and turned it to the light. "Aciphex? Do you have heartburn?"

"No. These is Morphine. This old guy gave em to me, who's dyin' of cancer."

"No, Hun. These are Aciphex. My dad takes it for his hiatus hernia. Look, it says Aciphex right on the pill."

Noleen threw the pills on the floor. "That damn, lyin', old fuck!" She started to laugh. "You won't believe what I almost did for these things, but don't you ask."

Carl watched as John and Noleen left together, hand in hand. "I wonder what's going on there?" he asked himself. Bill left shortly after, looking no more sober than usual. Carl shut off the lights in the kitchen first, and then he turned on the nightlights that illuminated the bar. Finally, he cut the main switch that turned off the rest of the lights in the bar and the dining room. He set the lock on the front door, wrapped his scarf around his neck, and plunged out into the cold night air. There was a large station wagon parked at the curb. The window rolled down partway on the passenger's side.

"Mariann?"

"Are you going to get in, or are you going to stand out there all night?"

Carl opened the door. "Are you crazy, coming out in this shit?"

"What? I'm going to let you take a cab home? I don't think so. This big cow can go places that Jeeps fear to tread. I've driven in snow. Remember? I grew up in Utica. Now, get in, you're letting all the heat out."

Carl got in and closed the door. Mariann rolled down the window so she could better see to pull out. There was little traffic at this time of night, and they had the roads pretty much to themselves.

"What prompted you to drive this moose into the city? Carl asked.

"I was going nuts, wondering if and when you were going to get home. The worse it got, the more I worried. I realized that I would be lost if anything happened to you. I said, to hell with it! If something is going to happen to you, it's going to happen while I'm with you. I guess I just finally realized just how much I love you, how much you mean to me, and how much I need you. I hope you can forgive me for being such a bitch, but from now on, things are going to be different."

"Mariann I . . ."

"Shut up, Carl! I'm spilling my guts! Don't interrupt me while I'm spilling my guts; not while I'm on a roll. I want to try to have a baby again. And if it doesn't work, I want to keep trying until it does. Please, Carl. Please find it in your heart to forgive me."

Carl snuggled close to his wife, put his arm around her, and kissed her softly on her forehead. He looked out the windshield as the steady onslaught of snowflakes continuously challenged the wipers. "God," he said, "I do love this weather.

Bill pulled up his collar against the sting of the blowing snow, as he walked the four blocks to his apartment. The cold air had a sobering effect; and he wasn't sure he liked it. He climbed the stairs to the second floor and let himself in. He made his way to the living room and sat down in his favorite recliner. Retrieving the remote, he found an old Greta Garbo movie. He didn't really care what he watched; the TV was on mostly for the noise and to supply the illusion that he wasn't really alone. Being alone at 3 a.m. can be frightening.

The morning's acquisition sat on the small end table beside him. The seal had already been broken and a double shot was already missing; his bracer before work. He poured a shot into a dirty water glass, swished it around and drank it. He told himself that this was to clean the glass. After all, what is better than alcohol to get rid of germs? He set the glass back down and filled it half way.

"Now, is this glass half empty", he asked himself, "or half full?" He downed the contents of the glass without stopping. "Empty, I'd say." He picked up the bottle and looked at the label. "This is good sipping whiskey, Billy boy, not guzzling whiskey. If you're going to guzzle, you should have picked up some Scotch." He filled the glass half way, again. This time he held the glass between his thumb and first finger and sipped it daintily. "Ah!" he said. "Much better."

He stood up suddenly, remembering the change in his pockets. He walked to the kitchen and crammed the change into a large piggy bank on the counter. He had to shake the bank to get it all in.

"Full," he said to himself, "now what?" He tried to lift the bank, but it was too heavy. He opened a drawer and removed a small hammer. He started to make sounds like a pig squealing. "Shut up Piggy!" he said. "You'll wake up the other tenants."

He swung the hammer hard, smashing the bank. The change strew across the kitchen counter, and onto the floor. He bent to retrieve the coins, but in his inebriated state he lost his balance, and fell back against the cabinet doors. He sat on the floor, and scooping the money up with both hands, began to pour it all over himself.

"I killed the pig, and I'm rich as a fig. I killed the pig with a hammer big," he sang to the tune of *How Dry I Am*. "I might have a hit song, here," he said to himself. "Let's see. The pig is dead, and I'm in the bread. I hit him in the head with a hunk of lead. No. That's not right. I hit him with a hammer."

He pulled himself to his feet, picked up the hammer and looked at it. "That's steel, not lead." He studied the hammer momentarily. "Tomorrow, I'll go find a hammer that's made out of lead. I'm sure as hell not going to change my wonderful lyrics because of a slight oversight. Then, I guess, I'll have to buy a new pig, too. I still don't know what I'm going to do with all this money." He kicked at it with his foot. "I guess I'll spend most of it on a hammer and a new pig."

He set the hammer on the counter, and retreated to the living room. He plopped into his chair and grabbed the glass from the end table. He downed it. He poured another glass, while scolding himself for not sipping.

He picked up the half-empty bottle. "You had better start sipping, Billy boy, or you'll be into your reserve stash before you know it."

Bill always felt that a good "drinker" should always have a stash. He would buy extra bottles and hide them all over the apartment: under chairs, behind shoes in the closet, under beds, or in the bookcase. He would hide them when he was more or less sober, and when he was really drunk, it became a game that resembled an Easter egg hunt. The problem was that things usually got thrown or destroyed when he couldn't remember where he had hidden them, and his frustration increased.

This always happen at the wee hours of the morning. The other tenants would complain about the noise, and Jacqueline Everhart who, of course, was his landlord as well as his boss, would chastise him like a wayward schoolboy. Somehow, she would always manage to smooth it over with the other tenants.

Other than a job and a paycheck, Bill had little use for Jacqueline. She was a self-centered, self-righteous, bitch, who was nearly always high on something. Sure, he was an alcoholic, but she was no more than a junky. She always looked down her self-righteous nose at him, but she had no right to.

Bill never got into any of that stuff. "One addiction at a time," he would always say, if someone offered him a pill, some powder, or some funny stuff to smoke. He was smart enough to realize that he had enough problems with his drinking; he didn't need any more problems.

He thought about Rowena. If he could straighten himself up, he would go after her with a vengeance. He would get a good job and woo her away from her lifestyle. *Fat chance of that happening,* he thought, *maybe if pigs could fly.* He thought about the piggy bank on the kitchen floor. "There's one pig that will never get airborne," he chuckled to himself. "I'll drink to that." He refilled his empty glass.

Bill was a victim of routine. He usually passed out between four-thirty and five a.m. He would be up by one p.m., take a long shower, shave, and dress. Then he was off to the liquor store. When he returned, he would try to eat something. At this, he wasn't always too successful. Keeping things down was always a problem. Most of the time a piece of toast, or a couple of stale crackers where the most he could hope to retain. He would be at work by ten minutes to six. He was only required to work until two a.m., but on Saturday, the busiest night, he was lucky to get out before three.

He wondered what Bess would think of his new life style. "Not much," he ventured, out loud. Bess was always the sensible one. She was even more wrapped up in Bill's dream than Bill was. She saw to it that there was always money for books and tuitions, even if it meant some major tightening of their belts, or doing without. They took the subway whenever possible, and almost never ate out. Bill would have to be at death's door, before Bess would let him miss a day of school. Bess was a nurse, and took the nightshift at the hospital, because it paid more.

She was coming home from work when she got hit. She was just crossing the street to the subway when a car ran the stoplight and ran her over. The driver never stopped, but someone got his license number. He turned out to be some businessman, coming home from a business dinner. She worked in the Trauma ward of the hospital, and ironically, it was her co-workers who fought desperately to save her life. She lived for two days in a coma. Bill never got to say goodbye, or tell her how much he loved her. He missed her.

All of those painful memories were now streaming through his head. He had started drinking to forget, and even that wasn't working. He poured another glass while the tears flowed steadily down his cheeks. The bottle was getting dangerously low, and he wondered if he should start looking for one of his back-ups. He looked at his watch. It was four-fifteen, still early. He pulled himself from the chair, and staggered toward his bedroom. *At least, if I pass out, I'll be in the right place,* he thought.

He tripped over a pair of shoes, as he entered the room, and fell against the bed. He lowered himself to the floor while he swept his arm beneath the bed feeling for a bottle. He came away with a handful of dust-bunnies. He got down on his hands and knees and searched farther under the bed. His persistence paid off; he brought out a bottle of cheap whiskey.

"God!" he said, squinting at the label. "I'm going to be sick, tomorrow."

Bill somehow made his way back to his chair. He drained the last of the good whiskey into his glass, and topped it off with some of the cheap stuff. By now, he couldn't tell the difference. The TV station went off the air, and Bill saluted as they played the National Anthem. After that he sat a watched white screen and listened to the sound of static. It worked for him. He hadn't been watching the movie, anyway. Noise is noise. Noise is good. Besides, he had dropped the remote, and was in no condition to get up and shut the TV off. He laid back his head and closed his eyes. Still, his tolerance for alcohol would not let him pass out.

Memories were streaming through his head again, memories of Bess. Somehow, he managed to pull himself up from his chair. He shut the TV off by pushing every button, nearly knocking it over in the process. Supporting himself with various pieces of furniture, he made his was to his stereo, and turned it on. Concert music suddenly filled the room. He made his way back to the chair and plopped down hard. The sounds and the whiskey swirled through his brain like a giant whirlpool. This was one of his favorite pieces. He tried to listen for the piano, but he couldn't control his concentration.

His mind kept wandering back to thoughts of Bess. He remembered what happened to the guy that took her life. He plea-bargained his way down to manslaughter, and got fifteen years. The thought of that asshole getting fifteen years for the lifetime of misery he had caused only made the pain more unbearable. "What ever happened to 'an eye for an eye and a tooth for a tooth'," he shouted out loud. He remembered the other tenants, and put his hand over his mouth.

He put his head in his hands and wept. The music changed tempo, and became more light and lively. Bill was no longer listening. His mind was racing from good times to bad times, from Bess to Rowena, and slowly settled upon the putrid, useless mess his life had become. He picked up the bottle and threw it against the wall.

When Jacqueline arrived at her office on Monday, she was inundated with calls. Bill was acting up again, waking people up in the middle of the night. She caught a cab and went to the apartment complex. She might have to evict Bill this time. As much as she admired him as a pianist, he was becoming a liability. She could easily find somebody to rent Bill's apartment. He would have to settle for an apartment somewhere where the tenants would accept his shenanigans.

She knocked at Bill's door, but there was no answer. She waited a few minutes, and knocked again. There was still no answer. She looked at her watch. It was eleven a.m. He was most likely still passed out. She opened the door with her own key. Crossing the kitchen to the bedroom, she found it empty. When she entered the living room, Bill was still sitting upright in the chair. There was blood everywhere, and the 32 caliber pistol was still clenched in his hand.

"My God," she screamed, "the shag carpet!"

The coroner released Bill's body on Wednesday and he was buried the next Saturday, next to his wife. Jacqueline Everhart was detained and questioned by the police after she was found on her hands and knees, crawling about the kitchen floor, picking up change. She claimed that Bill owed her money, and she knew that he would want her to have it. The police confiscated it as evidence, and eventually turned it over to Bill's sister, who had flown in from Chicago. She was his only living relative, at least, the only one at the funeral.

There were twenty-three people at the funeral, mostly patrons, and coworkers. John, Noleen, Carl, and Jacqueline were there. Rowena

Page came by cab. She wore dark glasses. She looked like she was taking it really hard. Jesse Werner came with his friend Martin Fraser. They held hands. Simon Rosenburg came with his wife Millie, and Harold Freed came alone. The rest were just a few of the regulars.

The weather was nice for a change: forty and sunny. The service was short and sweet. After a short eulogy, most everyone left, except Rowena. She stayed long enough to say a few words, and place something on the coffin. It looked like a letter.

It's been five years, now, since Bill died. Jacqueline sold the Rococo that summer. The new owners hired a piano player who specializes in modern jazz. They found him in a place on the island, called "The Pit", which might give you an idea of what I think of his playing. Needless to say, most of the old crowd is gone: moved uptown to a cozy, little nook, called "The Jubilee". The new crowd would never tolerate a show tune.

Carl is still here; he stayed on to manage the place. He received a letter from John and Noleen about a year and a half ago. Noleen opened a beauty salon someplace near LA, and from what John said in his letter, she had quite a following. She managed to clean herself up, and with the help of John, was staying that way. Noleen's daughter, Darian, was living with them, and John said that she was doing well in school. He sent pictures of Darian's birthday party. She had just turned seven. John was tending bar in some nightclub near Hollywood. He still hadn't given up on his hopes for a movie career. He had played a bad guy in one action film, and a bar tender in a beer commercial.

With a private eye, they traced Noleen's ex to some dump heap in Harlem. Bribed with enough pieces of silver to keep him in crack and whiskey for the next two years, he sighed off on both his wife and his daughter. Noleen and John had already made their wedding plans, and Carl informed me that the whole gang was invited. Adoption papers had also been filed.

Rumor has it that Rowena moved back upstate right after Bill died. It could be, because no one has seen her around, since. Maybe she decided to go back and face her demons. Perhaps she went back to finish college. I'd like to think maybe she did both.

David Wheat got transferred to the west coast. We got postcards, for a while, from Japan and Hawaii, simply addressed to the Rococo

Lounge. The last one was from San Diego. He said he was getting married. Go figure!

Paul Decker wrote a best-selling novel. This time he used his real name. It's about a real estate man who has affairs with the wives of his clients. You know what they say: write what you know. He's got a few lawsuits pending against him, even though he claims that the whole story is pure fiction. A jealous husband kills the hero, at the end. I sure hope Paul doesn't befall a similar fate. I wish him luck.

Martin Fraser succumbed to AIDS about three years ago. Jesse quit his job and began raising money to help those suffering from the disease. With the help of a couple of doctors and a motivated lawyer, he managed to put together a free clinic for those who had fallen through the cracks. It's called the Fraser Clinic, and with the help of Jesse's fundraising, it's been going strong for the last year and a half.

Simon Rosenburg suffered a heart attack two years ago, and died a month later. His wife followed him six months later. Some say she died of a broken heart. I know that they were very close, so it's possible.

Harold Freed contracted lung cancer. He's lost weight, and he looks very pale. It doesn't look good. I hate to say it, but chances are he won't be around next year.

Remember that "john" that raped Rowena? I read in the paper last year that a guy named Leonard Jones killed a prostitute in Queens. He killed her with her own knife while she was trying to defend herself. He's in Attica, serving a life sentence. You know what they say, "What goes around, comes around." Maybe he'll find himself a nice husky roommate who will show him what true love is all about.

Most of the old gang is here tonight; what's left of us. We meet at the Rococo on the Saturday following the anniversary of Bill's death and pay homage to the best piano man we ever met. The new regulars hate to see us come, but somehow, they manage to tolerate us. Paul Decker just asked the piano player to play "The Piano Man". His rendition leaves something to be desired, and I'm sure Paul didn't ask him to sing it. That's OK. I'm sure we can drown him out.

"I'd like to propose a toast. To Bill, I hope that wherever he is he has finally found peace."

"Who am I?" you ask. I'm nobody. You might say that I'm just a *barfly on the wall.*"

THE MATTRESS SALESMAN

"So, what are you saying, Simon, you're ashamed of your father?"

"I'm not ashamed of my father, just what he does."

"He sells mattresses. What is wrong with that?" She made that gesture with her hands that she always did when she knew there was no real answer. "He works hard. He puts food on the table. Because of him, you want for nothing. This is not a man to be proud of?"

"If he were an astronaut, or a college football coach, I would be prouder."

"Your father is good at what he does."

"I would rather he be a poor astronaut than a great mattress salesman."

"Tell me, son, what is so great about an astronaut. He flies above the world in his little bath tub?"

"It takes courage to do what he does."

"And it doesn't take courage to do what you father does; to get up every morning and go to work?"

"Yeah, sure."

"What do you know of courage? You're just a boy. Your father lived through the Holocaust. He survived the concentration camps. Don't you think that that took courage? He was younger than you. He works hard so you can have more than he ever did."

"Why doesn't he ever talk about it?"

"Who would talk of hell? You would not like what you heard. He has spared you that much. Now, finish your breakfast. You'll be late for school."

I remember these conversations now, as if it were yesterday. My mother and father are both gone, and I feel a ting of guilt for not having been a better son to them. Oh, I never got into any real trouble, a couple of pranks, and a brief brush with the law, but nothing serious. It was my relationship with them that was lacking. I feel that I never gave them the respect that they really deserved.

My father and I never talked about his youth. Growing up, a Jew in Germany during the Second World War, was probably too painful to talk about. I know he lost his father, his mother, a brother, and two sisters. There was only Aunt Sarah left from his family. They came here together as children.

I saw the tattoos. They both had them. Numbers tattooed on their arms. I often wondered why they never had them removed. After all, if the memories were so painful, why have a constant reminder forever on your arm? These are things I'll never know, as Aunt Sarah passed away two years ago.

It's no secret, what went on over there during the war. I've read accounts of the atrocities of the Holocaust. I try to imagine what it must have been like to be twelve-years-old, a Jew, and caught up in that madness. I can't. I can't because my father chose to spare me the horrors of his own life. He bottled it up and kept it to himself like some putrid cancer or flesh-eating bacteria that could destroy everything good. I know now how much courage that took. I still have my heroes, but my greatest one is a mattress salesman who once looked the devil in the eye, and spat.

Alas' the poor Neet

Have you ever chanced to meet a Neet?
    Have you ever seen them play?
'Neath prickly pines, on forest's floor,
    On a warm midsummer's day?
To play their prankish games
    On large but nimble feet,
The tireless play, the rules of which
    Known only to the Neet.
To leap about the forest floor,
    And frolic in the sun,
Thinking not of worldly woes,
    But just of having fun.
While man lurks in the nearby brush
    Poised with club and knife,
To pounce upon this timid beast,
    To snuff away its life!
Is their fur much sought for warmth?
    Nay! 'Tis not as warm as knit!
Does their meat then tempt the palate?
    Nay! 'Tis bitter and unfit!
'Tis for the feet they kill the Neet,
    With carcass left to spoil,
To boil them down in iron vats
    For making "Neet's Foot Oil,"
For softening boots and belts and such,
    And other leather goods.
For this the scampish Neet must meet
    Its sad fate in the woods?
A tear rolls slowly down my cheek.
    So sad my heart does beat.
For though man does have need for Neets,
    The Neet still needs its feet.